by
Marlayne Giron

"My tongue is the pen of a ready writer"

Psalm 45:1

DEDICATIONS

To my Messiah, Jesus. *"God is our refuge and strength, a very present help in times of trouble."* (Psalm 46:1)

To my true-life prince charming, Michael, who has stood by me through a horrific disease, two major surgeries, infertility, hair loss and most lately, breast cancer. You are the love of my life, my *Samuel,* my hero.

…and to Mary, who has been my greatest encourager and champion in my writing career. I couldn't have done any of this without you. *I love you dearly.*

Marlayne Giron

Also by Marlayne Giron

Second Chance Inn
The Victor
The Lesson Plan
Make a Wish
In Plain Sight

TABLE OF CONTENTS

Chapter One

Desperation

"*Es tut mir leid*[1], please go away."

Emma Lapp stared in disbelief at the door of her former home as her parents closed it in her face, completely devastated. She had come home utterly destitute and desperate, only to be turned away. Tears welled up and spilled over and down her cheeks as she turned around and fled back to her car, choking on her sobs.

She got in, slammed the door, and wept over the steering wheel; her last fragile wisp of hope decimated. She was unable to forget the look of horror on her mamm's face, staring at her as though she were a freak with tattoos, piercings, and green hair. But what really hurt was the fact that her father, the man she had looked up to and adored all her childhood, merely shook his head in disgust and shut the door in her face.

She had nowhere to go, no money and an unreliable car. It took several attempts to get it started and she drove out of her family's property, barely able to see the road because of her tears. She drove aimlessly with no destination in mind, not knowing what to do or where to go next.

She had gone about five miles when the car began to sputter.

"Oh, no, no, no, *NO!*" she wailed, pumping the gas in desperation. "Please *Der Herr*, help me!" The car rolled to a stop on the shoulder. She looked up and down the highway

______
[1] I am sorry

hoping to see a buggy or a passing car but there was none as far as the eye could see. The car had taken her from Philadelphia back to Lancaster and there it died and all her hopes with it.

She fumbled around in her trash and found a crumpled napkin and wiped her runny nose. Her cell phone was dead, and she had spent her last few dollars on gas. She rummaged around in her purse but all that was left of the crackers she had bought earlier was crumbs. Her head dropped onto the steering wheel. "I'm so tired, *Der Herr*, and *hungrig. Bitte hilf mir*[2]!"

A car horn blared; the driver was angry that she was partially blocking the road. She lifted her head from the steering wheel and looked around, hoping to find something, anything that would offer her some hope.

That's when she saw the sign. Emma's eyes widened and her mouth dropped open in shock. Her car had come to rest near the entrance to another farm with a lawn sign pointing to the farmhouse in the distance.

SECOND CHANCE INN

She got out of the car and began walking, desperately hoping that it was not just a coincidence.

Rachel was awakened by the pain from her fractured ribs. "*Owwwww,*" she moaned, clutching her sides. She looked about her room. From the angle of the sun, it looked to be late morning. She had returned home from the hospital just a week prior and had been bedridden the entire time. She could not sit up, stand, get out of bed or move without assistance but hated bothering Samuel and Karen when they both had their hands full with so much else. She was also incredibly lonely. Even though Ruth Beiler had betrayed her, she missed the friendship they had shared. She

---

[2] Please help me

had no other females to talk to or confide in and it was really getting to her. She had left all her friends and family back in California and a woman needed her girlfriends!

To make matters worse, she had a fully booked roster of guests coming the following month and had no idea how she was ever going to run an Inn when she needed help just to walk from one room to another. Samuel and Karen had both urged her to cancel the reservations, but she had steadfastly refused because they desperately needed the income. Samuel entered the room upon hearing her moan, sat on the bed, and took her into his arms. *"Was ist los, Liebling?*[3]*"*

Rachel buried her face in his chest. He smelled of hay and coffee. "Everything hurts! It hurts when I breath, it hurts when I move…Samuel, what are we going to do? We have two couples arriving May first and I can barely walk by myself. You cannot cook and Karen is still learning…your community has cast you out, so we have no help…" She knew she was panicking but couldn't help it. The situation was desperate.

Samuel lifted her chin and nodded, his eyes gentle. He cupped her cheek. "I know, I know. We will manage somehow. *Der herr* will provide a way. Right now, you need to rest and recover. It's a miracle that you are alive and suffered only fractured ribs and bruises!"

"Do you know what will happen if the guests come here and have a terrible experience? We'll get bad reviews; word will spread and then *POOF* – no more bookings or income. How am I supposed to rest when all I can think about is that?" Rachel exclaimed.

Samuel stood up and crossed his arms over his chest, shaking his head in dismay at her lack of faith. "What is it you always say? *Fiddle faddle…I'll think about it tomorrow?*"

"*Fiddle dee-dee,*" she corrected him, unable to resist cracking a smile at the sight of Samuel Miller attempting to

---

[3] What's the matter, darling?

mimic Scarlett O'Hara. A giggle erupted from her throat, causing her to wince in pain. "Ouch, that hurts!"

"*Jah*, that's more like my Rachel!" Samuel planted a lingering kiss on her lips that made her toes curl. "I need to see to the livestock. Karen will be close by if you need anything. *Won't you?*" He called out to Karen who was in the kitchen.

"Don't worry about me! I got it all dialed in!" she yelled back.

"*Gut*," Samuel turned about and went outside, the screen door slapping shut behind him.

Rachel lay back in bed and closed her eyes. She could already feel a migraine coming on from all the stress. She reached for her nightstand, but her pills weren't there. "*Karen?*"

No response.

"*KAREN!?*"

Still nothing. If she did not get those pills in time, she'd be completely incapacitated. She wrapped her arms around her ribs and braced herself.

"*KAAAAAAREEEEEN!!*"

"Coming! Geez, what *now?*" Her daughter reappeared in the door; her apron covered in *God-only-knew-what* substance.

"Do you know where my headache pills are?"

"No."

"Can you please find them?"

"Right *now?*"

"Yes now, unless you want to clean up barf…"

Karen dashed out of the room. Rachel grinned despite the pain. The imminent threat of vomit removal was obviously highly motivating. *I will have to remember that…*Rachel could hear Karen rummaging violently through her still unpacked suitcase that had been left in the family room for over a week.

"Found it!" She bounded into the room and dropped 2 pills into Rachel's outstretched hand. "There's a glass of water on your nightstand."

Rachel swallowed the pills and sank back into bed, covering her face with her arms. "Please close the drapes, can't take the light yet."

"Anything else? A tea cozy for your pepper pot perhaps?" Karen complained, repeating something her father, Barry, would have said when too much was being asked of him.

Rachel said nothing but was relieved when the room became comfortably dark. In moments she fell back into a deep sleep with a smile on her face; unaware of when Samuel returned to her room to watch over her and hold her hand.

"Rachel?" Samuel's voice brought her out of a deep sleep. She cracked open an eye to look at him. It was brighter now outside; It must have been high noon. "Do you think you can eat something?"

Rachel nodded, "I think so."

"*Gut*, I will bring it into you on a tray."

"No, please! I want to eat at the table like a normal person. I'm tired of laying prone."

"I don't think that's a *gut idea...*" he replied, gently pushing her back against the pillows.

"Why?" She stared at him, watching his face grow crimson with some unspoken secret. "Okay, spill the beans."

"I don't want anything upsetting you right now," he replied clumsily. *That did it.* Now she knew something was up. Rachel pushed the covers back and stood to her feet, ignoring her protesting ribs and Samuel who was trying to block her way. She stepped around him and limped into the kitchen.

There she saw Buddy happily licking the floor from one end of the counter to the other. Every pot and pan she owned was piled up two feet high across her beautiful ten-foot island with dried food stuck to them. The large farmhouse sink was stacked full of plates, cups and glassware and an ungodly stench was coming from the slop bucket.

"O.M.G.!!!!" she could not believe her eyes. Her once immaculate gourmet kitchen had become the stuff of nightmares. She leaned upon the kitchen table and slid onto a chair, dissolving into tears of frustration. "What have you been doing all these weeks while I've been gone? It looks like no one has cleaned anything in a month!"

"Karen and I have done the best we could under the circumstances…" Samuel protested.

At that moment Karen came in from the service porch and brightened up the moment she saw her mother standing in the kitchen. "You're up! Great! I'll have dinner ready in a jiffy."

Rachel buried her face in her hands. She had guests coming in a month and the Inn was an absolute wreck. She bit back the critical words that were rising in her throat. If she let loose it would just make everything worse. Karen would get upset then Samuel would get upset. They were helping as best they could but…

She pushed the accumulated crumbs on the table to one side in disgust. She could feel Samuel's eyes on her, waiting and watching for her reaction when Karen placed a plate full of plain noodles in front of her, oblivious to her distress.

"Let's pray!" They bowed their heads. "Lord – thank you for saving my mom and bringing her home safe so that maybe now we can have a decent meal around here!"

Rachel exploded with laughter then grabbed her ribs at the resulting pain, crying miserable tears at the same time. *I'm having a nervous breakdown.*

"What did I say?" Karen demanded, trying to spear a slippery noodle with her fork. It slithered off the table then down to the floor where a grateful Buddy lapped it up quick as a flash. He had taken up a strategic position underneath to catch all the droppings.

Rachel pushed herself to a standing position, Samuel hovering behind her. "I can't…I just can't!" She looked around the kitchen then the living room. Everywhere she looked, she saw a mess that would take days if not weeks to clean. It looked like a goat had exploded; the mess had reached critical mass. She didn't possess the energy or even motivation to deal with it. Her fractured ribs still hurt so bad that she couldn't laugh or cry without agony. She limped back to her bedroom and collapsed, sobbing into her pillow despite the pain it caused her.

Samuel was right on her heels. He gathered her gently into his arms and just allowed her to cry herself out for which she felt grateful. When her tears subsided, she looked up at him and for the first time noticed how much thinner he looked. "Karen not feeding you?"

"*Jah*, well she tries her best but she's not you in the kitchen. I've practically gone through all the canned goods in the root cellar."

Rachel sat up, her Jewish instincts kicking into high gear. "If you can help me, I'll try to make you a decent supper."

Samuel's eyes widened in a mixture of hope then apprehension, causing her to giggle despite herself.

"I don't think that's a *gut* idea…" he protested. It was fast becoming a very annoying mantra.

"Just do all the heavy lifting and I'll do the rest." Rachel got up very carefully and went to the service porch to get some eggs. The sight that met her eyes elicited a wail of despair. "*Oh, you've got to be kidding me!*" The service porch had a pile of dirty laundry that rose from the floor to above counter-height and filled the entire room. Every sheet, pillowcase and article of clothing had been dumped there for the past month just waiting for her return; it also stunk to high heaven. It was the last straw.

"Mom, what's wrong?" Karen entered the room, oblivious to the smell.

Rachel gestured to the room. "THIS! This is what's wrong!"

"Mom," Karen replied with as much patience as she could muster, "Mr. Miller and I have been up to our eyeballs just keeping the animals, garden and farm going, not to mention visiting you for over a month daily in the hospital! We honestly did our best..."

Rachel shook her head, "I could understand all that if we didn't have the high-capacity washers and dryers and you had to do it the 'old fashioned' way, but this. *THIS*??!! Didn't you try to do at least one load?"

At this Karen turned beet red with embarrassment. "Yes, I did, but everything came out pink,"

"Because you didn't separate the colors?"

Karen nodded. "Then Samuel tried."

"And?"

"Pink Barbie clothes."

Rachel was torn between laughing and screaming.

At that moment, a knock sounded on the front door.

Glad to escape her mom's ire, Karen dashed to answer. "I'll get it!!"

Samuel helped Rachel into a chair in the front room in the hopes of calming her down.

"Who is it?" they both asked simultaneously.

Karen opened the door wider to let them see. "I don't know."

Standing on the porch was a young woman in her early twenties. She was dressed in a torn black t-shirt and ripped jeans and covered in tattoos from her neck to her ankles with multiple piercings in her ears and nose. Her long hair was a tangled mess and slowly returning to its natural blonde state from a ghastly green shade. Her eyes were red and puffy as though she had been crying.

"I'm so sorry to intrude, but is this the Second Chance Inn?" Her face bore a look of utter desperation.

"Come in, please." Rachel gestured, feeling immediate empathy for her. She gestured to the chair beside her. "Sit."

She wiped her feet well on the mat and entered, obviously nervous.

Rachel smiled to put her at ease. "What's your name, honey?"

"Emma Lapp," she replied meekly.

Samuel's mouth dropped open "Emma Lapp, the daughter of Joseph and Susan Lapp?"

The girl nodded, her head dropping down as tears plopped onto her lap.

"You know this girl?" Rachel was shocked.

"I knew her family well," Samuel replied.

Karen offered the girl a glass of water and a box of Kleenex.

"I didn't know what else to do, I have nowhere to go..." she said plaintively. "I have no money; I haven't eaten since yesterday..."

"Let me guess," Rachel said, taking her quivering hand into hers. *Rumspringa* enticed you to leave the Amish life?" She had watched only one episode of the reality show, *Breaking Amish*, a long time ago, and had been horrified at what she had seen. The former Amish people on the show were absolute train wrecks.

Emma nodded, her shoulders beginning to heave with sobs. "I thought it was what I genuinely wanted and needed. I indulged in everything I wanted to and refused to be baptized, only...only,"

"It didn't work out as you planned?" Rachel finished for her.

Her words released the flood gates. Emma broke down in great gulping sobs, making Rachel's heart break for her.

"I couldn't stand the *Englisch welt* anymore. It's so horrible; darker, meaner and filthier than I expected. I do not fit in there and I can't return to being Amish. I went to my parents this morning and they shut the door on me. I have nowhere to go!" she gestured to her tattoos and piercings. "I don't fit in anywhere!"

At that moment Samuel caught Rachel's eyes, his eyebrows rising high into his hairline. "Are you thinking what I'm thinking?" he mouthed.

The 90's cartoon Pinky and the Brain sprang to mind, but Rachel resisted responding with the catchphrase, "...*try to take over the world*". Instead, she nodded. "You did say that *Der Herr* would provide..." she murmured out loud.

"I hoped that with a name like Second Chance Inn, there might be a second chance for me?" Emma continued, her teary eyes wide and heartbreakingly hopeful. "I just need a place to stay for the night and in return I'll do anything you need."

Rachel leaned forward and grasped both of Emma's hands in hers. Tears running down her cheeks as well. "Sweetheart, you are an answer to prayer!"

Emma looked back at her, shocked. "I am?"

Rachel nodded. "Can you cook and clean?"

"*Jah*, of course!"

"You're hired!" Karen piped up gleefully.

"Oh, I don't expect to be paid," Emma protested, unable to believe her sudden change of fortune. "Just a place to stay and some food would be *wunderbar*."

"Emma, this is an Inn and if you do your job well, of course you will be compensated. Not only with bed and board but also with a stipend. It will depend on occupancy but,"

Rachel was cut off as Emma flung her arms around her in relief.

"OUCH!"

Instantly mortified, Emma drew back, worried. "*Och*, did I do something wrong?"

Rachel waved her off, her eyes watering from pain. "Fractured ribs from an accident, it's okay. So, when can you start?"

"Is now too soon?" Emma asked, a tentative smile replacing her worried look. "I have been living out of my car for the past two weeks and just made it here before it died. This was my last hope…"

"Well, you're a Godsend!" Rachel smiled at her, a wave of happiness washing over her. "First things first. Let's push your car off the road and onto our property so it doesn't get towed, and two: I have two very underfed family members here that need a good home-cooked meal as I'm sure you do as well. After that, the kitchen is a disaster, there's a mountain load of laundry to be washed and an Inn to prep for guests."

Emma stood up, eager to start. She wiped the tears from her face with the back of her hand. "Leave it all to me!" She bent down and gently hugged Rachel. "*Danki,*" she said heartfully, looking gratefully into Rachel's eyes. "*Danki* for my second chance!"

Chapter Two

"Entertaining Angels Unaware"

In less than two hours, Emma had prepared them all a wonderful meal of oven-fried chicken, garlic mashed potatoes, and green beans. Samuel had helped himself to three servings of each and was now uncomfortably full and ensconced on the leather recliner in front of the glowing fireplace. Any doubts that Rachel might have had about welcoming Emma into the Inn were quickly extinguished as she set about scouring every filthy pot and pan in the kitchen with a vengeance. She loaded both dishwashers to capacity and then took on the mountain of laundry. By nine pm the worst of the mess had transformed into a gleaming kitchen and the mountain of dirty clothes into sweet smelling, neatly folded laundry.

Rachel felt like she had been gifted an angel from heaven in the form of a heavily tattooed, former Amish rebel. She wasn't sure how the Inn guests would react to seeing Emma, but she didn't care. Who was she to second guess God's methods?

With newfound relief, she could finally relax and indulge herself in her first hot shower in over a month instead of the tepid hospital sponge baths. She disrobed in her bedroom and for the first time got a good look at her body in the bathroom mirror. She was covered in bruises that were turning from blue to yellow, and which stretched from her collar bone down to her legs. She still couldn't remove the wrap that held her fractured ribs together so she wrapped saran wrap about her torso as best she could to keep herself dry, wincing with the effort. Her esophagus was still sore from being intubated but other than her ribs, bruising, and some minor lacerations she was in reasonably good condition considering what could have happened. She could have easily suffered serious head trauma, brain damage from almost drowning and/or paralysis.

"Could be worse…" she mused.

BOOM. Lightning flashed followed immediately by thunder rumbling over the house. The rain began to pelt down. She shook her head. Just like the running gag in all the movies she and Barry used to joke about whenever everything was going wrong for the characters. *Could be worse… could be raining.* It always did.

A twinge of pain squeezed her heart. She still missed Barry; that would never change, but Samuel's love, understanding, and affection had diminished the pain a great deal. Instead of waking up and dreading each day the way she had before she met him, she now looked forward to seeing his face each day and the way he looked at her. Just thinking about it gave her goosebumps.

She opened the shower door. Samuel had thoughtfully placed a plastic chair inside so she could sit while cleaning off. A large bath towel fresh out of the dryer lay over the towel warmer with a tiny sprig of lavender placed on top. Rachel smiled, Emma's attention to the minute details warmed her heart, and further confirmed that she had made the right decision.

She sat down on the chair and gloried in the feel of hot water running over her entire body, shampooing her greasy hair twice. She felt like a new person. When she exited the shower, she found Buddy stationed in the bathroom like a little sentry. He walked up to her and began licking the shower water off her feet and lower legs as though it was part of his job description. Rachel gingerly toweled the rest of herself off and watched him leave the bathroom; his job done. She wrapped herself in her robe then removed the saran wrap, using a hair dryer to dry out her damp rib bandages. While she showered, Emma had also discreetly placed freshly washed pajamas and a robe on the door hook. The girl was a wonder!

Rachel found Samuel and Karen in the living room, playing checkers before the fire. Emma was on the service porch, stuffing the fifth and sixth loads into the washing machines. Rachel went up to her and took both of her hands into her own.

"Thank you," she said.

Emma's eyes filled with tears. "No, *danki* to you!"

They embraced. "You must be so tired," Rachel said, looking her up and down. Emma's green eyes had blue circles under them and were still swollen.

Emma nodded, wiping away her tears.

"Would you mind sharing a room with Karen?"

"*Ach,* not at all! It will be good to sleep in a bed!"

"Well, it's a fold out bed, but we'll try to find you better accommodations tomorrow."

Rachel called over her shoulder. "Karen?"

"Yes mamm?"

Back to her Amish vernacular again?

"Did you get the fold out bed ready for Emma?"

"*Jah,*" Karen said, jumping her checker over several of Samuel's. "Crown me!"

"Did you put sheets on it?"

A long guilty pause ensued.

Finally, "There wasn't any,"

"Well, there is now in that basket!" Emma pointed, winking at Rachel.

Rachel grinned back. Emma already had Karen's number!

"While you're up there, could you strip all the guest room beds and bring the bedding down to the service porch?"

"*Jah, mamm,* coming." Karen complained.

Together she and Emma climbed the stairs. It wasn't even a few moments before she could hear Karen peppering Emma with questions.

"Karen, give it a rest, will yah?" Rachel shouted up the stairs. "The girl's exhausted! Just make up her bed and bring the dirty linens down."

She turned around to find Samuel right behind her. He gently encircled her waist and brought her close to him. He bent his head to her hair. "You smell gut," he murmured. It sent shivers down her spine. "Alone at last!" he sighed.

"Not for long," Rachel whispered before his mouth clamped over hers. Two pairs of feet descended the stairs. They separated instantly, their faces both flaming as though they had committed a felony offense.

Karen stared at them, not fooled for a second, frowned, then shrugged it off and carried the laundry basket into the service porch followed by Emma.

"You know what I miss?" Samuel said, taking her hand and leading her gently out to the front porch.

"What?" Rachel sighed, his kiss still uppermost in her thoughts.

He beckoned to the porch swing where they had spent so many healing moments together, holding hands and becoming so much more than friends. "This."

Tears sprung to Rachel's eyes. She had yearned in the hospital so many times to be where she was right now, here with him. The violence of the storm had calmed down to a steady rain with intermittent flashes of lightning in the distance. She had always loved watching thunderstorms because they were such a novelty in Southern California, but they had always freaked Barry out who would hide in the house while she sat under the back patio cover to watch. Samuel sat down and she cuddled next to him, her head upon his chest and closed her eyes in bliss.

Gently they rocked back and forth, silent for a long time, grateful to be in each other's company again after such a long and painful separation.

"Rachel?"

"Yes, Samuel?"

"I still want you to be my *frau*."

She turned to him, looking deeply into his eyes and cupped his clean-shaven cheek. "I still want to be your *frau*," she confirmed.

He took her in his arms and kissed her. "When, *mein liebling*?" His lips trailed from her mouth to nuzzle her ear lobe sending glorious shudders through her entire body.

"As soon as my ribs are completely healed and it doesn't hurt when I laugh, cry or burp."

His head dropped to his chest in defeat. "That could take months,"

Rachel caught his chin and lifted it to look her in the eyes. "Samuel Miller, do you honestly think that I can perform my wifely duties if my ribs aren't sufficiently healed?"

She could feel the heat of embarrassment radiating from his face when comprehension dawned on him. "Forgive me," he whispered. "I was being selfish, thinking only of myself. I'm a *dummkopf*!"

"Yes, but you are my *dummkopf*! All is forgiven!" Rachel pronounced, kissing him again. She shivered. "It's still chilly for early March. Want to go in and neck on the couch a little bit?"

He was unfamiliar with the term. "*Neck?*"

Rachel chuckled and winced with pain, grabbing her ribs. "Never mind, let's just build a fire and cuddle on the couch for a bit. I think I'm up to making hot chocolate if you'll help me."

"Always!" he grinned at her.

Samuel watched Rachel in the dying firelight. She had fallen asleep cuddled in his arms. He lifted her gently into his arms and carried her to her bed and shut the door. Thank goodness she was already in her pajamas and robe. He didn't want to have to be the one to change her out of her customary jeans and shirt so she could sleep comfortably. He silently marveled that she could even walk as though the accident had never happened. He had given up all hope for a life with her when he had found her trapped in the upended buggy. After a month of convalescing in the hospital, she was little worse for the wear with only damaged ribs as evidence of the accident that had almost claimed her life. He was curious as to how her injuries were healing, so he lifted her night shirt just high enough to see her abdomen area and was horrified to see the massive bruising and healing lacerations. Tears sprang to his eyes. He had come so close to losing her. It was truly a miracle she was alive and had suffered no brain damage after being fully submerged under freezing water for at least a good five minutes. Samuel had been told by the medics that the frigid water had worked in her favor by lowering her body temperature, thus preventing brain damage. They also had had to shock her heart back to life with the paddles. Surely *Der Herr* had a purpose greater than they both could see right now for her? The timely appearance of Emma at just the right moment gave him the chills now that he thought about it. He covered Rachel with the quilt and plucked her Bible off the nightstand and took it to the kitchen table. He hadn't read it much for himself, usually relying on the sermons and the elders in his community for spiritual guidance up until the day he lost both his family and his faith.

He opened it up randomly. A yellow highlighted scripture passage leaped off the page at him.

"Do not neglect to show hospitality to strangers, for by this some have entertained angels without knowing it." – Hebrews 13:2

He stared at the Bible passage, unable to believe his eyes. Never in his life had he experienced having the scriptures speak to him personally. Now he was convinced beyond all doubt that *Der Herr* not only had plans for Rachel and him but the Inn as well, and that Emma was just the start. For the first time in his life, he felt *Der Herr's* invisible presence in the room. An overwhelming sense of awe and unworthiness swept over him. He fell onto his knees, covered his face with his hands and wept.

"*Der Herr,* please forgive me. Forgive me. I have sinned greatly against you. You brought love and joy back into my life when I least deserved it. You returned Rachel to me even when I was secretly cursing you in my heart. I do not deserve Your forgiveness or Your blessings. I repent for blaming You…"

He dropped the bible. It fell onto the floor opening to another page from the Gospels. He was almost afraid to look.

"For if you forgive others for their transgressions, your heavenly Father will also forgive you. But if you do not forgive others, then your heavenly Father will not forgive your transgressions." Matthew 6:13-15.

His heart pounded as he read these words, thoroughly alarmed. *Der Herr* was speaking to him through His scriptures! Heavy conviction fell upon him so all that he could do was to prostrate himself face down on the floor, a godly terror coming over him. He had believed himself fully justified in his bitterness when he was excommunicated by his community. He had felt betrayed by his own kin (who had really had no other choice but to take part, regardless of their personal feelings). It had been festering inside of him like an ulcer for months.

The words poured out of his mouth of their own accord. "*Der Herr*, I forgive my community for excommunicating me. I forgive Sarah and Mark for shunning me. They were only doing what they thought was right and I have no right to judge them. Please forgive me, *Der Herr, please.*"

He wasn't sure what to expect next. The room was deathly silent, but a peace washed over him that he had never experienced before. The anger, hurt, and bitterness he had harbored against *Der Herr*, his family and community were gone. Completely gone! He sat up and leaned against the kitchen counter and wept silently with relief. Buddy appeared at that moment, climbed into his lap, and licked his neck; an honor the little dog had usually only reserved for his late wife and Rachel Winston. Samuel looked down into his soulful little brown eyes and cuddled him.

"I think we have more than one angel in this house," he said, stroking his silky head. Buddy offered him a doggy smile and thumped his tail.

Chapter Three

"Word Gets Out"

The smell of coffee, freshly baked bread, bacon, and cinnamon rolls greeted Rachel's nose. She stretched carefully, not wanting to aggravate her ribs. It was the best night's sleep she had had in over a month. Hospitals were no place to sleep with all the poking, prodding, beeping machines, fellow patients, and hourly checks. Her home was blessedly quiet in comparison. She got up, wrapped herself in a robe and went to investigate what was going on in the kitchen.

"Finally, you're up!" Karen greeted her. "We've been waiting breakfast for you."

"Good morning to you too," Rachel replied, gazing in wonder at the multiple loaves of bread that were cooling on the island. She smiled at Emma. "You've been busy!"

"*Jah*, it's gut to be back in the kitchen again! I used to work at the Yoder bakery in town before I left."

Except for the tattoos, Emma looked every inch the modest Amish woman. She had removed all her piercing jewelry, tied up her hair in a bun sans prayer kapp, and was dressed modestly with a black apron that was already coated with a fine layer of flour. She poured Rachel a cup of steaming hot coffee. Samuel came in from the service porch where he had been washing up from his morning livestock chores.

"Smells *wunderbar!*" he grinned, taking a seat at the table. He looked at the heaping platters of bacon, country-fried potatoes, scrambled eggs, and cinnamon rolls and rubbed his hands in glee.

"So much better than cold cereal and milk!" Karen exclaimed, equally as pleased.

Emma and Rachel took their seats at the table and bowed their heads. Before Rachel could utter a word, Samuel beat her to it.

"Der Herr, thank You for all Your marvelous blessings. For the gut food you provide, for the rain in due season, for the bountiful harvest but most of all, for Your unfailing love and forgiveness, we give thee thanks! Amen."

Rachel stared at him; gob smacked. She had never heard Samuel pray aloud like this: with such heartfelt earnestness. Something in him had changed dramatically. She laid her hand over his, her eyes questioning.

I'll tell you later he mouthed with a smile that was suffused with a joy she had never seen before. His entire face was lit from within!

Karen groaned with pleasure. "Emma, these potatoes are so good! Would you teach me how to make them?"

"*Jah*, of course. Anything you want to learn; I'll be happy to teach you." Emma smiled.

Rachel bit her lip, a little hurt. Karen had never asked her to teach her how to cook.

"So, Emma. How did you hear about our Inn?" It's only been open since last December. How did you know how to find us?" The mystery had been niggling at Rachel since Emma's arrival.

"I didn't hear about it. My car broke down on the shoulder just outside your property. I saw your sign on the road right when the motor died. It said, "Second Chance Inn" and it was just like an answer to prayer and a sign from *Der Herr*."

"Lucky for both you and us!" Karen said, stuffing a cinnamon roll into her mouth. "OMG these are so GOOD!!!" She got up from the table, taking another roll with her. "I'm off on my egg rounds then I'm going to go visit Willis."

Rachel cast a nervous sideways glance at Samuel but instead of his usual glower he nodded and gave her a smile. "Send them all our love," he said.

Karen froze and stared at him. "Really?"

"*Jah*, is that a problem?"

"*Noooo*, but I thought that…well never mind, I'll tell them!" She left the room, shaking her head and muttering under her breath to herself.

Emma said nothing but her perplexed look was obvious.

"It's a long story," Rachel said.

"*Och*! No need to explain anything to me, *geht mich nichts an*!"

Rachel looked over at Samuel wondering what had just happened to alter him so. She gave him a good once over. She loved his clean-shaven face, but his hair had become overgrown and unruly. "You need a haircut," she announced.

He ran his fingers through the thick curls that were well past his earlobes. "*Jah*, I need a cut. Just get out the bowl and hack away."

Rachel shook her head. "Umm no. I think we should go to a men's barber in town and get you a *manly* cut."

He was about to object, citing the rules of his community, then remembered he was no longer compelled to follow them anymore. He was intrigued.

"My treat," Rachel added. We can also get some supplies while we are in town for the Inn guests. You can get the full VIP treatment while I get a much-needed mani/pedi and then we'll do some shopping, deal?"

Samuel nodded; it was almost like a date.

"I'll drive," Rachel added.

Samuel opened his mouth to protest but her hand halted his objections.

"My ribs can't take the jostling of the buggy, it's still cold outside and I'll belt a bed pillow around my torso, okay?"

"Okay," he acquiesced.

"Just let me get changed, make a list and then we'll head out."

"I'll take care of getting the rooms ready while you're out," Emma volunteered.

Rachel's heart filled with gratitude for her. She gave her an embrace then held her at arm's length. The dark circles under her eyes were gone and so was the worried crease between her brows. "Looks like you had a good night's sleep. Anything I can get you while we're out?"

"Maybe some skin makeup to hide all this?" Emma looked down at herself. "I don't know what I was thinking but once I started, I couldn't stop. It became an obsession."

"There are treatments that remove tattoos, but they are costly and painful."

"*Ach*! It couldn't be any more painful than getting them in the first place!" Emma snorted.

Rachel patted her hand. "Leave it to me," she smiled.

Samuel was waiting for Rachel on the service porch, dressed in his traditional Amish clothes, and looked very Old Order except for his beard. He was still holding onto most of his life-long habits and saw no need to spend hard earned dollars on *English* clothing. He did not have a driver's license, so he was acting as Rachel's co-pilot.

She shifted her purse and pillow in her arms. "Ready?"

He gave her a nod, clearly nervous.

"Just hope the car starts after sitting idle for over a month!" she muttered, more to herself than him. They walked slowly together to the green VW with the matching miniature toy in the rear window that said MINI ME on it and climbed in. Samuel's hat brushed up against the sloped roof of the car. Rachel positioned the pillow over her front and wrapped it around each side, then belted herself in.

"Fingers crossed!" she grinned at him, turning the key. The VW revved uncertainly for a moment then came to life as she gunned the engine.

She backed away from the barn, turned and carefully drove down their long driveway, looking both ways down the two-lane. An Amish buggy went by first. Was it her imagination or were they all frowning at them in disapproval? She waited for another car to pass then pulled out, driving slower than normal. Samuel said nothing for the entire ride, his face unreadable. Whenever they passed an Amish buggy, she noticed that he would slide down as low as possible in his seat or avert his gaze away. She started paying closer attention to the Amish passengers and without fail, every single one of them either shook their heads at them, frowned or ignored them completely.

She took hold of his left hand and held it, squeezing it every so often as an expression of solidarity with him. He had done nothing to be ashamed of. The reactions of his community were grating on her nerves even though she had been expecting it.

They finally arrived at a local barbershop. They walked in together.

"Just take a seat, there, I'll be with you in a jiffy," the barber gestured to a vinyl chair. Samuel sat down and gazed around the room, looking at the posters of differing hairstyles for men on the walls and the other patrons as if trying to figure out what kind of cut he wanted. The more he looked the bigger his frown became.

Rachel had to stifle a laugh. Too many weird hairstyles for him. She leaned over and whispered in Samuel's ear. "Just tell him you want it short all around but not a bowl cut."

He nodded, clearly nervous as to what was about to happen to him when a customer next to him got out of their chair with initials shaved into his head.

Rachel walked up to the barber and slipped him a ten-dollar bill. "Give him a very conservative, *manly*, old-fashioned cut."

He gave her a wink and pocketed the cash. "Not to worry!" he assured her.

Rachel left Samuel, hoping she had not misplaced her faith and $10.00.

She found a local nail salon not too far down the street from the barbers and indulged herself with a French manicure and pedicure. Her dried cracked feet were soft and silky once again. She returned to find Samuel leaning back in the vintage barber chair with a hot towel covering his face, snoring.

The barber gently removed the towel and gave him a refreshing splash of aftershave that jolted him awake. His hair was cut short on the sides and in the back with just a bit of a wave at the top. The barber twirled the chair around so Samuel could get a good look at himself. The barber was rewarded with a happy and relieved smile.

"A real *maaaannn!*" Rachel squealed in her best Leena Hyena voice. Barry would have "gotten it" instantly but movie anecdotes were lost on Samuel.

He removed the barber cape. "*Entschuldigung*[4]?"

"I'll explain later," Rachel replied.

The barber was chuckling despite himself. "Who Framed Roger Rabbit, right?"

"Yup,"

"I thought so, love that movie! I gave him the works: straight edge shave, so that will be $35." She was happy to pay him. Samuel looked amazing.

Rachel and Samuel exited the shop. "*Was sagst du mir nicht*[5]?"

"It's not something I can explain, I'll just have to show you, but not here…in the car."

Samuel ran his hand through his newly cut hair and across his face. "I liked this very much, but my face feels raw."

---

[4] Excuse me?
[5] What are you not telling me?

"You are a bit pink but that will calm down. Okay, are you ready to be initiated into the world of cartoons?"

Samuel shrugged and watched in silence as Rachel played a YouTube video of Who Framed Roger Rabbit and Lena Hyena cackling about a REAL MAN. He shrugged, nonplussed, the humor not registering with him.

Rachel dropped the phone into her purse in exasperation. "No sense of humor!!! Barry used to call me at work and put Loony Toons on over the phone and coworkers would wonder why I was giggling in hysterics."

They drove to a local eatery frequented by both Amish and tourists alike for lunch. If Rachel had thought the cold shoulder treatment was bad on the road, it was nothing compared to what they received at the restaurant. As soon as all the Amish saw Samuel, they turned their backs on him in unison as if they had rehearsed. It was so overt even the tourists took note of it and twittered amongst themselves.

Rachel's face began to burn with anger, but Samuel remained calm and serene where she might have expected him to get up and walk out.

"Are you okay?" she whispered over her menu, her eyes darting around the room.

He nodded and smiled at her. "*Jah, Der Herr* and I have come to an understanding," he replied. They quickly ordered, finished their meal, and left, looking neither to the left nor the right, the disapproving silence of his former community deafening.

Shunning was no small matter and she had just experienced the full brunt of it on his behalf. *What must he have endured these past few months because of me?*

They got into the car.

"Where next?" Samuel was looking at her and smiling, no trace of the hurt, anger, or resentment that she would have expected of him after their treatment.

"Are you going to tell me about this new and improved understanding between you and the Lord?"

"*Jah*, all in gut time." He picked up her list and looked it over. "*A handful of patience is worth more than a bushel of brains*," he quoted.

"Oh, is that some kind of Amish saying?"

"*Jah*," he pointed at the list. "Bicycles?"

"Yes, the guests coming next month have specifically requested four touring bikes so they can ride the backroads and see the countryside."

"We have several bicycles in the barn which belonged to my *frau* and *kinner*[6]...I could get them cleaned up and tuned in time."

Rachel stared at him. His voice was steady, but the sadness in his eyes was unmistakable. "Are you sure you want to do that? I can easily rent bikes in town if it's too painful for you."

Samuel nodded and patted her hand, too choked up to say anything further. He dashed the tears from his eyes and looked out the window, embarrassed by his emotions.

"All right, then I just need to get some toiletries and some nonperishable snacks for the goodie baskets then."

When they returned from their errands, Samuel and Rachel were surprised to find several young men in various styles of dress standing near the front porch. One had hair spiked in every direction and dyed purple. Another looked like a biker with the Harley Davidson leather jacket and heavy chain necklaces that could have doubled as offensive weapons and the last was a young man who looked semi-Amish except for his expensive but ill-fitting wool suit.

"*Gutten tag*[7]!" all three of them said respectfully.

The blonde in the Harley Davidson biker jacket came forward and introduced himself. "I'm Amos Yoder, may I

---

[6] Wife and children
[7] Good day

help you with those?" He indicated the numerous shopping bags in the trunk of the VW.

Samuel stopped dead in his tracks. "Amos?! *Was machst du hier*[8]?"

"You know this young man?" Rachel was not yet inclined to entrust total strangers with her things yet.

"*Jah*, I know all of them," Samuel nodded. He pointed at the one in the wool suit, "That's Abram Troyer," he pointed at the one with spiky purple hair and tattoos, "and that's Aaron Schruck."

"The three A's," mused Rachel. She studied the young men up and down and relaxed. They looked harmless despite their garb. "Is there something we can do for you?"

The lads exchanged nervous glances amongst themselves, silently hoping for one of the others would be first to volunteer.

Abram stepped forward. "We heard that there might be a place for us here. We've all been excommunicated, but we can't go back to the *English* world either."

"Heard from *who*?" asked Rachel, already figuring out who the culprit was.

"Emma Lapp," all three responded in unison. They held up their cell phones. "She texted us that you might need some additional hands around the place late yesterday. We don't expect to get paid…"

"*Jah*, well that's gut," snorted Samuel, obviously peeved at being put on the spot. "How did you three all get here?" There were no other cars besides Rachel's and Emma's.

"We pooled our money and took an Uber from the train station," Amos explained.

"We're happy to help out in any way we can." Aaron offered, then as if on cue, his stomach rumbled loudly.

Rachel's Jewish upbringing kicked into high gear. "You're hungry," she stated. She could feel Samuel's indignant eyes boring invisible holes into her head, but she plowed forward anyway. "Yes, we can use the help, but we're going to

---

[8] What are you doing here?

have to discuss it privately and pray about it first. In the meantime, we can offer you a hot meal. Do you have any place to stay?"

All three nodded yes to the hot meal and no to the any-place-to-stay questions simultaneously. It was almost comical.

Rachel turned to Samuel. "Can you vouch for these fellow's characters?"

Samuel looked at them up and down, rubbing his newly shorn head in consternation. "*Jah,* they are basically all *gut kinner... dumme jungs*[9] but harmless."

"Well, since Emma invited you all here, she's going to have to be the one to rustle you all up some grub."

Emma appeared on the porch. No doubt eavesdropping in the hopes that Rachel and Samuel would welcome her friends as they had her. "I have some sandwiches and Kool-Aid on the back picnic table," she said, gazing hopefully at Samuel and Rachel.

"We'll help you carry everything in first," Amos offered, grabbing two heavy grocery sacks. The other boys followed suit and followed Emma around to the back porch where they deposited the groceries.

Rachel shut the door, so they could talk in private while putting away everything.

"What do you think, Samuel? Could you use more help around here?"

"Can you use more mouths to feed?" he replied. "Those boys will eat us out of house and home and where will they sleep?"

"As far as sleeping, they can use the barn just for tonight, but you didn't answer my question. Can you use more help? I know you sold a lot of your acreage before we came here, but you still have quite a bit and it's been lying fallow because there isn't enough of you to go around. You have your hands full with the garden, livestock, Inn, and general repairs..."

---

[9] Stupid boys

Samuel nodded. "*Jah,* I could use the help. My *kinner,* Sarah, Mark and his family and our community used to all help me out, but they are all gone now." It was still a painful topic.

"Didn't you say that "*Der Herr*" would provide?" Rachel reminded him gently. "Maybe it's not just to help me but you as well?"

"Where are we going to put them all? They can't sleep in the barn indefinitely; especially in the winter months."

"Aren't Amish all carpenters? The four of you could easily enlarge the *Dawdi* house into a bunk house once we're legally married."

At this Samuel grinned and pulled her close. "Are you saying that as soon as we have a bunk house we can marry?" He bent down and kissed her until her knees went weak, wrapping his arms about her.

"…and my ribs are healed," Rachel murmured against his chest. She looked up at him. "We should *also* pray and ask for God's wisdom and guidance before we make a decision."

He continued to nuzzle her neck while he whispered his prayer. "*Der Herr, we come to you humbly and ask you to lead and guide us in this decision. We want to be faithful to Your Will and gut servants. Please show us plainly what Your will is.*"

"Amen," Rachel shuddered, gooseflesh spreading all over her body from his attentions. "I'll tell them that we'll sleep on it tonight and that they can bunk in the hay loft."

Samuel's grin was wolfish. "We'll sleep? He teased. She gave him a playful push. "Yes, you in the *dawdi haus* and me here in the Inn, like good Christians!!"

Chapter Four

"A Fresh Start"

It was still dark when Rachel was awakened from a deep sleep. Outside their rooster, Henry, was crowing.

"*Shut uuuuuuuup!*" came the muffled voice of Karen from the second story bedroom she now shared with Emma. It had become a daily routine since they had moved here but Henry never took the hint. Sometimes he crowed so hard and long he passed out and tipped over from lack of oxygen. It was an endless source of amusement when it wasn't at the crack of dawn.

Rachel lay in bed, the last vestiges of her dreams still vivid in her mind. She had been dreaming about the Inn. Where the *Dawdi haus* had been stood a lovely bunkhouse that could sleep 20 with a sign over the lintel that said *A Place of Refuge*. It was so vivid she had to believe it had come from the Lord as her answer to prayer. She seldom, if ever, remembered her dreams unless they were spiritually significant, like right after Barry had died. He appeared as he had looked in his youth, wearing a plaid flannel shirt, arms crossed. In her dream, he had greeted her with his customary "*Hey sugar, what's cooking?*"

She had run to him and made to hug him, asking what heaven was like and Barry had become tongue tied in his attempts to describe it. "It's more amazing than you can imagine," dream Barry had told her.

But she was going to need more than just a singular dream to go by if she was going to take such a risk. She decided to lay out a fleece. "Lord, if you want us to build this bunkhouse and take these wayward youth in, you're going to have to provide a confirmation from someone else in this house, I leave the details up to You but I'm saying and deciding nothing until I get it." With that, she flung off the duvet and carefully got dressed. She could already smell the wonderful smell of baked goods and coffee coming from the kitchen. Saying "yes" to Emma had been a no brainer but three strapping young men who could eat through their food stores was entirely different.

Karen stomped downstairs. "I'm going to kill that rooster and roast him one of these days!" Every day she threatened the same thing and Henry always lived to see another day. Karen had a soft place in her heart for all animals, no matter how annoying.

She grabbed a biscuit off the cooling rack to tide her over until breakfast and followed Samuel out to the barn to take care of the livestock and collect the day's eggs.

Rachel sat carefully on the barstool in front of the kitchen island that Samuel had made for her, watching Emma knead dough. Three other loaves were already cooling as well as a variety of biscuits. On the stove a large cast iron pan contained what had to be an entire slab of bacon, in another was fried potatoes and another scrambled eggs. Rachel helped herself to a biscuit and poured herself a cup of coffee. "We could have our own little bake shop here and call it Emma's treats!" She remarked casually, lifting the bun to her mouth.

"*Jah!* And a place of refuge for all the other kids like me who left and have no other place to go anymore." Emma nodded.

Rachel froze in mid-bite. "What did you say?"

"A half-way house for ex-Amish," Emma replied.

"No, what did you say before?"

"A place of refuge?"

"Yeah, *that*. Where did that come from?"

"*Och*, it just popped into my head…"

The service porch door opened and slammed shut. Karen reappeared. "They beat me to it," she grumbled.

"Who did what?" Rachel wanted clarification.

"Larry, Moe, and Curly…they were already in the barn tending to the animals when I got there. They said to tell you that they're starving. I got up before dawn for *nothing!*"

"You mean Abram, Aaron and Amos?" Emma was trying not to smile at the Three Stooges reference.

"Yeah…*them*."

"What about the eggs?" Rachel asked.

"They did that too."

Rachel stifled a giggle. She knew that collecting eggs was a woman's job in the Amish community and the fact that the boys had done it themselves was further proof of just how desperate they were to make a good impression.

Samuel reappeared, followed by the three boys to clean up on the service porch. They had finished the morning chores in record time and were famished. They stood awkwardly, waiting to be invited in, eyeing the kitchen table that only had four places as well as the platters of steaming food.

Rachel carefully slipped off her stool and beckoned to them. "You can all sit here for the time being until we have a larger table," she pointed to the kitchen island.

They all nodded and took their seats obediently.

Samuel removed his hat, bowed his head, and offered up a vocal prayer. "*Der Herr*, thank you for these boys and the hard work they put in this morning. We thank you for the food You provide so generously and that You would give us wisdom on making Second Chance Inn a place of refuge for these wayward *jungen und mädchen*."

The instant she heard "refuge" come out of Samuel's mouth a wave of euphoria swept over Rachel. The Lord had heard her prayers and had answered swiftly, leaving no room for doubt! She was bursting to tell Samuel but decided to wait until they were alone after breakfast.

Every ounce of food was swiftly consumed without the usual leftovers.

Rachel handed Karen a dishtowel. "Well, Karen – since you got deprived out of your livestock and eggs duties this morning, you can help Emma clean up from breakfast before you go on your delivery rounds."

"Oh, *may I?*" Karen opined sarcastically, imitating her late father. Samuel gave her a warning look and cleared his throat loudly. Karen made no further comment and began collecting the plates.

Rachel grabbed his hand and led him out to the *Dawdi Haus.* "We need to talk!"

He followed her in and as soon as the door was shut, gathered her into his arms and gave her a kiss that melted her insides to butter.

She kissed back then pushed him away gently. "I was being serious!" she smiled.

"So was I," he murmured and gave her another swoon-worthy kiss that almost rendered her incapable of thought.

"Will you please *stop*! I can't think!"

Samuel chuckled warmly but still held her tightly in his arms. "*Och*, go ahead now, *mein liebling*[10]. You are walking much better!"

"I had a dream last night, a dream I remember vividly and that isn't usually the case."

Samuel's face grew serious. "So did I."

"No! Really?"

"*Jah.*"

"You go first, then."

"I was dreaming about the *Dawdi haus,* I was working with the three lads on expanding it only it was much larger than I thought we should make it."

Gooseflesh rose all over Rachel's body and the hairs on the back of her neck were standing up. "And?"

---

[10] My darling

"We put a sign over the door, but I can't remember what it said…"

"Let me guess, did it have the word refuge in it?"

Samuel stared at her, his eyes going wide, his eyebrows climbing into his hairline. "*Jah*," he choked. "A place of refuge."

They stared at each other in shock and awe for a long moment. "I believe *Der Herr* is trying to tell us something."

"Ya think?" grinned Rachel, "we're going to have to really think this through if it's going to work. We will have to have rules set up in advance, what we expect of them in exchange for a place to live, food and what will happen if they don't fulfill their end of the bargain."

"You forget that we now have three young men and a young lady added to this number. We can't put them all under the same roof."

"Well, for now, Emma and Karen can continue to bunk together. They seem to get along well, but you're right. We should have expanded living quarters!"

"For the time being, I can clear out most of the furniture to make room for additional beds." Samuel offered, looking around at the small dwelling. "I'll have the boys get started on making frames for the bunk beds."

"I think we should take the spring wagon into town to do some shopping, you are going to need to get mattresses and bedding. I can follow in my car."

Samuel tipped his hat to her and went to the barn to get Molly hitched up to the wagon.

Rachel sat down and started making a list of what they needed when Abram, still in his ill-fitting suit, approached her. Rachel looked up and smiled at him.

"*Mamm*, I guess we'll all be going now," he said miserably.

"No need," Rachel replied. "We believe the Lord wants you here so all three of you can stay."

At this Abram's eyes went wide and filled up with tears of relief. "Really?" he choked, unable to believe his good fortune.

"There will be rules and boundaries you will all have to agree to in writing first, of course," Rachel replied.

"Anything! Everything!" Abram grinned, wiping the tears away with his knuckles.

Rachel looked at his suit. "Do you have any other clothes to wear besides those?"

"*Jah*, but they are all filthy and smelly," he replied, obviously ashamed. "I have them in a trash bag.

"Well bring it onto the service porch and tell Aaron and Amos to do the same. I'm going to teach you how to use the washer and dryer."

Abram looked terrified as though she had asked him to slay a dragon. He wheeled around and went in search of the other two young men who soon returned with their own trash bags filled with smelly clothes.

Rachel led them to the service porch. "Dump all your clothes onto the floor in separate piles," she instructed. As soon as the clothes were out of the bags her eyes began to water from the smell. "Sort them into groups: whites, darks, and colors. Now each one of you will take turns washing first your white clothes and put them into the washers. Whites are washed with hot water with nonchlorine bleach." She showed them where to put the soap, fabric softener and bleach. They watched then did as instructed. "When those loads are done, you will put your dark clothes into the other washers and wash them in cold water. The machines will beep when they're done. Then they go into separate dryers on the "normal" setting." There are hangers on that pole you can put the shirts on, so they don't wrinkle. The pants, socks and underthings get folded and put into those baskets. Just make sure you keep your items separate from each other." She glanced at each one of them. They each resembled a *deer caught in the headlights*, overwhelmed by the complicated instructions, but they nodded obediently. "If you aren't sure, then ask Emma."

These words elicited sighs of relief.

Samuel reappeared. "Ready?"

"Yup, let me grab my purse, coat and pillow." She pointed at the boys. "Do you need anything while we're out?"

They all shook their heads "no."

"Okay, but if you think of anything here is my cell phone number. We have a landline you can use over there."

Samuel helped her out the door and Rachel wondered if she would return to find the boys had turned all their clothing into pink, Barbie-sized clothes when she returned.

They returned hours later. Samuel's spring wagon was loaded with wood, fasteners and mattresses and Rachel's car was crammed with several sets of twin sheets, pillows and men's pajamas, robes, slippers and winter coats she had gotten on sale. She didn't want the young men traipsing around in the cold *dawdi haus* or barn freezing to death. In their vast pile of clothes, she hadn't noticed anything of the kind and decided to augment their attire.

They were quick to help Samuel unload his wagon and even Amos, the toughest looking of the bunch, had to wipe away a tear from his eyes when he saw his new clothing, not expected to receive such generosity from a total stranger.

"How did your laundry turn out?" Rachel asked them.

They all grinned triumphantly at her.

"*Gut*! Emma showed us how to fold them and they are sitting in laundry baskets until we have someplace to put them." Aaron volunteered. His eyes looked hopeful.

Rachel gave them a smile. "We have some good news for you, but we'll discuss it after dinner. Right now, I need you three to help Samuel build some bunk beds and get some bicycles cleaned up and do some additional maintenance for our Inn guests."

They all stared at her, as if not believing in their good fortune. "We can stay?" asked Abram.

"That will depend on whether you agree to our rules," Samuel said.

"Absolutely! Whatever you want!" Amos replied.

"We will be putting them in writing for each of you to sign as a contract later today." Rachel said, looking each one in the eyes kindly. "Right now, go ahead and have lunch and then you can all start helping Samuel on those bunk beds."

Hours later, with the input of both Emma, Samuel and even Karen, Rachel had a contract typed up for each of the boys as well as for Emma to sign.

In exchange for room and board and compensation determined by Samuel Miller and Rachel Winston, I ____________________________ do hereby promise and agree that I will abide by the following rules:

1. *I agree to fulfill all requests for work required of me in a timely and thorough manner.*
2. *I agree to do my very best in everything I am asked to do.*
3. *I agree to refrain from using foul language (in either English or German) while on the premises.*
4. *I agree to never profane the Lord's name in either word or deed.*
5. *I agree to refrain from fraternizing with the opposite sex while on the premises and to never enter the dwelling of the opposite sex.*
6. *I agree to dress modestly and respectfully and that my hair will be well groomed and of its natural color.*
7. *I agree to knock before entering the Inn and only during business hours while guests are present.*
8. *I agree to never say or do anything that would make the Inn Keepers or Second Chance Inn look bad in the eyes of its guests.*
9. *I understand that any use of tobacco and drugs except as prescribed by a physician will result in immediate expulsion.*

I understand that any failure on my part to abide by both the letter and intent of these rules will result in my immediate expulsion from the property of Second Chance Inn.

Signed: _____________________________________

Emma, Abram, Aaron, and Amos read their contracts over carefully, asked their questions and when they felt that they completely understood what was expected of them, signed, and dated each one without hesitation.

Chapter Five

"A New Season"

It took Samuel and the boys just one week to rearrange the *Dawdi haus* and finish the furniture to accommodate all four of them.

The Inn was thoroughly cleaned from top to bottom and all the guest rooms filled with goodies and toiletries customized to each guest.

Rachel was feeling better and stronger every day, but she still could not do the amount of baking, cooking, and daily prep that was needed to keep the seven of them well-fed in addition to taking care of her Inn guests, so she delegated the lion's share of those chores to Emma who was more than happy to fill her shoes in that capacity. Every day that passed, Emma seemed happier, and more content. Rachel would frequently hear her humming or singing hymns under her breath as she worked dough or folded clothes.

Rachel awoke to the sound of hysterical laughter coming from the kitchen. She looked at the clock. Seven am.

What could be so funny at this hour? She got out of bed and slipped into her robe, curious.

She found Karen and Emma sipping coffee at the table; a paper map spread out before them.

"You have got to be kidding me!" Karen was choking on her laughter, tears running down her face.

"What is so funny?" Rachel wanted to know, pouring herself a cup of coffee.

"OMG, Mom – you won't believe the names of the towns around here!"

Emma stood up and shook her head at Karen, wiping her hands on her apron. "There's a *gut* explanation for each of them," she said.

"Oh, I bet!" Karen choked.

Rachel sat down. "Why are you looking at a map?"

Karen wiped tears from her eyes. "I wanted to see where I could expand my egg route around here and when I saw the names of the nearby towns, I just lost it!" She pointed to one on the map and Rachel's eyes got as big as saucers.

"Blue Ball?" She grabbed the map, unable to believe her eyes and put her hand over her mouth to suppress her own laughter.

"*Intercourse?*!!" Karen screamed with laughter, pounding the table and making the coffee cups jump. "*Fertility! Mount Joy? Lickdale?*!!! No wonder the Amish have so many kids! They're obsessed!"

Rachel was having a tough time suppressing her own laughter. She got out her phone and did a Google search then shoved it under Karen's nose, showing her the news article[11] about the explanation for lewd town names in Lancaster. "Look, they all have rational explanations just like Emma said! Get your head out of the gutter!" She glanced over at Emma whose shoulders were also shaking with laughter. "You're no help!"

Samuel chose that precise moment to enter the kitchen and found them all dissolved into giggles. "*Was ist so lustig*[12]?" He stared at Rachel, waiting for an answer.

She opened her mouth but all that came out was a scream of pain mixed with laughter, as she held her ribs; tears run-

---

[11] How did Intercourse, Bird-in-Hand and Blue Ball get their lewd-sounding names? | Local News | lancasteronline.com
[12] What's so funny?

ning down her face. She waved him off. "Explain later," was all she could manage.

"See! See!" Karen declared to Samuel. "I'm not the only one with my head in the gutter!"

He stared at her, thoroughly confused, "What are you talking about? *Was ist gutter?*"

Rachel abruptly changed the subject, hoping to spare her ribs any further strain. "Our guests will be arriving this afternoon at the train station from Philadelphia. Will they all fit in your six-seater with their luggage?"

"*Jah*, but you might want to follow in your car just in case,"

"Emma, rooms all ready?"

"*Jah*, Rachel. I was waiting to put fresh cut flowers in the vases until today."

"Great! You have the chickens dry brining?"

"*Jah*," Emma nodded, handing her the breakfast plates stacked high with hot pancakes and sausage. This was followed by a large bowl of fresh berries.

The boys came in from the barn, washed up on the service porch and took their seats.

Together they all bowed their heads in prayer and gave the Lord thanks.

"Starting this afternoon, you will all have to start taking your meals in the *Dawdi Haus*," Rachel said, while Emma loaded up their plates with fried potatoes, eggs, and sausages. "We have guests arriving today and the dining room is reserved exclusively for them."

The boys, Emma and Karen nodded. "*Jah, mamm*" came the chorus of agreement around the table.

When everything was eaten, Karen collected the plates without being asked.

"Rachel, I made a list of groceries we will need, we're going through them like crazy. You might want to start buying in bulk." Emma handed her the list.

Rachel looked it over then checked her bank balance. "This is coming close to cleaning me out for the month," she murmured. Her guests had paid their balance half up front, but the rest was not due until they checked out in week. At the rate the boys were consuming food, she was going to run out before she knew it. She shoved the list into her jeans pocket and gathered her canvas shopping bags, wondering where and how she was going to store all the food needed to sustain seven adults and four Inn guests.

"We need to do something about your car, Emma, it needs to be pushed off our driveway closer to the barn," said Rachel on her way to the door.

"We can push it there and I'll take a look at it," volunteered Amos. "I have some experience working on farm equipment and cars." He gave Emma a wink which made her blush.

"Alright, see what you can do. It would be good to have a second working vehicle around here."

Samuel was waiting in the driveway with the large buggy. Rachel got into her car, belted the pillow around her waist and headed out for the train station with Samuel following behind. It was a beautiful spring morning. The fields were turning green from the recent rains, the air was cool, and the sky was a forget-me-not blue with big puffy clouds.

"Thank you, Lord, for this beautiful day to welcome my guests," Rachel breathed. The beauty of the rolling hills and farmlands of Lancaster County never ceased to impress her with God's creative handiwork. She soon arrived at the train station parking lot and was getting the SECOND CHANCE INN sign out of the trunk when Samuel pulled up in his buggy and parked in the Amish section where he could tether his horse. He was wearing a blue work shirt and blue jeans and with his new haircut and clean-shaven face and could have easily passed for an *Englisch*. His appearance was in stark contrast to his mode of transportation, which was garnering many confused looks from both the Amish at the station as well as non-Amish.

Rachel linked her arms through his, further complicating the matter, and giggled. "They don't know what to make of either of us," she murmured. They walked out to the train platform and waited for the train.

"Why are you so fidgety?" Rachel whispered. Samuel was bouncing up and down on his heels and pacing quite a bit.

"Just anxious," he said, trying to smother a smile.

"Anxious about what?"

He smiled at her and shrugged which only made her that much more suspicious. Rachel had a notorious reputation in her family for being impossible to surprise and she could spot subterfuge a mile off.

"Okay, what's going on?"

Samuel refused to look at her. "Just waiting for our guests," he replied unconvincingly.

Rachel was given no further opportunity to cross examine him because a train horn sounded in the distance, signaling its arrival. The train soon came into view and rolled to a stop before them. Samuel held up the sign and pointed it towards the disembarking passengers.

A familiar face exited the train. Rachel could not believe her eyes. Screams of excitement erupted from her throat. "Janet! Janet!!" She hopped up and down, waving her arms frantically, running to close the distance to her best friend while holding her ribs. In her excitement she had forgotten all about her Inn guests. "Janet! Over here!" A tall, willowy brunette waved and walked over, her tall lanky husband, Ben, following behind. Rachel and Janet grabbed each other and embraced; both bouncing up and down with glee.

"*Ouch! Ouch! Ouch!*" The bouncing was not good for her ribs, but she did not care. "Oh, my gosh what are you doing here?" Rachel was crying and laughing at the same time.

At that moment, another couple ran up to them.

"*Rhonda*!!" Rachel screamed again, turning to embrace her very first Inn guest and her husband Charles.

Janet, Rachel, and Rhonda formed a joyous circle with Samuel, Ben and Charles looking on with smiles.

"Surprise!" Rhonda sang out. "We are your Inn guests for the next week too! We loved it so much in the winter we wanted to come back in the spring, just the two of us. We met Ben and Janet on the train and when we found out we were all staying at your Inn we became good friends!"

Rachel turned to Samuel. "Did you know about this all along?"

His grin was answer enough. Rachel threw herself upon him despite the pain and peppered his cheeks with hero kisses then turned back to her best friend of over ten years.

"The reservations said Mr. & Mrs. Jones and Smith!" She accused.

"We wanted to surprise you!" Janet smiled. We knew about the Inn opening and booked the first available week." Janet looked Rachel up and down, her face concerned. "How are you feeling? Are you all healed from your accident? We have been really worried about you!"

"Just some cracked ribs and bruising, praise the Lord!" Rachel replied, hooking her arm through Janet and Rhonda's while the men collected the suitcases. "Which would you rather ride in, my V-Dub or the wagon?"

"Oh, us girls need to catch up," Rhonda said. "The men can ride in the wagon with Samuel. I think I am just short enough to fit comfortably in the rear of your car."

The men returned with the luggage and helped Samuel to get everything loaded. The smaller suitcases went into the trunk or the backseat of the VW next to Rhonda. The bulk of the remaining suitcases were loaded onto the wagon.

"I can't believe you're both here!" Rachel said as they got into the car, wiping happy tears from her eyes. "You have no idea how much I've missed you both!" Rachel grabbed

Janet's hand. "And the weather forecast is supposed to be cool and sunny this week."

"So, tell us about Samuel," said Janet. "He can't seem to take his eyes off you. Is he Amish? He doesn't look like it. Don't they all wear beards? Start at the beginning and don't leave anything out!"

"I could see he was smitten with her during our visit last winter," Rhonda exclaimed.

"Where are your boys and Vivi?" Rachel asked Rhonda.

"We left them with my in-laws in Connecticut for Spring break," Rhonda replied. "Stop stalling and spill the beans!"

"Yes! Inquiring minds want to know!" Janet seconded.

"Okay," Rachel groaned then launched into an abbreviated summary of everything that had happened since she and Karen had arrived over nine months ago. She was just getting to the part about Samuel proposing to her when they arrived at the Inn.

Janet stepped out of the car. "OMG it's *tots adorbs*!!" she exclaimed. "I love the wrap-around porch with the hanging flower baskets and window boxes! And that red barn!!!"

"We hope to start serving afternoon tea on the porch soon," Rachel replied. "I have an Amish girl who used to work in a bakery helping me out and she's amazing!" Rachel opened the car doors and trunk. "I'm afraid I can't help you with the luggage, I'm still in a lot of pain."

Janet waved her off, "don't worry about it! The men can all take care of it!" She continued looking about, taking in the Inn, *Dawdi Haus*, barn and fields. "You know this would make a fabulous wedding and events venue!"

Janet and Rachel had met as students in the college program and had become fast friends. Rachel had earned both hospitality and culinary degrees while Janet had gone on to build a fabulously successful event planning business, focusing mainly on "platinum weddings" for those willing to spend a lot of money and was in high demand.

"I can see the wheels spinning in your head," Rachel commented as Janet took in the property.

"You could hold weddings in that barn, you know?" she said.

Rachel shook her head. "Out of the question, it houses our livestock and farm equipment and stinks to high heaven."

Janet turned around to face her. "Then why not build one just for weddings and events? You certainly have the property to do it! There's a lot of untapped potential here!"

Rachel blinked at her. She had not thought beyond just getting a successful Inn up and running and then the accident had happened.

Janet put her arm around Rachel's shoulder and pointed. "Right there is the perfect place for a wedding barn, outdoor patio, and wedding arbor! You can have string lights, decomposed granite on the ground, a portable dancefloor, it would be amazing!"

"You forget one thing," Rachel said. "I simply don't have the money to build all that. I'm just keeping my head above water as it is and…I just took on a young, former Amish woman and three young men who are eating me out of house and home!"

"Rachel, Janet is right! You need to think bigger!" Rhonda agreed.

"But the expense," Rachel protested.

"You let me worry about the expense," Rhonda said, taking Rachel into her arms. "I'm filthy rich and would just love to partner with you on this if you're willing!"

"Me too!" Janet seconded, "We could both partner with you to make this a wedding, event and resort destination!"

Tears sprang into Rachel's eyes. "Really? You would really want to take that big of a risk on me?"

"I already have the client base," replied Janet with a teary smile.

"…and I have a lot of wealthy friends who would love to come here if there were more rooms and amenities!" Rhonda added.

Rachel shook her head. "This is all moving too fast for me to keep up! First getting engaged to Samuel, then taking on these lost Amish youth and now this!"

"Speaking of marrying Samuel," interjected Janet. "Have you set a date yet?"

Rachel shook her head. "We've been waiting until I'm healed and then we were just going to go to the courthouse and get married there…"

"*Absolutely not!*" Janet exclaimed, horror-stricken. "Your BFF is a wedding planner extraordinaire! I forbid you to do this! Getting married in a deary courthouse, indeed! *UGH!* You are going to have a proper wedding! None of this courthouse stuff. How fast can those men of yours get a barn built?"

Rachel stared at her, confused. "I think Amish can raise an entire barn from start to finish in a week but that takes hundreds of them all working together," she replied, "We only have Samuel and the four boys. It would take months and months!"

"*Hmmmm*," Janet murmured. "Let me think about this a bit and discuss it with Ben. "He's part of a carpenter union, we may be able to get the labor you need."

"I could not afford to pay them," Rachel said. "…neither could I possibly let either of you shell out that kind of money for me."

Rhonda put her arm gently around Rachel's shoulders. "You let us worry about that, honey. In the meantime, let's start planning!"

Chapter Six

"Barns, Baked Goods and BFF's"

Rachel, Janet, and Rhonda entered the Inn.

"This is absolutely wonderful!" Pronounced Janet, looking around in admiration at the kitchen and large living room. Dried herbs hung from the wood ladder over the kitchen island, filling the room with the earthy smells of lavender, thyme, rosemary, oregano, and sage. The living room had a cozy river rock fireplace with comfortable seating all around and a large, tufted ottoman perfect for putting one's feet up on. On either side of the fireplace were built-in bookcases filled with books and on a nearby buffet table was a charcutier spread of various crackers, dried fruits, fig jam and a variety of soft and hard cheeses to welcome her guests.

Rachel summoned Emma from the service porch where she was loading the washer. "Emma, please welcome our guests. This is my best friend, Janet, from my college days and Rhonda. Rhonda and her family were our first guests here last Christmas."

"So nice to meet you!" Emma smiled, grasping their hands with a smile.

Rhonda sniffed the air. "What is that wonderful smell coming from the oven?"

Emma smiled, pleased. "Fresh popovers I've made for supper later," she replied.

Janet turned to Rachel. "If they taste as good as they smell, I think you're going to need a small bakery as well," she grinned. "And a commercial kitchen."

"My thoughts exactly," Rachel replied. "But my current priority is making you all comfortable. Let me show you to your rooms. The men should be arriving shortly with Samuel."

Rhonda and Janet followed Rachel up to the second floor to their respective rooms. Each room had a King-sized bed covered in a handcrafted Amish quilt, crisp white sheets, and goose down pillows. A vase full of fresh cut flowers stood upon each dresser. Next to the dresser was a large wicker hamper filled to the brim with toiletries and sundries specific to her guests. There were Amish, triple milled lavender and lemon soaps, bath salts, lotions, body butter, organic toothpaste as well as bottles of water and other Amish-made goodies. On the door hung two soft, white terry cloth robes and slippers.

Janet inspected the contents of her room hamper. "You thought of everything! I can't wait to try it all!"

"If I can impress you, I can impress anyone!" grinned Rachel, remembering what a stickler Janet was for perfection in their mutual classes together. Even the water bottles on display had to have all the labels facing in the exact same direction at meetings.

"I'm dying to dig into that charcuterie table," Rhonda enthused, leading the way back downstairs to the living room. "Let's fill up and take our plates out onto the wrap around porch and brainstorm about your wedding!"

Samuel, Ben, and Charles arrived half an hour later and found Rachel, Janet, and Rhonda ensconced on the front porch, deep in conversation, eating cheese, and crackers. They were giggling convulsively.

Rachel went to greet Samuel as he lugged several suitcases out of the large buggy and set them on the pea gravel walkway. She gave him a peck on the cheek. "Thank you!" she said as Ben and Charles joined their wives on the porch.

Charles admired the contents of his wife's loaded plate. "This looks great! Where do we get some?"

"Just inside there, please help yourselves!" Rachel pointed. "There's also iced lemonade and water."

The men needed no second invitation and went inside. Aaron, Amos, and Abram appeared and without being asked to do so, helped to carry all the luggage into the Inn and up the stairs to the guest rooms.

"Where did those strapping young men come from?" Rhonda wondered, chewing on a dried date. "They weren't here at Christmas."

"Long story," Rachel replied, "…but they and Emma were all godsends! I believe the Lord brought them all here just in the nick of time to help us. I would have had to cancel your reservations if it wasn't for them!"

"You just need about 93 more and you can have that wedding barn built in no time!" Janet commented.

"Wedding barn?" asked Emma.

"Yes, I think there is a lot of untapped potential here," Janet replied. "This property is perfect as a destination wedding venue contingent upon significant additions. I think Rachel and Samuel should be married here instead of at a dismal, courthouse counter, don't you think?"

Emma looked at Rachel. "Why the courthouse, if it's okay for me to ask?"

Rachel shrugged, "well, because I don't know anybody here; all of my family and friends are back in California. Samuel became an outcast because of me and has been shunned by his family so we were just going to keep it very informal and quick."

Emma nodded, "I understand." "But if you're serious about building a barn to have weddings in, I know a *gut* way you could get the help you need," she added.

Janet, Rhonda, and Rachel all stared at her in shock.

Janet leaned forward. "How?"

"Social media. I belong to a Facebook group of ex-Amish and Mennonite just like me who don't like the *English* world much either. There must be a couple thousand of them. I could create a post asking for craftsmen…"

Rachel held up her hand. "That sounds wonderful, but I don't have the means to pay them…"

"You could always set up a GoFundMe page and crowd fund it," Janet suggested.

"What is that?" Rhonda wanted to know. The term was unknown to her.

"It's like a charitable giving site where people can donate towards a cause, only it isn't tax deductible." Janet explained.

"Well, what are we waiting for?" Rhonda said, standing to her feet. "Let's get started!"

Rachel pulled Rhonda back down to her chair and grinned at her. "You forget that no technology is allowed at Second Chance Inn! I still need to confiscate your cell phones and laptops for the duration of your stay!"

"*But*" Rhonda protested.

"You did sign the consent form to do so, right?" Rachel grinned, wagging a finger at her.

Rhonda visibly drooped then brightened up and turned to Janet. "We'll just have to make a trip to the local library then, won't we?"

Janet nodded. "We aren't' giving up this easy, Rach! You're going to have a fabulous wedding no matter what! No BFF of mine is getting married at the courthouse! *PUH LEESE!*" She rolled her eyes in horror.

Rachel's guests sat back in their chairs with groans of delight and no small degree of discomfort. They had just finished a glorious dinner of roasted chicken, garlic popovers and broccolini. Even the women had eaten two each of the popovers.

Rachel gestured to all of them. "If you all want a special treat, follow me out to the front porch!"

Curious, her guests followed her out with Samuel bringing up the rear. The sky was deepening from violet to a deep blue on the horizon.

Rachel pointed down at the grass and bushes that banked up against her porch. "Look!" she whispered.

"Fireflies!!!" Rhonda exclaimed in delight.

"Oh, they are so beautiful!" Janet agreed, watching the tiny lights rise and wink out over and over.

Ben and Charles watched mesmerized. Samuel slid his arm gently about Rachel's waist and pulled her close, remembering the first time they had watched the fireflies together.

"It's so quiet here," whispered Janet. "So peaceful!"

There was a snort behind them. "Just wait until 5:00 am when Henry starts blowing his horn!"

"Karen!" Janet exclaimed in surprise, turning around to give her god daughter a hug. "How are you liking life here so far?"

Karen beamed, "much better than I expected to! I've gotten good at tending to the livestock, have my own egg delivery business and I'm seeing a cute Amish boy!" She leaned in and whispered the next part in Janet's ear. "Have mom show you the names of the towns around here!"

"Okay, Karen!" Rachel said, overhearing. "Let's not spoil the magic of the moment!"

"See you all at the crack of dawn tomorrow!" Karen sang out with a grin and went back into *the* house.

"Who's Henry?" asked Rhonda, thoroughly confused.

"Our rooster," Samuel replied. "*Kein Grund zur Sorge*[13], I put him somewhere out of the way when we have guests so they can sleep in."

"Could you do that on a regular basis?" Rachel grinned at him.

"…and deny Henry the satisfaction of doing his job?" Samuel smiled back.

"Feel free to sit out here on the porch or in the living room before the fire, I believe Emma has something special for dessert later, and of course freshly ground decaf coffee to go with it." Rachel went back inside, followed by Samuel.

"I don't think I could eat another bite," Rhonda said, sitting on the porch swing with Charles.

"Me either," Janet agreed, going to a rocking chair, next to her husband. "I'm not a sweets person."

Rhonda leaned towards her. "So, do you really think this could become a destination wedding venue?"

Janet nodded. "Absolutely, with the right amenities and staff." She gazed at the rolling farmland in the distance, the gardens, and the barn. "It's a beautiful setting and it's being underutilized."

"I don't know much about crowdfunding, but I have plenty of wealthy friends with children of marriageable age that would love to book a place like this!" Rhonda replied.

"Just leave all the details to me," Janet smiled at her. "As soon as everything is set up, I will give you the information and the online links you'll need to spread the word! I'm going to have a talk with Emma about that ex-Amish Facebook group she's a member of."

Rachel and Samuel stood side-by-side at the kitchen sink, rinsing and loading the dishes into the dishwasher while Emma served up her dessert of Apple Dumplings with vanilla ice-cream to the guests on the front porch.

---

[13] Not to worry

"None for me, Emma" smiled Janet, "but when you get a chance, I'd love to talk to you about that Facebook group you mentioned."

"*Jah*, of course," Emma smiled. "Let me just serve the boys some dessert and I'll come right back."

Emma returned to the kitchen and brought over a large pan of apple dumplings and a tub of ice cream to the *Dawdi haus* so the boys could have some. She returned to find Janet and Rhonda deep in discussion on the front porch while their husbands gorged on the dessert.

"Please sit," Rhonda gestured to another chair.

Janet spoke in hushed tones so Rachel could not overhear from the kitchen. "We were curious to know about this Facebook group of ex-Amish you told us about. How many are on there and what percentage of them do you think we could get to help build a wedding barn?"

Emma reached into her apron and took out her phone. "I can check for you right now," she said. After a moment she held up her phone so they could see.

"Whoa!" Janet exclaimed, her eyes going wide. "Really? Over 6,000?"

"I can't believe there are that many ex-Amish people!" Rhonda chimed in. "How many did Rachel say you needed to build a barn?"

"About one hundred," Emma replied. "If you can pay them for their work, I could create a post calling for laborers that are local. I'm sure they'd love the wages and camaraderie they used to enjoy from barn raisings."

Janet grinned at Rhonda and Emma. "Operation Miller Nuptials has officially begun!"

The following morning Rachel had scheduled her friends for a baking session with Emma as part of their accommodation package. The day had dawned grey with clouds that soon began to dump rain over the entire area. They all enjoyed a hearty breakfast of vegetable quiche, berries, piping hot coffee and orange juice. Samuel had taken the men with him to go turkey hunting earlier. They were all clad in camouflage outfits and loaded up with thermoses of hot coffee, hearty chicken sandwiches and apples while Aaron, Abram and Amos tended to minor repairs and the livestock. Karen had already left on her egg rounds.

"I'm going to see Willis when I'm done!" she informed her mother with a happy wave.

Since the men would be gone for a good part of the day and the weather was so miserable, Rachel thought Janet and Rhonda would appreciate learning how to bake Amish recipes.

The women took seats opposite Emma at the large kitchen island.

"Ben just loved the apple dumplings you made for us last night," Janet commented, sipping her coffee. "He wants me to learn to make them."

"I want to know how to make those orange glazed cinnamon rolls!" Rhonda added. "My kids specifically asked me to get the recipe."

Rachel handed out aprons. "I think we should have time for both with this weather," she replied.

The ladies donned their aprons. Janet put her hair into a ponytail, but Rhonda's short curly hair had become a glorious mound of curls from the humidity which were untamable. For the next several hours, they mixed, kneaded, and baked; talking and laughing together the entire morning while classical music played softly in the background and the fire crackled in the hearth. Emma was a wonderful teacher and soon the results of their efforts were baking in the oven.

Janet stared at the old-fashioned wood stove. "I'm amazed you're still using that!" she marveled.

"It was tough going for quite a while until an Amish woman taught me how to regulate the heat," Rachel replied then fell silent. The recent betrayal from Ruth Byler whom she had thought of as a friend, still smarted.

"What's wrong?" Janet asked, sensitive to Rachel's emotions.

Rachel wiped a tear away and waved off the question. "Another long story…"

"Oh, we're all ears!" Rhonda said, leaning forward on her elbows.

At that moment, the service porch door opened and slammed shut with a loud bang. Buddy ran and hid under the coffee table as Karen stomped into the room, her face blotchy red from crying.

They all turned to look at her. Karen was dripping wet, a puddle of water forming about her feet. The look of devastation on her face was clear to all.

"What's wrong, honey?" Rachel asked, approaching her with arms held out. Karen held up a hand to stop her, obviously not wanting to be hugged or comforted.

"It's Willis," she said, fighting to control her emotions. She was trembling from head to foot.

Rachel got a towel from the service porch and wrapped it around her. "What about Willis?"

Karen grabbed her sodden prayer kapp and flung it angrily to the floor. "He broke it off with me!" Her bottom lip was trembling, but she refused to give into her tears in front of them.

Rachel crossed her arms and just stared at her, saying nothing, waiting for Karen to elaborate. Secretly she was relieved, Karen was far too young to be serious with any boy.

"He says that I was taking too long to learn German and a bunch of other things. He broke up with me and then told me that he had formed "an attachment" (she held up quote fingers) with some other Amish girl called *UH MAN DUH!*" She spat the name out with disgust. Clutching the towel about her, she ran up the stairs and slammed her bedroom door. The room felt quiet.

Janet, Rhonda, and Emma all stared at Rachel who just shook her head.

"*Ummm,* what was that about?" Janet asked Rachel.

"It's *another* long story," Rachel sighed. "We probably shouldn't discuss it with Karen upstairs where she can hear me."

"Okay, then change of subject!" Rhonda said brightly. "Janet and I have been brainstorming with Emma and we think the wedding barn is entirely doable."

"Huh?" Rachel said a bit lost. She plopped down on a seat next to her friends and poured them all another cup of coffee.

"If you will grant me temporary internet access so I can use my laptop, I'm all prepared to set up a GoFundMe account for the wedding barn. Rhonda has already made up a healthy list of potential investors and future clients. Emma will post for Amish labor on her Facebook group as soon as we have the funding. I already did the preliminary calculations last night and I think you would need about $70,000 for a basic barn, more if you include a commercial kitchen and add guest accommodations in what would normally be the hayloft, which you should *definitely* should! If all goes according to plan and weather permitting, we all figure the barn could be ready in a few months and you and Samuel can be married in it!"

Rhonda bounced up and down in her chair with excitement, "Oh, Rachel! Please say yes!"

"You could invite your family and friends to stay here and have a family reunion for the wedding." Janet added.

Rachel stared at the two of them, tears flooding her eyes. "You would really do all this for me?" she wiped at her eyes, deeply touched.

Both women stood up to hug her. "Well of course, we're BFF's right?"

Rachel was overcome with gratitude. "If you really think it is doable, then let's go for it. I also think we should include a separate bakery for Emma. She told me she used to do wedding cakes for *English* customers so we can be an almost full-service wedding venue and Inn."

"…and I could learn to do flower arrangements," said Karen's voice from the stairs. "You have a great cutting garden, mom. I could take some online courses and watch YouTube videos…it will give me something to think about besides *Willis*." She joined them in the kitchen and helped herself to a freshly made cinnamon bun.

Rachel looked at each of them in turn, grateful for their friendship and determination to make her marriage to Samuel a memorable event. Then she had a sudden epiphany.

"Why don't we have the wedding in late November and combine it with Thanksgiving? It only makes sense if all my family and friends are going to come here anyway."

Rhonda went to the wall calendar in the kitchen and flipped it to the month of November. "The Sunday after Thanksgiving falls on the 22nd this year."

"You do realize that's the anniversary of JFK's assassination, right?" Karen piped up. Rachel stared at her daughter, not knowing how to respond. Karen shrugged and bit into the bun. "Just saying…"

Chapter Seven

"Heartache"

Karen entered the chicken coop, a dark cloud of misery hanging over her head, and allowed herself the luxury of a good cry away from questioning eyes.

It was bad enough that Willis had up and dumped her without any warning and in front of his entire family; but even worse that he had admitted to glomming on to another Amish girl without a second thought. It also didn't help that her mom and her friends were now planning a wedding when it should have been her and Willis planning theirs!

She plunked down onto an empty egg crate, put her face in her hands and finally succumbed to the sobs that had been welling up in her throat. *How could he do this to me?* She had really cared for him and thought he had loved her in return. She had shared things with him she had never told anyone else: deep emotional hurt, her feelings of abandonment that lingered because of the circumstances surrounding her adoption; the pain of losing her father. She had entrusted her heart and soul to him; thinking they would be together forever…and he had stomped all over it.

Karen's sobs became wails. She didn't know what to do with herself. She paced around in anguished circles inside the coop, crying and cussing a blue streak. She was heartbroken, betrayed, and angry all at the same time. She had put on a brave *I couldn't care less* face for her mom and her guests but deep inside she was unraveling. She had lost all hope and purpose. Her once bright and happy future with Willis now looked bleak and uncertain.

"I wished I'd never come here!" she spat. "I wish I was dead!"

"*Ach, du lieber*[14] don't say that!" said a male voice from the doorway.

Karen jumped, startled. "Who's there?" she demanded, wiping her eyes with her apron. A large male figure was silhouetted in the doorway.

"It's Aaron," he replied, stepping into the dim light of the kerosene lantern hanging from the roof hook.

"It's not nice to eavesdrop!" Karen snapped, mortified that she had been discovered. "What are you doing here? It's my job to take care of the chickens, you know, and I don't appreciate you horning in on my territory!"

Aaron chuckled, amused at her indignation. "It's *homing in* not "horning in" and wasn't eavesdropping," he said gently, stepping towards her. "I was just passing by and heard someone crying and wanted to make sure they...uh you are okay?"

His voice was kind and warm in contrast to his appearance. He was dressed in jeans and a work shirt, but his hair was still spiked and fading from purple to brown.

Karen shrugged, "thanks, but I'm fine!"

Aaron stepped closer, he was a good head and a half taller than her and very broad in the shoulders. "You didn't sound *fine*."

She reluctantly looked up at him and was surprised to see twinkling blue eyes, long lashes, and dimples. "Yeah, well, I just got dumped by Willis Hochstetler!"

Aaron snorted at the mention of his name. "*Ach*! Willis has a reputation for courting lots of girls and then moving on to someone else when he gets tired of them. You were just the latest shiny object...I wouldn't bother you're pretty

---

[14] Oh dear one

little head over it; you're in good company. *It's better to suffer wrong than to do wrong,*"

Karen felt insulted by the *pretty little* head inference and rolled her eyes. "Is that supposed to be some kind of Amish wisdom to make me feel better? Right now, I'd like to go back over there and let him suffer a little wrong!" She balled her fists and tried to march out of the coop, but a human wall stood between her and the exit.

"What?!" Karen screeched at him when Aaron refused to budge.

He threw his hands up in the air as if to surrender but he didn't move. "If it were me, I wouldn't give him the satisfaction,"

Karen frowned at him, but he continued to look down on her with kind eyes. "Yeah...well you're not me!" She stomped out of the chicken coop and back into the house, slamming the screen door behind her.

Her mom and guests all jumped at the sound and stared at her.

"Men!" Karen spat out by way of explanation and stomped up the stairs to her room, slamming the bedroom door.

"Should we wait while you go see if you can talk to her?" asked Rhonda.

Rachel shook her head. "If she wanted to tell me she would; Karen is pretty tight-lipped when it comes to her feelings, especially with me."

They all heard the service porch door open and shut and the voices of Samuel, Charles, and Ben all chuckling. The men had returned home from turkey hunting.

Rachel went to greet them. "I see you were all very successful today!" she smiled, eyeing the three wild Spring gobblers that Samuel held up with pride.

"We bagged our limit!"

"Roast turkey for dinner?" asked Charles hopefully. "We're starving!"

"Oh, I think we can accommodate that!" Rachel grinned as Emma arrived to collect the turkeys. She eyed the men whose camouflage attire was covered in mud. "We stowed some robes and slippers on hooks in the service porch so you can get out of your muddy camo gear. Just leave your dirty clothes and shoes on the porch so we can wash them." She shut the door behind her to give them privacy.

Rachel turned to Rhonda and Janet. "I'm going to set out some cheese and crackers to tide everyone over until dinner is ready,"

"I'm going to head upstairs for a nap, while the men shower," Janet smiled. "See you in a bit."

"Me too," said Rhonda with a yawn. "I never get naps at home, but it sounds divine!" She followed Janet upstairs.

Samuel entered the room and looked around clad in his robe and slippers. "I put all the dirty clothes into the washer," he said. "But I didn't start it."

Rachel exhaled in relief, "Thank goodness! That's all I need is for that expensive camouflage to be shrunk down to GI-Joe size. "What about the boots?"

"They're outside, the boys are hosing them down. I'm going to take a shower."

"Good idea!" Rachel looked him up and down and pinched her nose with a grin. His face was painted in camo colors, and she could smell him from a distance.

Samuel closed the distance in two strides and took her in his arms.

"*Ewwww*, you stink!" she laughed as he nuzzled her earlobe, "and you're making me stink!"

"*Du riechst lecker*[15]," he murmured, his lips closing over hers. Despite his rank odor Rachel could not help but melt into him. His kisses turned her spine into jelly.

She gently pulled away, "Go wash up, I've got to get the afternoon charcuterie spread set up."

"Ach, you mean the cheese and crackers?" Samuel chuckled. Such a fancy word!"

---

[15] You smell delicious

"Fancy word for fancy cheese!" Rachel replied. "This isn't cheese whiz I'm serving!"

"I like cheese whizz," Samuel threw over his shoulder as he exited the house.

Rachel found her guests out on the wrap around porch again at sunset, munching on cheese, crackers, and dried fruits in anticipation of another firefly show.

The four of them were seated on the rocking chairs, talking quietly amongst themselves.

"Supper should be ready in a couple of hours," she said. "We are serving roast turkey, of course, along with sauteed green beans, and home-made egg noodles. For dessert we have chocolate whoopie pies."

Ben chuckled. "Whoopie pies?" He had never heard the term before. "Did Whoopie Goldberg invent a dessert?"

Charles turned to him. "Trust me, you'll love them!"

Rachel consulted her phone. "Tomorrow should be a good day for your bike ride, the weather is supposed to be clear and cool, and the bikes have been tuned up and are ready to go. I have a route all mapped out for you with places of interest including the Kurtz's Mill Covered Bridge. I can pack you a picnic lunch if you want. If you get too tired or have any problems, just message me and we will come pick you up."

"That sounds great," Janet said then hushed as the fireflies began to come alive and float above the grass. They all watched in rapt silence until the sky grew dark and one by one the little lights winked out.

"Charles and I are going to do a little shopping in town, tomorrow" Rhonda said. "Any recommendations?"

"Well, if you like the toiletries in your room the Garden Path Soap and Herbal shop is right here in Bird-in-Hand. There's also Kettle Kitchen Village in Intercourse,"

Rhonda's eyes went as big as saucers. "I beg your pardon," She stared at Rachel. "Did you say *Intercourse?*"

Rachel could feel her face flaming. "That's the name of the town," she managed.

Rhonda burst into screams of laughter so loud that Buddy went to hide under the porch.

They all stared at her, but her laugh was so infectious the rest of them could not help but laugh along with her. Karen came running downstairs.

"What's so funny?"

Rhonda was unable to respond. Karen's question just made her double over and laugh louder.

"The name of the major town nearby," Rachel replied.

Karen's face instantly lit up with a big grin. "That's not all!" she said, "there's also Blue Ball, Mount Joy—"

Rhonda's screams of laughter became deafening. She rushed from the room, up the stairs and into the bathroom, slamming the door behind her. They could still hear her laughing and choking from downstairs.

"She has a weak bladder," Charles said with a grin. "Three kids."

"I'm going to check on dinner," Rachel said, wiping tears of mirth from her eyes. Samuel followed her into the kitchen which was filling with the savory aroma of roast turkey.

"It didn't seem to hurt when you laughed just now… progress!" he murmured into her ear as he exited through the service porch. He favored her with a wink and a smile that made his meaning clear. "The lads and I will eat in the *Dawdi Haus*,"

Rachel looked at her large farmhouse table, pleased with the setting. It had a fresh white tablecloth on it, pale green plates, cloth napkins tied with raffia string and sprigs of lavender. Small white candle votives flickered bathing the room in a soft, golden light. The turkey lay on a large oval platter, golden brown and smelled mouth-watering.

"This looks amazing!" Janet enthused, taking her seat, and inhaling deeply. "It smells even better!"

Rhonda and Charles came downstairs and sat across from them at the communal table while Rachel brought the green beans and noodles over.

Rhonda addressed Rachel. "So, in addition to building a wedding barn and additional accommodations, we need to discuss your wedding dress!"

Rachel placed the food on the table and stared at her. "I honestly have not given it any thought. I don't think it would be appropriate to wear white under the circumstances, since it's our second marriages."

"Well, I want to design one for you," Rhonda smiled.

"Design?" Rachel repeated.

"Didn't I ever tell you?" Rhonda replied. "I'm not only a master seamstress, but I'm also a clothing designer. I'm based in New York, of course, but also have fashion houses in Paris and Milan."

Janet stared at her. "I thought you looked familiar! I've seen your clothes featured in Vogue and Marie Claire!" She turned to Rachel and pointed at Rhonda. "She's *famous*!"

"Also highly in demand," Rhonda grinned. "I have been wanting to start a wedding line and your dress could be the first! We can call it the '*Rachel*'!"

Rachel's head was spinning. "I can't afford you!" she bleated.

Rhonda caught Rachel's hand in hers. "Who said anything about money? We're friends, aren't we?"

"Yeeesss, but…"

"No buts! You'll ruin all my fun! I brought my sketch book with me and have been doodling, but you will need to let me know what you do and don't like."

Rachel was overcome with emotion. "Um, okay but first things first; let's just eat dinner first and we can talk about it on the porch afterwards." She knew that Rhonda came from money but had just assumed it was Charles that was the breadwinner. Rhonda James. She would have to *Google* her when she got a chance.

Rachel led grace and while her guests dug into the meal, went to her computer in her small office and did a quick search. She got almost 10,000 hits on Rhonda James + fashion designer. She clicked on images of her designs and her mouth dropped open. Just one of her pieces sold for over $10,000!!! Now she really felt uncomfortable! She re-entered the dining room to find Janet and Rhonda with their heads together, deep in conversation. She made a U-turn and went out the service porch over to the *Dawdi haus*. There she found Samuel and the boys around their table, consuming their turkey and sides as only ravenous men could.

"Samuel, could I have a word with you?" she beckoned.

He wiped his mouth and stood up, visibly concerned.

"*Jah, was is los*[16]?" He took her hand, and they went outside. It was a bit chilly, so he wrapped her in his arms.

"I don't know what to do," she murmured against his chest. "Rhonda wants to design me a wedding dress and they both want to help us build a wedding barn with additional accommodations, maybe even a bakery for Emma. They want to crowd fund everything…and…and… things are just moving too fast for me! I had no idea Rhonda was a famous and rich fashion designer! I feel weird letting her design a dress for me and not allow me to pay for any of this either."

Samuel tilted her chin up to him so she could look him in the eyes. "Do you count these women as clients or friends?"

"Oh, definitely friends!" Rachel replied. "I just don't want them to ever feel like I was taking advantage of them,"

"Did you ask for these things?"

Rachel shook her head, "Of course not!"

---

[16] What's going on?

"Then they are doing it out of the kindness of their hearts because they love you, *jah?*"

Rachel nodded. Samuel pulled her closer. "Kindness when given away, keeps coming back," he whispered into her ear. "Allow your friends the joy of doing this for you… for us. They do it out of love,"

"You make it sound so simple," Rachel replied, snuggling closer. She looked back up at him. "So, what do Amish brides wear?"

"A simple dress in blue or lavender, but you would not be an Amish bride."

"Well, I can't wear white, and blue is my favorite color…" She smiled up at him, suddenly shy. "Am I your bride?"

His answer was to close his mouth over hers and kiss her tenderly. "Soon you will be," he whispered.

Chapter Eight

"Haute Couture"

The next morning, Rachel's guests were up early.

A magnificent spread of scrambled eggs, country ham, a variety of muffins, cottage fried potatoes and melons greeted them as well as coffee and orange juice. Samuel and the boys had already eaten theirs while it was still dark after tending to the livestock. Now they were out in the fields with Samuel for the spring planting. Karen was already gone on her egg rounds.

Janet heaped her plate high while Rachel poured coffee and juice all around. "Did you sleep well?"

Janet nodded. "I slept really well! I usually toss and turn for hours at home. I wish I could bottle this place and take it home with me!"

Rhonda and Charles came downstairs and ogled the food. "I'm going to have to go on a diet after this," she proclaimed. "Your food is just too good! I never eat like this at home. I usually subsist on black coffee and protein bars."

She filled her plate and sat down. "You disappeared while we were eating dinner last night. Is everything okay?"

Rachel nodded. "I'm just a bit intimidated now that I know that you're a bigwig fashion designer," she laughed. "I knew you were wealthy, but I had no idea that you're also world renown!"

"I'm just Rhonda to you, Rachel. Now…have you given any thought to your wedding frock?"

"Let's discuss it after you've had your breakfast, okay?"

Rhonda wagged a finger at her. "Okay, but no more procrastinating after that!"

The bicycles were waiting for Janet and Ben on the front porch and outfitted with baskets, panniers and a mount for their cell phones so they could use GPS to navigate. A picnic hamper and thermos were strapped to the rack over their back fenders. They came out in their bike riding gear including the helmets provided for them by Rachel. The sky was a brilliant blue, with puffy white clouds.

With happy smiles and waves, they pedaled off down the long driveway and out onto the small two-lane road with a warning to beware of the deep drainage ditches on the side of the road.

Rhonda grabbed ahold of Rachel's hand and led her out onto the porch. She laid her sketch pad on the table and took out a black marker. "The shops don't open for another couple of hours so that will give us some time, while Charles reads the Wall Street Journal," she grinned. "Tell me what you envision,"

Rachel shrugged. "Well, I did some research, and I although I am not Amish, I think I would like the dress to honor Amish brides, I think Samuel would like that."

"What do they wear?" Rhonda asked, instantly curious.

Rachel held up her phone to display photo images; most of them were from various book covers of Amish fiction since the Amish did not take photos of themselves, even at weddings. "It would be similar to this only they wear blue or purple for their weddings."

"The most chaste people on earth wear blue *not white?*" Rhonda exclaimed in disbelief.

"Yup, but since I don't plan to wear white either and blue is my favorite color it all works out."

"Let's discuss design, the fabric choice will come later and depend upon the final design anyway."

"Definitely modest!" Rachel said. "Nothing too low cut and below the knees, maybe ¾ length sleeve?"

Rhonda began sketching. "You have a very small waist! How did you manage that?"

"I could never get pregnant," Rachel blushed. "We adopted Karen when she was a little girl."

"I never would have guessed, she looks a lot like you," Rhonda replied, still sketching. "The design should accentuate your waist. I think an A-line dress would really suit you. Something very fitted around the bodice with a full skirt; something very Grace Kellyish. Will you be wearing a hat?"

"I hadn't thought of it, the Amish wear *prayer kapp*s so I suppose a hat wouldn't be out of line."

Rhonda sketched faster, her enthusiasm for her craft bubbling to the surface. Rachel waited patiently, and then Rhonda turned the drawing pad around to show her.

Rachel was speechless. Rhonda had created a dress that could have been on Audrey Hepburn in Breakfast at Tiffany's or Funny Face. She had even hinted at Rachel's features in her drawing and topped it with a small but stylist hat with a netting covering just the eyes. "What do you think?" Rhonda grinned.

"I think it's amazing!" Rachel replied, leaning forward to hug her. "I believe Samuel will just love it! I just hope I will do your creation justice!"

"One thing about my designs," Rhonda said, adding a few more details to the sketch, "the woman wears the dress, not the other way around! You will look absolutely fetching my dear friend! Next, I need to take your measurements and then we will go shopping for the perfect fabric. I'm going to sew this myself! It has been an age since I've gotten behind a sewing machine and I miss it!" She held up a cloth measuring tape. "Never leave home without it," she grinned. "Stand up!" she commanded. "We will need some privacy for this next part; where's your bedroom?"

Rachel led her inside, closed the door then stripped down to her bra and panties so Rhonda could get accurate measurements. For the next fifteen minutes, she measured, re-measured and took copious notes on every square inch of Rachel's body until she was satisfied. "I'll work on the pattern when I get back to New York and make a muslin first to fit on you before I cut the actual fabric back in my workshop."

"Rhonda?" called Charles from the living room. "Almost ready to go?"

"Coming!" Rhonda said and gave Rachel a hug. "You're going to be a beautiful bride!" she said, kissing her cheek.

"I'm going to need bridesmaids," Rachel smiled, tears of gratitude filling her eyes. "Better include yourself and Janet in the wedding party!"

"*Ooowww* how fun! I'll just have to make dresses for us to compliment yours as well. Do you have a color in mind?"

"Sage green?" Rachel replied.

"My absolute favorite!" Rhonda smiled, gathering her things. "Are there fabric stores nearby?"

"Tons of them," Rachel nodded. "The Amish make all their own clothes and some pretty fabulous quilts so you should have no trouble finding material."

"We'll see," replied Rhonda over her shoulder. "I have something in particular in mind and it's not cotton poplin!"

Karen returned from her egg rounds late that morning, depressed. Her route took her past the Hochstetler farm where she could see Willis in the fields with his father and brothers. She rode past without stopping, her heart still smarting from his rejection.

Aaron met her in front of the barn. "Hey," he greeted her, tying Molly up to the hitching post. "I can take care of her from here," he offered. His smile was kind.

Karen shifted uncomfortably. "Well, okay, thanks!" She turned and went to get the empty egg crates.

"I'll take care of those too," he said.

"Thanks," Karen replied again, not knowing what else to say.

He tipped his hat to her and removed the buggy shafts from Molly's harness.

Karen turned and went into the house to see what Emma was up to but snuck a glance over her shoulder. Aaron was still smiling at her. *Dang! Caught me!*

She found Emma in the kitchen, preparing more popovers and loaves of bread.

"Can I help?" Karen asked, removing her cape.

"*Jah*! You like to bake?" Emma smiled.

"I'm not sure, I haven't done much baking, but I would like to know how. I sure love to eat it!"

"Me too! Go wash up and you can help me with the popovers."

Karen swiftly washed up on the service porch and came back, tying on an apron. "I overheard that you've done wedding cakes too for people like us."

"*Jah*, I've done quite a few. I took lessons in fondant and icing and got to be highly creative with cakes once I got the hang of it," Emma smiled.

Together they mixed the ingredients and poured the batter into the popover tins and set them into the oven.

"So, are you going to make my mom's wedding cake?"

Emma wiped her hands dry on a clean dishtowel and floured the board for the loaves that had been proofing. "She hasn't asked me yet, but if she does, I would be happy to. She has done so much for me! Now, do as I do." She took her fist and punched it into the dough that had risen in the greased bowl. Karen followed suit. "Now we turn it out and knead."

They kneaded in silence for a few minutes.

"I think I want to make her bouquets," Karen announced. "I've been watching YouTube instructional videos, and it doesn't look too hard. Maybe I can take an online course..."

"I think that would make your *mamm* very happy," Emma whispered with a catch in her voice.

Karen watched tears flood Emma's eyes. "Did I say something wrong?"

Emma shook her head. "I just miss my family so much," she whispered, wiping the tears before they could plop onto the dough.

"What happened?" Karen asked.

"I was excommunicated," Emma replied.

"Oh," replied Karen. She knew what that meant because of what had happened to Samuel. "But you haven't done anything wrong, have you?"

"*Ach jah!*" Emma stepped away from the island, her shoulders beginning to convulse with sobs. "I left on *Rumspringa* and never returned to get baptized, breaking my *eltern's* hearts. I did things I'm not proud of, knowing I would be shunned. The last time I saw my parents they shut the door in my face and said they had no *tochter!*"

"That's so harsh!" Karen replied, shocked. "Can't they just forgive you if you ask them?"

Emma shook her head. "It doesn't work that way in our community. Unless I repent and return to obeying the *Ordnung* I am not welcome. I just can't live like that anymore and I can't make it in the *English welt either!*"

"Which is how you wound up here?" Karen asked.

Emma nodded, dabbing at her eyes with the corner of her apron. "*Der Herr* lead me here. It was a miracle, Karen, a real miracle! I had no money, no place to go, no food or water, and my car died on the road outside your driveway. I was pleading with *Der Herr* to help and that's when I saw the

Inn sign. Your *mamm* took me in, no questions asked! She is a very rare and kind person especially considering how I look."

Karen took this all in, her head spinning. She had always heard her mother spouting off about the Lord and the Bible and had never taken it very seriously, thinking her mom was just a bible thumper, but Emma's account had her rethinking everything. It could not just be only mere coincidence that Emma had showed up right when her mom returned home unable to do anything. She and Samuel had been at their wit's end waiting on her mom to return home and continue on as before and disheartening when she couldn't because of her injuries.

They returned to their kneading. Emma tried to concentrate on baking and Karen on processing what she had heard.

"So are Larry, Moe and Curly excommunicated too like you?

Emma snorted at Karen's description, smiling through her tears. "*Ach*, yes. The led even wilder lives than I did and that's saying a lot."

"Even nerdy Abram?" Karen asked.

"*Jah*, even him, don't let appearances fool you. He got into a lot of trouble before coming here."

Karen leaned in, curious. "What *kind* of trouble?" She loved gossip.

"Never you mind, now…tend to your kneading!" Emma retorted, squashing the topic.

"Spoil sport," Karen grumbled.

They finished the bread and soon had the loaves baking in the oven.

"Let's make the men some sandwiches and take them out to the fields," Emma suggested. "They're probably hungry again."

"Okay," Karen agreed. She was curious to see Aaron again.

Together they made two hearty meatloaf sandwiches for each, a thermos of ice-cold Gatorade, grapes and left-over whoopie pies from the night before. They got everything packed up and walked out to the nearest field where the men were planting corn. Although it was cool out, they were sweating profusely as they poked holes in the newly turned earth and dropped corn by hand into each row.

"Lunch!" Karen announced, holding up the hamper. She gazed at the vast field, ogling the number of rows they still had left to plant. "Isn't there an easier way to do this?"

Samuel mopped his neck with his kerchief. "*Nein*, I don't own mechanized farm equipment. Planting by hand ensures proper placement."

Aaron reached for the picnic hamper and gave her a smile. "*Danki* for the food, did you help make it?"

Karen nodded at him, suddenly feeling awkward and not knowing what to say.

Aaron winked at her and walked away, the other boys following in his wake, trying to get at the food.

Emma grabbed her arm, "let's go, Karen, we have laundry to take care of and we need to get the rooms made up."

"Oh...*joy*." Karen dead-panned, allowing herself to be pulled back to the house. "More housework! I wish my mom was back to normal!"

"*An ounce of work is worth a ton of wishing*," Emma replied automatically. "Your *mamm* is still recovering; it is my honor to help her! *Tag*! You're it!" She poked Karen and took off at a run to the house, Karen on her heels, laughing despite herself, having no clue that behind her in the field Aaron was watching her as he ate his lunch.

Janet and Ben returned late in the afternoon from their bike ride, sweaty but exhilarated.

Rachel met them on the front porch and poured lemonade into tall glasses. "How was your ride?"

"It is so beautiful here!" Janet exclaimed, parking her bike. The route you gave us was wonderful and those covered bridges! It reminded me of that book, *The Bridges of Madison County*! We took dozens of photos but I'm tired and need a shower."

"Me too," Ben said, joining them on the porch. "I can see why you love it here, it's so peaceful."

"Your rooms are all made up with fresh sheets and dinner will be early tonight so there will be no afternoon appetizers. We're having roast lamb, rosemary popovers, and roasted Brussel sprouts with butternut squash."

"What about dessert?" Ben asked eagerly.

"An Amish specialty, Shoofly pie."

Janet wrinkled her nose.

"It's not what you think!" Rachel exclaimed.

"I'm game for anything," Ben replied, mounting the stairs. "After that ride the more carbs and sugar the better!" He grabbed Janet's hand and pulled her up the stairs. "Shower time, then a nap before dinner!"

Janet followed him upstairs, smiling despite herself.

Rachel's guests meandered out onto the front porch to watch the nightly dance of the fireflies. It had become a favorite ritual at the Inn after a long day and a great meal.

"I'm going to have to let all of my pants out after this trip," Rhonda sighed.

Rachel handed her and Janet both glasses of red wine and the three of them sat down in the rocking chairs to chat.

"Well, I've done a lot of thinking today while Charles and I were out shopping, and I think Janet's plan to crowd-fund the barn and Emma's bakery is a fabulous idea. When do we get started?"

Janet looked at Rachel. "Just say the word, BFF."

Rachel squirmed a bit, uncomfortable with the enormous generosity of her friends. "Are you sure you want to do this? This is going to take a lot of time and effort on your part! What about your businesses?"

"This will be a boon to my business," Janet assured her. "My clients have been clamoring for wedding barns and there just isn't enough of them to go around."

"And I'm going to launch my own line of wedding dresses in my couture business," Rhonda assured her. She leaned forward and grasped Rachel's hands in hers. "Please let us do this for you…it will be so much *fun!*"

A large lump of emotion stuck inside Rachel's throat; moved by their selfless offers. She nodded "yes;" grateful tears swimming in her eyes.

Chapter Nine

"Wedding Plans and Rope Swings"

For the remainder of their stay, Samuel took the men out for horseback riding, fishing, and another round of hunting while Janet, Rhonda, and Rachel brainstormed.

Despite the rules of her Inn, Rachel granted them one day of internet access so they could set up the GoFundMe page, contact prospective donors and create a post on the Facebook group to find local construction help. The response was almost immediate, and they were all busy fielding responses for raising the wedding barn. Rachel scheduled an appointment with her general contractor to start on the plans.

It was a blur of activity with the week ending all too soon for all of them.

Rachel stood on the front porch, unable to staunch the flow of tears as Janet, Ben, Rhonda, and Charles made ready to depart.

She gathered her friends into her arms and the three of them hugged. "I can't tell you how much it has meant to me to be with you all again," her voice was muffled against Janet's shoulder. "I wish you didn't live so far!"

Janet nodded, her own eyes welling up. "You never know what life may bring," she smiled. "At least we will have your wedding in November to look forward to! You can make it a huge family and friend reunion and once the barn and the extra accommodations are set up, they will have a place to stay!"

"And I will have to come back a few more times to fit and alter your dress," Rhonda reassured her.

Charles and Ben offered Samuel a warm handshake goodbye.

"Thanks for everything," Ben said. "We really enjoyed ourselves!"

"Especially the great food!" Charles added, patting his tummy. "I'm going to have to hit the gym hard when I get back!"

Samuel grinned, laying his arm across Rachel's shoulders. "We look forward to seeing you all again for our wedding. Now, let's get you to the train station!"

The women followed in Rachel's car once again while the men rode in the large wagon which had a few more suitcases than before because Rhonda and Janet needed extra stowage for all the items they had purchased.

Once at the station and everything unloaded, they all stood together on the train platform next to the pile of luggage to say their farewell. "Goodbye! See you in a few months, BFF!" Janet smiled. "Keep me updated on the barn raising."

Rachel nodded. "I will!"

The train arrived moments later, and the two couples climbed aboard with tearful waves.

Rachel and Samuel returned to an empty farmhouse. Samuel unhitched the horse from the buggy and led her into the barn.

Rachel entered the house, sad now that her friends were gone. She found Emma on the service porch, loading the washer and dryer with sheets for the next set of guests that were due in another week. Karen was nowhere to be seen.

"Thanks for all your help, Emma." Rachel gave her a hug.

"*Ach, no*! I should be the one saying danki to you! I have gut news!"

Rachel bent down and helped her to load the dryer. "What?"

"My post to that Facebook group of ex-Amish and Mennonite calling for local workers has gone viral. I think we're up to over 100 right now who are willing to come and work for wages."

"Really?" Rachel was shocked. The post had only been up for a couple of days.

"*Jah*!" Emma nodded with a big smile. "More than enough!"

Rachel stuffed the dryer with more sheets. "Now we just need the funding to pay them all, buy the materials and figure out how to feed them all!"

"We had just as many women volunteer to help as the men, so we'll have the help we need to feed them all," Emma replied.

"I guess I better go check on the GoFundMe page and see how we're doing and catch up on my emails." Rachel went to her small office and logged in. When the GoFundMe page popped up her eyes got as big as saucers.

"Samuel!" she screamed. "Samuel! Emma! Hurry!"

Emma came running in. Samuel arrived a few moments later along with Karen. They all stared at the screen in shock.

"Wow," was all Emma could muster.

Karen pointed at the numbers on the screen. "Holy cow, mom…I can't believe it's already that high!"

"Well, I definitely have enough to get the process started!" Rachel agreed. She checked her inbox. There was a message from Rhonda James with the subject line all in caps:

MY CLIENTS AND FRIENDS CAME THRU IN SPADES!

Rachel opened the email and they all listened as she read it aloud. "*Rachel – I couldn't wait until I got home to tell you that*

I'm just over the moon! I sent out an email blast over my phone while on the train to all my colleagues and friends before we left about your wedding barn and Inn, and they are all just buzzing about it! You should start seeing a ton of donations coming in. I have started a wait list for those who have donated that want to use your new venue for their events! I'll be in touch! Heal up and much love…Rhonda James."

Rachel and Samuel looked at each other and then embraced in celebration. For the first time in weeks, it didn't hurt her ribs. "I'm going to give Daniel Gold a call and let him know I have the deposit he needed! Samuel, could you help Emma coordinate the workers for the barn raising?"

He nodded, "*Jah,* it will be good to feel like I'm part of the community again,"

Emma gave Rachel a quick hug before returning to her chores. Only Karen lingered behind.

"Hey mom…" she began in that lilting voice of hers.

"No!" retorted Rachel with a grin, reviving their old childhood game.

"Mom…stop! I want to say something!" Karen was in earnest.

"Okay, sorry! I just said it out of habit. "What's up?"

Karen shuffled her feet. "Well, I was thinking that I would like to make wedding bouquets for you, Janet and Rhonda."

Rachel sat back, both stunned and deeply touched. She examined her daughter's face. "Oh honey, I would just *love* that!"

Karen's face brightened. "I've been watching YouTube videos on flower arranging and enrolled in an online course. I've also found a local florist shop that's willing to let me apprentice for nothing on the weekends so I can learn. The only problem is that in late November it will be slim pickings from the garden. We'd have to order and ship in what you want."

"Sweetheart, whatever you need we will get. It might have to wait until we see Rhonda's final design for my dress, is that okay?" Rachel was determined to let Karen shine in her small gesture of kindness.

Karen nodded, "*Jah*," she said, slipping back into her Amish vernacular. She bent down and gave her mom a little hug. "*Danki!*" she added, then skipped out of the office, her face wreathed in a smile. Rachel savored the rare display of affection.

Rachel, Samuel, Emma, and the boys looked over the architectural renderings of the Wedding barn with Daniel Gold, the general contractor.

He pointed out the various components. "I suggest we include the commercial kitchen/bakery and florist area on the bottom level of the barn as one unit and use the entire upper level for room accommodations. That way all the plumbing and the electrical can be centralized into the single building rather than separate buildings, which will save you a lot of money."

Rachel examined the blueprint. "How many rooms and bathrooms do you think we can fit up there?"

"You will want to keep the center section of the barn free with a vaulted ceiling, but I think we could easily accommodate 2 king rooms, 2 double queens and 2 rooms with multiple bunkbeds as well as bathrooms and a common area with the size of the barn."

Rachel sat back and looked around at Emma, Samuel, and the boys. "We're going to need more staff," she commented. "But where on earth are we going to put everyone?" She looked over at Samuel. The look on his face was making her nervous.

"There's also public parking to consider," Daniel continued. He pointed to an area adjacent to the proposed wedding barn and outdoor arbor. There should be at least room for twenty vehicles to park according to the City's zoning requirements.

"That would mean tearing out a great deal of my remaining farmland," Samuel said, rising abruptly to his feet. "Ach, I need some air," He left the room.

An awkward silence ensued.

"Should I come back at a later time?" Daniel finally asked.

Rachel shook her head. "It's too late for that, we're committed now that I've already given you ⅓ down so there's no turning back. When should I let everyone know on the start date for the barn raising?"

"As soon as we pour the foundation and it's cured, you can commence. I have scheduled it for the first week in June and it should take at least another week to cure if the weather cooperates, so I would suggest late next month."

Rachel stood up and shook his hand. "Okay," she said. "Emma, could you give everyone a heads up on our Barn Raising Facebook page?"

"*Jah*, Rachel," Emma nodded.

"You might also want to put out a call for new staff. It will have to be on a contractual basis per event. We will need servers, laundresses, cooks, maids as well as some manpower,"

"You just leave it all to me," Emma smiled.

Rachel gave her a grateful smile. "Emma, have I told you what a blessing you have been for us, lately?"

"*Jah*, at least three times today," Emma chuckled. "The feeling is mutual!"

Daniel rolled up the architectural plans and made his way to the door. "If the weather holds, the cement trucks should be here first thing next month. In the meantime, I'll order the materials you'll need for the barn raising."

Rachel escorted him to the front door. "Thanks!" Worried and concerned, she went in search of Samuel who had left so abruptly. She tried the *dawdi haus* first, but no one came to the door when she knocked. Next, she went to the barn.

"Samuel?" she called out.

"Up here," came the faint response.

She looked up and found him in the hayloft with Buddy on his lap. "Samuel, can we talk?"

He nodded, avoiding eye contact.

She climbed up slowly and sat down next to him. Buddy left Samuel and nestled in her lap. "I know all this change is bothering you, please talk to me."

Samuel shrugged but still refused to look her in the eyes. "It's your property now,"

"What is that supposed to mean?" Rachel demanded. "It's ours, not *mine*…unless…"

Samuel looked up at her. "Unless what?" Now he was frowning.

A feeling of dread came over Rachel. "Unless you don't want to marry me anymore…"

"*Ach*! Whatever put that idea into your head?" He looked insulted. When she didn't respond, he lifted Buddy out of her lap and pulled her onto his. His strong arms completely enfolded her, sending delicious thrills through her body. His breath was warm on her face. "Of course, I still want to marry you! The waiting is driving me *verrückt*[17]!"

His mouth closed over hers and for a few intense moments, he made her forget about everything else.

When they finally broke apart, she felt lightheaded. "Then why are you up here sulking?"

He frowned at her, "I'm not sulking, I just needed someplace quiet to think. All these enormous changes so suddenly, it's a lot!"

Rachel nodded, instantly sympathetic. "I know, for me too, but it seems to have become par for the course with us. It was the same way when Barry died, and I had to leave California. Do you want to call it all off?

He stared at her. "The wedding? The new barn? The bakery?"

She shook her head. "No, not our getting married but the rest of it?"

---

[17] Crazy

Samuel stared at her for a long time, and she could tell that he was struggling. No doubt, he just wanted to go back to his former, quiet life but circumstances seemed to conspire to change all of that. He cupped her face in his hands, his eyes suddenly soft. "Maybe we should pray and ask *Der Herr* about it?"

Rachel nodded, mesmerized by his blue eyes. Their foreheads met, they closed their eyes and she let Samuel lead the prayer.

"*Der Herr*, we need your guidance and wisdom. Please let us know what thy will is in all these matters." He said simply. If these changes are not what You want, please make it clear to us."

"Amen," Rachel whispered. She opened her eyes and found him staring at her longingly.

"As long as I have you as my *frau*, I will be content." His mouth claimed hers again and she melted into him until a cold nose nudged her. Buddy whined.

"I think he wants some of your affection," Samuel smiled as the dog climbed back into her lap. "I know how he feels!"

Rachel plucked Buddy off her lap and put him back onto Samuel's as she stood up. "Well, I know what I want right now," she gave him a teasing smile.

"What?" Samuel asked, his mind drifting to their wedding night.

"A nice big swing!" Rachel grinned. She grabbed the rope swing that was lying across one of the nearby hay bales.

"Are you sure about this?" he asked nervously, watching her pull the swing back to its' maximum length.

She grinned at him. "Absolutely!"

He held the rope while she climbed onto the seat. "Ready?" he asked.

"Let go!" Rachel cried.

He released the rope and Rachel went sailing through the air, screaming with delight as she arched out of the barn doorway, twisting madly. "*Wheeeeeeeee!!!*" The swing arched backwards, and she easily slid off onto the floor, laughing with abandon, clutching her ribs as it dragged her across the floor. Samuel was at her side within moments carrying Buddy. He set him down onto the floor and kneeled next to her. The dog ran up to her face and began licking earnestly.

Rachel continued to laugh with helpless abandon.

"Are you okay? Rachel, answer me!"

"I'm okay!" she managed to get out in-between giggles. "It just hurts to laugh!"

Samuel shook his head at her, relieved she wasn't hurt and chuckled despite himself. He gently pulled her up to a standing position and held her close. "No more swings for you until you can laugh without pain."

She grinned up at him, "Yessir!" She wiped her backside. "Ugh, I'm an absolute mess now, I better go change clothes!"

Samuel wrinkled his nose at her. "*Jah,* you *stinken!*"

Chapter Ten

"Barn-Raising"

Sarah Hochstetler confronted her husband, John, the moment he walked onto the service porch from a long day in the fields. "Have you heard?" she demanded, her hands upon her ample hips.

John removed his filthy shoes and dropped them outside so as not to trail dirt on Sarah's clean floors. "*Nee*[18], heard what?"

"There's to be a barn raising on Samuel's property!"

John stared at her, confused. "Why would Samuel build another barn when he has one?"

"The talk is that it's to be a barn built for weddings." Sarah retorted. "I told you that woman he left us for was *narrish*[19]!"

"A wedding barn?" John repeated. "Where is he getting the workforce to raise a barn like that? It would take at least a hundred of us."

Sarah shrugged. "I don't know, but I saw cement mixers pouring the foundation yesterday when I was out running errands."

John fell silent. He missed his bruder-in-law; it had been months since they had last seen or spoken to each other. Not since the day their Bishop and elders laid down the ultimatum that Samuel forsake Rachel Winston or risk excommunication. It had been abundantly clear to him how Samuel cared for her and how her love and care had brought

---

[18] no
[19] Cuckoo

him out of the dark hole he had been in since he lost his family, but it had been a heavy price to pay.

"John? John! Are you listening to me?" Sarah demanded. "There's also talk that they plan to be married in that new barn!"

John stared back at his wife, his heart plummeting. He had long held out hope that Samuel might change his mind and return to all of them but if he married the *Englisch* he would forever seal his doom with his community.

"I heard you," was all he could manage.

"Welcome to Second Chance Inn!" Rachel greeted her new guests.

The couple was in their mid-fifties. The woman had beautiful waist-length brown hair and twinkling eyes. "Oh, I'm so excited to be here!" chirped Mary. "Thank you so much for letting us bring our boys with us!" She held up two tiny Yorkshire terriers. "This is Luke, this is Skyler, and this is my husband, AJ. He's a volunteer firefighter."

Samuel carried the luggage upstairs as their guests admired the cozy living room.

"Who's this?" AJ asked, kneeling to pet Buddy who was thumping his tail on the ground and staring at the Yorkies curiously.

"This is Buddy," Rachel said, picking him up in her arms. "He's very gentle and sweet, aren't you?"

Buddy licked her nose to confirm her description of himself then leaned forward, sniffing and whining to get closer to the little terriers.

Mary juggled the dogs, who were every bit as anxious to meet Buddy. She set them on the floor, and they all watched the dogs greet and smell each other. They scampered around the room, tails wagging furiously.

"I apologize in advance for any noise that disrupts your visit," Rachel said. "We've already had a cement pad poured for the new wedding barn this week and following that will be a barn-raising."

"Oh, I've always wanted to see an Amish barn raising!" Mary replied excitedly. "Could we watch?"

Rachel smiled at her; Mary's enthusiasm was infectious. "Of course, but from a safe distance. I can set you up on the porch with snacks and lemonade where you can get an unobstructed view. Every afternoon except Sunday, we have snacks and beverages on the porch followed by a late supper and big farmhouse breakfast the next morning. Sundays we have an early supper. The Inn offer lessons in Amish bread-making, quilting, and woodworking for the men."

"Also hunting, fishing, and horseback riding," Samuel added, coming down the stairs.

"Let me give you a little tour," Rachel continued. She gestured to the large living room with the deep comfortable couches, recliner, banquet, and rustic fireplace. "This is where we serve afternoon snacks, but you are welcome to take them out to the front porch." She led them into the large kitchen.

"Oh, I just love your island and herb ladder!" Mary gushed, running her hands over the smooth butcher block and marble surfaces, and admiring the bundled herbs hanging overhead. She pointed at the old fashioned, iron woodstove. "Do you actually cook and bake with that or is it just decorative?"

Rachel grinned at her. "Yes, but it took many burnt buns and loaves before I learned how to use it properly. It's a real workhorse! Now, let me show you to your room."

She led them up the stairs where they admired the framed images of her red barn in all four seasons: fall, winter, spring and summer.

"Oh, it's just a cozy as I imagined it would be from your website!" Mary went in and set the Yorkies down on the floor so she could admire the beautiful Amish quilt on the bed. It was mostly white in a lone star pattern made with pale blue and yellow patchwork and had a scalloped edge in pale blue polka dot bias ribbon. On the nightstands were bottles of water and on the dresser was a vase of flowers.

"There are Amish toiletries and sundries in the bathroom for you and here on your table are some goodies from the local shops to enjoy. Please don't hesitate to let me know if you need anything or of any arrangements for local amenities you'd like to enjoy."

"She has quite a list," AJ grinned. "Me? I just want to sit on that rocking chair on the porch and relax!"

"I'll let you unpack," Rachel smiled, closing the door so they would have some privacy. She went downstairs where Emma and Karen were preparing the afternoon charcutier board.

Emma looked up and smiled. "*Gut nachrichten*, the last count I got for the barn raising is a little over 150!"

"How many men, how many women?" Rachel asked.

"125 men and about 30 women."

Rachel sat down at her computer and brought up her Go-Fundme page. "Wow!" she exclaimed. "Wow! Wow! WOW!"

Emma and Karen came running to look.

"WOW!" they both agreed.

"Mom, you have over $50,000 in there!" Karen pointed.

"Once we start ordering materials, paying the workers, and making food to feed them, it's going to go pretty fast!" Rachel replied.

"You should really post pictures on the progress so everyone can see," Karen suggested. "Maybe even have a weekly blog post on the Inn website!"

"As well as a remaining balance and what is still needed to finish," Emma added.

Rachel nodded. "All very good ideas," she agreed. "I'll get started on that right after I call the GC and find out when the materials will arrive and then we can post a date for everyone to come."

Rachel, Emma, Karen, Mary and AJ watched in awe from the front porch as the workers began to arrive on the barn site early in the morning. Instead of the usual line of Amish horses and buggies, there were large trucks filled with workers and small commuter buses entering the new parking lot of pea gravel, depositing dozens of workers in all manner of dress. Each one checked in first with Rachel at a small desk with a laptop where she recorded contact information, social security numbers and hours worked so she could accurately track wages. Samuel and the boys had set up sawhorses and laid planks over them to serve as tables under shade trees to feed the multitude of workers who had come to help raise the barn and had also constructed bench seats in preparation. Porta Potti's had been set up and a temporary wash station near the outdoor water pump. The construction materials had been delivered the day before and lay meticulously organized nearby. His workforce were all former Amish and Mennonite with prior experience in barn raising and carpentry and were well versed in what to do. Once they all were all checked in and gathered together, Samuel stood in the center of the cement pad and raised his arms for attention. Everyone fell silent.

"Let us pray," he said, removing his hat. Everyone fell silent and did likewise. "*Der Herr*, we ask for thy favor upon this endeavor. We ask that you protect each of the workers who have come to help us, so that they will accomplish their tasks without injury. We ask for thy blessing upon the weather, that it would hold fair for us as we labor, and we also ask that you bless this barn for all those who will come here in the future to celebrate, amen."

"Amen!" murmured all of them. With the prayer concluded, the men strapped on their leather toolbelts and got to work while the women followed Emma and Rachel to the Inn.

Emma quickly had them all organized at various food prep stations for sandwiches, salads, beverages and chicken.

Soon Rachel's kitchen and service porch were filled with the wonderful smells of baking bread, cookies, fried chicken, and muffins. Many of the women seemed to already know one another, having made friends through their social media group and the air was filled with lively chatter and laughter.

Mary was over the moon with excitement. "I want to help!" she informed Rachel, snatching an apron off a peg.

Rachel grinned at her, amused by her enthusiasm. "Are you sure? After all, you did come here for a vacation."

"Are you kidding me? All my life I've had to be satisfied with just reading about the Amish and *now* I actually get to be part of the story! Just put me to work!"

Rachel pointed to the sandwich station. "Have at it!" Mary scampered over and introduced herself to the other women. Soon she was up to her elbows in meatloaf sandwich prep. Rachel went to her phone and piped out Maranatha praise music from a Pandora station into her Bluetooth speakers. Soon the women all joined in singing together as they worked.

AJ was content to sit on the rocker and watch as the teams of men framed out the barn with hand tools and constructed the joists. A crane had been rented to lift each joist into position once the walls had been framed out. The men swarmed all over the structure like worker ants. The sound of hammers pounding nails and men calling out to one another filled the air. By noon quite a bit of the framing had been completed and although it was cool and breezy outside, everyone was sweating profusely from their labors.

"Look," Sarah gave Rachel a gentle nudge in the waist with her elbow and pointed to the nearby road.

A small line of Amish buggies had pulled over; their passengers climbing out to watch the barn-raising.

"Why would they do that?" Rachel wondered aloud. "Surely they've all seen a barn raising before."

Emma grinned at her. "I guess they're wondering where all the manpower came from."

"HELP!" yelped a voice, catching everyone's attention.

Rachel and Emma watched in horror as someone yelled out in pain and collapsed onto the ground. Samuel called a halt, and the men left their tools on the ground and went running to the downed man. Rachel and Emma ran to where the man was, Karen on their heels.

They found Aaron on the ground, twisting in pain and moaning.

"My back! It's my back," he groaned.

Karen knelt beside him. "What's wrong with your back?" Rachel looked at her daughter, surprised to find her looking so worried.

"I lifted something the wrong way and it went out." He grimaced. "It's happened before."

"Can you stand if we help you?" Rachel asked him; secretly relieved that it was not the result of an accident that she could be held liable for.

Aaron nodded. Together she, Emma, Karen, and Samuel eased him carefully onto his feet while he groaned and winced in pain.

"I'll take it from here," Karen volunteered. "I'll get him inside and ice his back."

"Are you sure?" Rachel asked her.

"I'm sure," Karen replied and slowly walked Aaron away from the site back to the *Dawdi Haus* while they all watched.

"Well, that's interesting!" Rachel remarked to Emma, watching her daughter walking with Aaron. "I'm just glad it wasn't anything more serious!"

"*Jah*," nodded Samuel. "I think now is a good time to call a halt and let the men eat some lunch."

"I'll ring the bell," Emma called over her shoulder, running back to the house. She picked up the iron rod and banged the iron triangle until she had gotten everyone's attention on the barn site.

"*ZEIT FÜR DAS MITTAGESSEN!*" Samuel called through his hands.

The men who had already paused when Aaron went down, lined up and stood before the make-shift picnic tables, all eyes upon Samuel.

He removed his hat, signaling that they should do the same. Baseball caps, hardhats and Amish straw hats came off and they all bowed their heads respectfully and fell silent.

"*Der Herr*, we thank you for blessing our efforts today and keeping the men safe. We thank you for the food you have provided and ask for Thy blessing upon it and these men and women who have come to help us. Amen."

"Amen," came the response.

"This way," beckoned Emma, pointing to the wash station where they could clean up. As the men washed, the women brought out platters of food and arranged them on the serving tables while the men lined up. The famished men heaped their plates high and took seats on the benches under the shade trees and tucked in while Emma, Rachel, Mary, and the other women went down the table line filling glasses with sweet tea, lemonade or iced water.

"I'm having so much fun!" Mary called out to Rachel; her face lit up with happiness as she poured tea. "I feel like I'm in one of my favorite novels!"

Rachel grinned back at her.

AJ stood up and hurried to meet Karen as she helped Aaron to the *Dawdi Haus*. "I'm a volunteer fire fighter and have some medical training, perhaps I can be of help?"

"I threw out my back," Aaron moaned as AJ helped to support him. "It's a long-term problem," Aaron gritted out, trying not to yelp each time he moved in the wrong way. "Some heat and a day in bed should help."

"Oh no, not heat!" AJ replied, shaking his head. "You need ice to bring down the inflammation and take Ibuprofen." He and Karen slowly walked him up the stairs and into the house. "You should also see a good chiropractor."

They got Aaron into the house and laid him on his bed.

"I'll get some ice," Karen said, leaving the room. AJ didn't miss the fact that Aaron's eyes followed her out of the room.

"You like her." He stated. Aaron's eyes widened and he nodded silently. Before AJ could say anything further, Karen was back with a soft icepack made especially for the human body. She pushed it gently under Aaron's lower back in the sore spot.

She held out her hand and gave him three Ibuprofen which he downed all at once. "I'll go back and get you some food."

Aaron nodded and offered her a little smile. "*Danki*," he said. Karen smiled back and left, glancing over her shoulder for a last look before exiting.

AJ took a pillow off another bunk and pushed it under Aaron's knees, so Aaron's lower back was flat on the bed. He pointed his finger at Aaron. "If you need to get up, this is how you do it, so you don't reinjure your back." He demonstrated by laying down. "Now watch me, you roll onto your side then swing your legs gently off the side of the bed and push yourself up to a sitting position with your arms against the bed while your legs rotate towards the floor. Once you're in a sitting position in bed, you can slowly get up by pushing up with your legs, got it?"

Aaron nodded. "Thank you, AJ, I'm sorry if all this has ruined your vacation."

AJ grinned at him. "Are you kidding? Mary is over the moon, and I get to relax and do next to nothing while eating great food; it's my ideal vacation!"

By the end of the day all four sides of the barn had been framed out. The workers had already collected their day's wages and left for their respective homes. Samuel stood with his arm around Rachel's waist as the sun set.

"If the weather holds it should be all done within two weeks."

Rachel nodded, taking photos with her camera so she could upload them to the GoFundMe page and update all the contributors on the wedding barn's progress.

Samuel turned her around to face him and carefully embraced her. "Does this still hurt?" he asked tenderly.

Rachel looked up at him and shook her head no.

Samuel pulled her against him and tightened his arms. "What about this?"

Rachel grinned up at him and again shook her head "no". He tightened his embrace and bent his mouth to hers.

She closed her eyes and succumbed to his kiss which deepened and grew more intense as she kissed him back, melting into him. Reluctantly he broke away and ran his fingers through his hair.

"It's going to be a long six months," he murmured aloud.

"We could still go to the courthouse in the meantime and make it official sooner," Rachel offered, sharing his frustration.

Samuel shook his head and gave her a crinkly smile. "The longer I wait, the sweeter the reward will be."

Rachel's breath caught in her throat, "Am I your reward?"

Samuel closed his mouth over hers again and kissed her even more passionately. She finally had to give him a little push away. "You're killing me, Larry!"

His brow knit in consternation. "*Ach!* Who is this Larry?"

Rachel stared at him for a moment, then laughed. "It's from a commercial, there is no Larry."

Samuel shook his head at her. "I don't understand half of what comes out of your mouth," he complained.

"You will learn," Rachel grinned back at him.

Chapter Eleven

"New Ventures"

Karen carried in a breakfast tray to the *Dawdi Haus* and set it on the table. She walked down the hall and knocked on the bedroom door. "Aaron? How are you feeling today? How is your back?" Without waiting for an answer, she opened the door and found Aaron swiftly recovering his lower half with the blanket, his broad chest, and arms still bare and which were turning a bright shade of red to match his face.

"Oops!" Karen backed out and shut the door swiftly. "Sorry about that! I brought your breakfast." Although she had gotten only a brief glimpse of him, Aaron's broad shoulders and muscled build had not escaped her notice.

"Give me a minute," his voice came through the door. She could hear him grunting and yelping a bit as he tried to dress. It was taking forever.

"Oh, for goodness' sake!" She burst into the room and saw him trying to pick up his shirt from the floor while seated with his toes. She snatched up the shirt and held it out for him. "Here."

Aaron took the shirt and tried not to twist his back as he put his arms through the sleeves. "Thanks," he murmured, mortified by his helplessness.

Karen reached forward and supported his forearms while he slowly stood up.

"It's a little better today," he told her, padding barefoot down the hall to the small kitchen table.

"It sure doesn't seem like it," she commented. "Mom made you some eggs and grits."

He sat carefully down at the table and sniffed appreciatively. "You're *mamm* is amazing," his eyes filled with tears. "My *mamm* was a wonderful cook too, I really miss her…"

Tears dripped into his grits and his shoulders drooped. Karen did not know what to do. She felt bad for him. She reached out her hand and gently patted his shoulder, but words failed her. Aaron dragged his arm across his wet eyes and collected himself. "*Danki*," was all he managed to choke out.

Karen shuffled her feet. "I gotta go help with the food," She beat a hasty retreat, uncomfortable with his display of emotions.

Rachel came into the kitchen early and found Emma already organizing all the women into food prep groups. The air was filled with lively chatter, laughter and *bon homie*.

Emma greeted her and introduced her to three young women. "Rachel, I'd like you to meet Annie, Ruth, and Naomi. They are all very accomplished cooks and bakers and are extremely interested in joining our team when the wedding barn is finished."

Rachel smiled at the young women. They were all a bit on the plump side. "Nice to meet you!" She held out her hand and shook theirs in turn. "The work will be on a contractual basis for each event. Does that work for you?"

The young women all nodded enthusiastically. "*Jah*, we will be glad for the work!" Annie said.

"Great, if you give Emma your email addresses, I'll send you an agreement and W-9 forms to fill out."

Rachel then went in search of her Inn guest, Mary, and found her up to her elbows in macaroni salad. "Mary, are you sure you really want to work instead of sight-seeing to-day? I have a small list of places I thought you might enjoy…"

"Oh, I can shop at any time," Mary grinned at her. "This is my first barn raising and I'm having the time of my life!" She lowered her voice so that only Rachel could hear her next words. "I had no idea there were so many young men and women who had left the Amish and then found themselves stuck between two worlds where they don't fit in anywhere but here. You've created quite a haven for them! I've been talking to Emma and the boys, and you have no idea how much your Inn means to them! Second Chance is so much more than an Inn, Rachel, or a place to vacation for people like me, it's a place of *refuge* for all these poor *lost sheep*!"

Goosebumps spread all over Rachel's skin when she heard these words. *Another confirmation.* All the doubts that had been creeping back into her heart dissipated. She had been experiencing increasing guilt over the fact that total strangers were funding the building of the wedding barn to help her and Samuel, but Mary's words made her think that maybe God had much bigger things in mind than just her wedding and financial success.

She put her arms around Mary and gave her a fierce hug. "You have no idea how much your words mean to me!" she whispered into her ear. Mary grinned at her and wiped a tear from her eyes and nodded.

By the end of the day all the roof trusses had been lifted into place and secured. Rachel and Samuel stood with AJ and Mary on the front porch at twilight, watching the fireflies and admiring the barn that had seemingly sprung up in one day.

"We should be able to get the metal roof on tomorrow as well as the outer walls finished." Samuel remarked.

"Why a metal roof?" asked Mary.

"It has heating elements in it so if we have a heavy snow-fall, we can heat the roof and lessen the weight on the struc-ture." Rachel replied. "It was the contractor's idea." She turned to Mary and AJ. "I can't thank you enough for your help these past few days! You've become good friends and like family to us. If it isn't too presumptuous to ask, I would love to invite you both to our wedding in November."

"Oh, I would just *love* that!" Mary gushed, hugging Ra-chel carefully. "I was hoping you would invite us! I would have been so disappointed if you hadn't!"

Emma appeared on the front porch. "Supper is ready," she announced, wiping her hands on her apron. "Tonight, we're having brisket, cheese biscuits and collard greens. Dessert is apple dumplings."

AJ patted his tummy. "I'm going to have to go on a diet after this trip," he opined.

"I need to have that put on as a sign over the door," Ra-chel giggled. "Every guest that has come here has said the same thing."

They all walked into the kitchen together. Emma had laid a clean white table runner across the large wooden ta-ble. On a large platter was the steaming brisket with root vegetables surrounding it. She had also lit little white tea lights in glass canning jars, so the room was filled with the flicker of candlelight and the smell of savory meat.

"I'm going to miss all this when we go home," Mary snif-fled, dabbing at her eyes. "I wish we lived closer! It's just the two of us and we have no family."

"Perhaps you could move closer?" Rachel asked.

AJ shook his head. "I'm afraid my job is too far away for us to relocate here but I'll make sure to schedule time off for us to come to your wedding in November." He looked over at Samuel. "You're a lucky man."

Samuel put his arm around Rachel's shoulders and gazed down lovingly into her face. "*Ach,* luck had nothing to do with it. *Der Herr* was our matchmaker."

Rachel stared up at him in mute amazement. Samuel's words deeply touched her; she had never heard him ascribe the cause of their relationship to the providence of God before. Nor, she realized, had she, until this moment.

Mary and AJ left the following day, waving tearful good-byes. Rachel felt like she was losing a sister but soon she was distracted by preparing food for the workers who had returned to work on the barn.

It took another month of dedicated work to finally finish the barn and when it was done it was truly a beautiful sight. The outside had white siding and the roof was black steel. Unlike a regular working Amish barn, there were windows letting in light all the way around and a split HVAC system that would cool both the vast common area on the bottom floor where the events would be held, but also the upper floor with the numerous bedrooms and bathrooms. Adjoining the bar was the large commercial kitchen and small bakery/florist rooms in the rear as needed. The front had large, sliding ornate barn doors set on black rollers and inside were large, rustic support beams which ran from one end of the 20-foot ceiling to the other. Hanging from the center beam was a large crystal chandelier. Market lights were also strung crisscross inside and there was ample storage behind large doors on each side for the tables and chairs that would be needed for future events. Outside was a generous parking lot made of decomposed granite, a fenced area for a portable dance floor with market lights strung all around and a beautiful wooden arbor under which people could take their vows. Rachel had planted bareroot pink Cécile

Brünner climbing roses that were tiny in size but smelled heavenly. She had had them in her garden in Southern California and missed them. She could hardly wait until they bloomed.

Rachel, Samuel, Emma, Karen, and the boys walked into the gleaming new kitchen and admired it in awe. There was a large walk-in freezer and refrigerator, several commercial ovens, and a large, French cooking suite outfitted with a gas chargrill, double Plancha's, induction and open burners and refrigerated drawers. All the counterspace was stainless steel except for one counter that was marble for making pastries. There was storage, baking, nesting, and cooling racks for the mass production of baked goods. There had even been enough money to fully stock all the pots, pans, and commercial grade food prep utensils and appliances they would need. Next to the commercial kitchen was a small shop that had an exterior door and display window that had the words EMMA'S BAKERY stenciled on it. The interior was all gleaming white and pale pink with a refrigerated case and marble counters. Rachel had made it as a surprise for her. The moment Emma laid eyes on it, she covered her mouth to suppress her outcry and burst into happy tears. She flung her arms around Rachel's neck.

"*Danki! Danki*!" she wept. "I just can't believe it! It's a dream come true!" She drew back and looked Rachel in the eyes. "Months ago, I was at my very lowest point. I thought my life was over then Der Herr brought me to you both." She clasped Rachel and Samuel's hands in hers. "*Danki, danki*!"

"You are every bit as great a blessing to us, Emma." Rachel replied, her eyes swimming.

Next to the bakery was a smaller area that had been set aside for Karen to use for a florist shop complete with a Floral walk-in cooler. She had spent the last couple of months both apprenticing and taking an online florist course and had just recently received her certificate.

"This is for you, Karen." Rachel said to her daughter, wondering what her reaction would be.

Karen stared at the stocked shelves, large stainless-steel sink, walk-in cooler, and stainless-steel counter in amazement, completely surprised.

"Well, what do you think, honey? Will it work for you?"

Karen nodded silently, awestruck and did not know what to say but she did give Rachel a smile that spoke volumes.

Rachel had been taking both still shots and video on her phone as they walked through the barn so she could upload them to the *GoFundMe* page, the Facebook Group where her laborers had come from as well as her official website which had been augmented with a new tab for booking events at the barn.

"Well, I guess we're officially open for business," Rachel looked up at Samuel. "I'm going to get these uploaded and let everyone know that they can start booking their events. I should think we could fit in at least one or two before our wedding?"

"I thought yours was to be the first event?" Emma said, looking surprised.

Rachel shook her head. "We could use the revenue; we've practically gone through our entire *GoFundMe* account."

"Not until we have dedicated it to *Der Herr*," Samuel replied. "He has granted all our prayers for the safety of our workers and provided gut weather, so it is only proper that we acknowledge Him and dedicate it to His purposes first."

"Too bad we can't host weekly church services," Rachel replied. "I really miss going to church and having that support system."

"Well, why couldn't we?" Emma replied. "Many of those who came here to work are still believers and have nowhere to go since they've been excommunicated from their communities."

Rachel and Samuel exchanged looks that plainly said *why didn't we think of it first?* "We'll need a pastor, someone who really knows the Bible and not just a set of *do's* and *don'ts.*" Rachel replied. They all fell silent for a moment, thinking of anyone they might know that would fit the bill.

Rachel shrugged after a long pause. "We will pray and leave that up to the Lord to bring them," she finally said. He has been faithful about everything else so let's pray and leave this in His hands."

They all clasped hands and bowed their heads.

Samuel spoke first. "*Der Herr,* we give thee thanks for all thou hast done for us. Restoring Rachel to health, bringing Emma, Aaron, Abram, and Amos to us in our hour of need. We also thank thee for providing the funds for this event barn and keeping the laborers safe. We dedicate it first to Your use. We ask that all who come to this Inn and Barn are blessed and that You will fill it with Thy holy presence. We also ask that You provide us with a wise and godly man who will look over this flock of displaced sheep with nowhere else to go. We leave all these great matters in Thy hands."

"Amen!" Everyone agreed.

Chapter Twelve

"A Surprise Visitor"

"It's about time!" Janet exclaimed the moment she answered Rachel's call. "I've had people texting and calling me for the past two weeks wanting to know when the barn is going to be available. My clients have all been chafing at the bit to book it for weddings, vow renewals, bar mitzvah's, quinceañera's, anniversaries…you name it!"

"The site is going live today," Rachel replied. "The barn was completed just a few days ago. I was just uploading the last of the pictures to the website."

"Well, hang onto your pantyhose because I can tell you right now, you're going to be booked solid as soon as you click 'publish'. Just make sure to keep Thanksgiving week blocked off for your family reunion/wedding."

"Done," grinned Rachel.

"When is Rhonda coming back down for a fitting? I want to be there so she can fit mine as well."

"September 9th," Rachel replied.

"Okay, I'll book my flight now, consider this call a request to book our rooms.

"You got it," Rachel grinned into the phone. "BFF – I just can't thank you enough for all you've done! I hope the barn exceeds all your expectations."

"Oh, I'm sure it will! So, what are you doing for staff?"

"We've found several young men and women who are willing to do contract work so we're good there. Now all we need is a pastor."

"To perform weddings?" Janet asked.

"No…well, yes, that too." Rachel's words stumbled over themselves.

"What else?"

"We want to also use the barn for holding church services. These young men and women who left the Amish have no place to go for fellowship."

"Really? That's a marvelous idea! You really are providing a place of refuge for all these kids."

A thrill shot up Rachel's spine. "Another confirmation!" she exclaimed.

"What are you talking about?" Janet replied.

"We've been getting that phrase from everyone for the Inn and taking on these excommunicated kids. We prayed and asked God for confirmation, and this is the word that keeps coming out of everyone's mouths! It's starting to freak me out."

"That's amazing!" Janet replied. Rachel could hear her phone beep that a text was coming in. "I need to go, just be prepared for the floodgates to open!"

"Taking a deep breath!" Rachel replied. "See you soon!"

"Can't wait!" Janet replied. "Love you!"

Rachel signed onto her website and gave it one last good look over to make sure everything was set up properly. The booking calendar system was ready to receive dates except for Thanksgiving week. "Okay, Lord. Here goes!"

She pressed publish and then went to her Facebook page and the *GoFundMe* site and posted that the Second Chance Inn events barn was now open for business. She had set up an audible alarm on both her phone and the computer to let her know when a request came in so she could respond quickly. It hadn't even been ten minutes before it started beeping like crazy with requests for booking dates. Janet had not been exaggerating!

She spent the next three hours on her computer accepting reservations and deposits. The first event was a 40th anniversary party and following that was a wedding. By the time it was afternoon, the Inn and Barn were solidly booked for every Saturday starting in two weeks through the end of December and into the following spring and summer. Rachel purposely kept Sundays set aside for Bible study and Christian fellowship just in case the Lord provided a pastor. She called Emma into her office.

"You won't believe this, but I just opened up the reservations and we're booked solid for events in the barn and Inn for the next year and a half!"

Emma's eyes went wide. "*Ach*, that's amazing!!" She looked over the first event. "Only two weeks to prepare! I'll call Janet right away and start working on the details."

"Be sure you coordinate with Karen as well so she can order the flowers ahead of time. Can you also text Ruth, Naomi, and Annie as well the young men and give them all a heads up their days are going to be filled for the foreseeable future?"

"I'm on it!" Emma grinned at her. "They will be so happy for the work!"

Rachel and Samuel sat on the front porch swing, enjoying a rare moment of uninterrupted peace and privacy. Rachel snuggled into him, her head upon his shoulder, watching the fireflies float above the grass.

"The calm before the storm," she murmured. "This will be our last week without any guests, so enjoy it while you can."

"I intend to," he replied softly and tilted her chin up to his. His lips pressed gently upon hers and his arms wrapped tightly about her. After a very long and passionate kiss he drew back reluctantly. "It's a *gut* thing we will be busy and have lots of guests; otherwise, I'm not sure how I could wait another six months for you," he whispered, then sat straighter when he realized that his embrace had not elicited a painful response. "Are you all healed now?"

"Getting there," she smiled shyly up on him. "Are all Amish men as ardent or is it just you?"

"Why do you think we have so many *kinner*?" he grinned at her.

"And here I thought it was mostly because you're an agrarian society," Rachel replied. Samuel leaned in and nibbled her earlobe and left a trail of kisses upon her jawline and neck.

"Samuel, you're not making the wait any easier," Rachel groaned into his chest.

He embraced her gently and patted her back. "I'll try to be *gut* until November," he murmured into her curly hair. "But after we are wed…"

Rachel placed her finger over his lips. "After we are wed, I'm totally and completely yours."

He lifted her hand to his lips and kissed it tenderly. "Until then, *mein Liebling*."

Emma was up to her eyeballs in cake batter when a soft knock came upon the new bakery's door. She was preparing a three-tier cake for the anniversary party that was to be held at the barn that coming weekend. She paused and listened; not sure she had heard correctly. The bakery had only been open for less than a week, so she was not expecting any customers yet. The knock came again, sounding more urgent. She turned the mixer off, wiped her hands on her apron and went to the door and opened it.

Her heart clenched the moment she beheld the woman on the other side.

"*Mamm?*" she whispered. Her mother stood before her, casting nervous glances over her shoulder at the driveway as if fearful of being caught. Her buggy was parked outside. They had not seen nor spoken to one another since the day her *daed* had shut the door in her face.

"May I come in?" Susan asked, clearly nervous. Emma nodded and stood to one side, her emotions in turmoil. Her mother entered the shop and looked around. "Emma's bakery?" she said, pointing to the letters etched on the window.

Emma nodded silently, fighting back her tears. *Why is she here?* She wondered. Her *daed* had made it clear that they were to have nothing to do with her anymore.

"Yes," she finally gulped out. "Rachel Winston hired me the day you and father shut the door in my face." She was unable to keep the pain out of her voice. "She gave me a place to stay in exchange for helping her with the Inn. She was grievously injured a few months back."

Susan nodded. "I remember reading about it in the paper," she said, looking around the shop. She offered Emma a little smile. "You always did love to bake, when you were a *boppli* you were always making mud pies..." her voice trailed off and then a sob erupted from her throat. She covered her mouth with her hands as tears streamed down her face. "I'm not supposed to be here, you see," she mumbled. "Joseph has forbidden me to ever contact you or speak of you again...but...but...I had to know that you were okay."

Emma's hurt and anger dissolved in the face of her mother's pain. She held out her arms and her mother rushed into them and sobbed uncontrollably. "You were my first-born," she wept. "You were the light of your *daed's* eyes; he has suffered greatly too."

"He has?" Emma was surprised.

Susan nodded. "He misses you, but he won't admit it." She wiped her eyes with a handkerchief. "I'm violating the *Ordnung* and your *daed* by coming here but I had to know...I haven't slept in weeks for worrying about you."

Emma gulped, fighting to control the emotions overwhelming her. She looked around the small bakery and picked up some muffins she had made fresh that morning and put them in a pink bakery box. She handed them to her mother. "No one has to know," she said. "Just tell him you went to a bakery in town and picked these up for him."

Susan's blue eyes fastened upon Emma, then she slowly looked her up and down as if really seeing her for the first time. "Your hair is it's natural color again," she whispered, tucking a loose blonde tendril behind her ear. "And all that horrible jewelry is gone but you still have," she waved her arms up and down, indicating the tattoos, "...all those."

"They are harder to get rid of and very expensive." Emma replied. She gave her mother a small smile. "I wish I had never gotten them in the first place."

"Did Rachel Winston ask you to change all this?"

Emma shook her head. "No, she just offered me food and shelter in exchange for my help. She will be hosting events at the new barn and built this bakery for me."

"She built this just for you? She is a very generous woman to do such a thing for a stranger," Susan marveled.

"Yes, much more so than my own people." Emma replied, unable to keep the bitterness out of her voice. "She has opened her home to others just like me who needed a place to stay. A place we can call home since we belong nowhere else."

Susan's eyes filled with tears, and she nodded then bowed her head with silent weeping again. "I'll come when I can," she whispered, giving Emma a last hug. "I'm glad you have found a refuge my *dochder*."

Emma watched her go, her heart aching but also somewhat lighter. The surprise visit had done much to heal her aching soul; she just hoped it would not be the last of such visits.

Rachel, Emma, Samuel, Karen, and the boys watched the barn from a distance as their first clients celebrated. It was twilight but the barn was illuminated from inside and without by market lights as well as the crystal chandelier. The sound of laughter continuously erupted from the guests, many of whom had also booked rooms in the loft area and the Inn for the special occasion. Music from the 1980's filled the night air with selections from Footloose by Kenny Loggins, Thriller by Michael Jackson and other top hits as guests took to the dance floor.

"Well, I'd say our first event here was rousing success!" Janet grinned, who had flown in the day before. "I made sure to mingle and could overhear everyone raving about the food, service, ambience and the rooms so we should have some great reviews to post on YELP and our websites."

"We couldn't have done any of this without you," Rachel said, giving her friend a grateful hug.

Janet squeezed her back. "This is nothing, I can't wait for you to see what I have planned for your wedding!"

"Just something simple," Rachel responded, worried that her friend would go overboard in her enthusiasm. At that moment, the music cut out and the DJ came on and asked everyone inside the barn to gather outside on the dance floor for a special treat. Rachel, Janet, and the rest all turned their eyes to the sky as the lights were dimmed.

The crowd quickly gathered and hushed as George Benson's song, "Nothing's Going to Change My Love for You" came out of the speakers. Then a drone display began that synchronized with the music.

Rachel felt Samuel's arms go around her as they watched the spectacle in the night sky to the *oowwws* and *aaawwws* of the admiring crowd. When the show concluded, there was a loud round of whoops and applause from the appreciative audience.

"Let's hear it for our guests of honor, Mike and Marilyn! Forty years of marriage!" announced the DJ when the fireworks and music had stilled.

Another burst of applause rang out and the music silenced, which signaled the end of the festivities. Rachel was strictly abiding by an 11:00 pm curfew so as not to disturb her closest neighbors. Shuttle buses had arrived an hour earlier to pick up the guests that had booked rooms elsewhere while the main party retired happily to the barn loft. The staff that Rachel had hired to service the event quickly went into high gear quietly washing up and putting everything away while Emma, Naomi, Ruth, and Annie prepped everything for the morning breakfast.

"I don't know about you, but I'm whooped," Rachel remarked to Samuel as they bid each other goodnight on the porch. "And I didn't even do the lion's share of the work!"

Samuel nodded in agreement. "The staff all performed wonderfully. We have much to be thankful for." He put his arms about her waist and kissed her on the forehead. "*Gute Nacht meine Liebe,*"

Rachel raised her face to his and put her hands on each side of his clean-shaven face, staring deeply into his eyes. "I love you, Samuel. I didn't think I could ever love again the way I loved Barry, but you have filled my heart with such joy I can't even express it."

"*Ich liebe dich auch*[20]," he whispered back and kissed her sweetly on the mouth.

Karen was working in her new florist shop, assembling corsages for the next event that was to be held at the barn when Aaron walked in.

"Hi!" he said, watching her work with the florist wire and delicate orchids. He nodded towards her handiwork. "You're getting really good at that," he commented.

---

[20] I love you too

Karen felt a hot blush creeping up her neck, but she shrugged, playing it cool. She wasn't ready to trust her heart so easily again. "Thanks," she mumbled, "how's your back?"

"*Ach*, much better since I started seeing that chiropractor your mom recommended! He gave me stretching exercises that have really helped a lot. See?" He stretched one arm over his head and down to the floor, bending at the waist.

"All the other doctors I saw just handed out pain pills."

Karen nodded. "A good chiropractor makes a huge difference; they fix the problem; not put a drug Band-Aid on it."

Aaron came closer and placed his elbows on the counter and his face in his hands.

He looked intently at Karen. "So, you've had personal experience with a chiropractor?"

His physical nearness was making Karen nervous. She nodded. "I had a curved spine so my mom has been taking me to one since I was little so I would not have to get corrective surgery. She always told our chiropractor back home that he could not retire until she was dead because he fixed everything that was wrong." She giggled nervously.

Aaron continued to stare at her as if memorizing her facial features. A long awkward silence ensued.

"Well, I need to get these done and start on the bouquets," she announced. "Don't you have something better to do than to hang around a florist shop and harass the shop keeper?" she gave him a smile to demonstrate that she was kidding.

Aaron stood up and broke into a brilliant smile, pleased at her teasing. "*Jah*! Time to go a-choring!" He turned around and started to leave but not before turning back and giving her a wink while tipping his straw hat. Karen watched him leave. His hair had grown out of the purple spiked style he had arrived in. It was now dark brunette and cut short, tapered at his neck. His piercings had also disappeared, just like the others but he still had his tattoos.

Rachel sat at her computer, putting the final finishing touches on the wedding invitations she had created for herself and Samuel's nuptials in late November using Canva. The invite was a fall template with colors of red, orange, yellow and even eggplant tastefully displayed. A small rivulet of perspiration slid down her back despite the air conditioning being at full blast. The weather had become very warm and muggy; hovering into the high 90's for most of the week. *My electric bill is going to be sky high just trying to keep the Inn cool, not to mention the barn!* It was now early August and the Inn and Barn had been teeming with guests attending numerous events since it's official opening in early summer.

She mopped her sweaty neck with a bandana. "So glad I blacked out the last week of August or the electric bill would bury us!" she muttered aloud to no one in particular. The expense of cooling such a humongous structure in such miserable weather would not be offset by the remunerations she took in, so it was better all-around to just close in hot and humid weather. She and her staff also all deserved a much-needed break. "Just like they do in Palm Desert,"

She heard Samuel enter from the service porch; the screen door slapping shut behind him.

"*Ach* it's beastly hot out there!" he commented, helping himself to ice-cold lemonade from the refrigerator. "I gave the boys the afternoon off so they could swim in the nearby creek. What is *Palm Desert?*"

"You heard that? It is a place in Southern California that people retire in to find out what hell is like before they die." Rachel replied.

Samuel stared at her, his mouth agape, not sure whether she was kidding or not.

Rachel giggled. "It's an old saying. It's so expensive to run the air conditioning in Palm Desert during the summer

116

that all the businesses just shutter because it's cheaper. Hey – do Amish homes have air-conditioning like we do?"

Samuel shook his head, "Nee, but it makes it easier for us to manage the heat while working outside, because we get used to it. Your ways are going to make me soft!" he patted his tummy that had filled out quite a bit since April.

"The boys are in the creek? Maybe we should have installed a swimming pool while we were at it," Rachel opined. "Too late now,"

"What about an above-ground pool?" Karen entered the room having heard the last few sentences. Her face was flushed red from the heat. "They aren't as expensive. I would kill to go jump in a pool right now!"

Rachel sat back and thought about it. "Me too, let me check and see what our account balance is and if we have the funds for it. She looked up her bank balance and then totaled the outgoing bills that were stacked up neatly on her desk. "I think we could do it. We're doing pretty good right now." She went onto Amazon and searched for above-ground pools. "Here's an 18' round, 6' deep one for a couple of thousand."

Karen hopped up and down. "Get it mom! Please?!!"

Rachel looked up at Samuel. We would need an area of level ground." She informed him.

He mopped his neck with his kerchief. "Leave that to me and the boys. If I tell them, it is for a pool for their own use, they'll have it prepped in no time. We can work on it in the afternoons or early mornings when it's cooler."

Karen peered over Rachel's shoulder to read her computer screen. "It says it can be delivered within a week!" She looked up at Samuel. "Can they get it done in a week?"

He nodded, "*Jah*, it shouldn't be a problem unless we have a summer storm."

Karen then pointed to a tab she saw on Rachel's computer screen that read *wedding invite*. "Mom, can I see it?"

"Sure," Rachel nodded and brought the screen up, wondering how her daughter would react now that the wedding was becoming more of a reality. She watched her face for a moment then Karen nodded.

"I like it," she said. "That will give me inspiration for the kind of bouquet I make you,"

Rachel lightly touched her daughter's hand. "Karen, I have to say that you have really shined these past few months with your floral skills. All the guests have commented on how creative and beautiful they are. You are natural at it! I didn't realize you had such an amazing talent!"

Karen looked into her mom's eyes for a moment before blushing and looking away, clearly uncomfortable. "Thanks, I'll do my best to make you something beautiful." She changed the subject. "So, when are the invites going out?"

"As soon as they arrive from the printers," Rachel replied.

"Who are you inviting?" Karen wanted to know.

"Well, everyone!" Rachel replied. "All your aunts, uncles, and cousins. Do you have any friends you'd like to include?"

Karen's smile instantly disappeared. "I don't have any friends," she muttered, shuffling her feet, her face darkening with hurt. "Willis' sisters and the other Amish girls stopped inviting me anywhere since he broke up with me and none of the girls I knew back in California would respond to my texts once we got internet back." She turned away and stomped off, her happy mood over the pool completely obliterated by her lonely reality.

Rachel sat back, staring at Karen's retreating back in consternation. "I had no idea," she bleated, appealing to Samuel. "We've all been so consumed with the new barn and all the events, I never stopped to think about Karen having any friends."

Samuel nodded, "I have been neglectful in this area too," he admitted.

"Girls need good friends," Rachel said. "I don't know what I would have done without mine all these years, but I can't make friends for her and she's so isolated here. Normally she'd make friends in school, but I've been home-schooling her since we got here, I just don't know how to help!"

"Let's pray about it," Samuel said, clasping her hands. "When we have no resources, *Der Herr* has ample."

"Great idea!" Rachel replied. They clasped hands, and closed their eyes, unaware that Emma was watching from the kitchen.

Rachel spoke. "Lord, please forgive me for neglecting Karen in this regard. In addition to a pastor for our youth, we also ask you to provide good friends for my daughter. This new life hasn't been easy for her so we both ask that you would bring wonderful girls near her age into her life not only to befriend her but also to mentor her."

"Amen," agreed Samuel.

Samuel greeted the boys on the porch of the *Dawdi haus* when they returned from the creek. They were all looking more normal now that their hair was cut short, and back to its natural color and they had removed the heavy jewelry.

Samuel affected a grim face. "*Jungen,* I have *gut* news and *schlecht*[21] news for you. Which do you want first?"

He stifled his laughter as Aaron, Amos, and Abram exchanged worried glances amongst themselves.

"Are you letting us go?" Abram asked fearfully.

Samuel shook his head, then broke into a smile. "Of course not! I'm immensely proud of all of you! We have all of you, Emma, and the others to thank for making the Inn and Barn successful!" He watched in silent amazement as tears welled in their eyes. He'd had no idea this place had come to mean so much to them or that his words would impact them so deeply.

"Bad news first then," Aaron piped up, looking a little bit relieved.

---

[21] bad

"We need to level out a patch of land twenty by twenty feet in one week." Samuel replied.

The boys groaned.

"In this heat?" bleated Abram.

"What for?" Amos wanted to know.

"Rachel is getting you an above-ground pool to swim in." Samuel grinned at them.

Their eyes all went as big as saucers and their jaws dropped; utterly shocked.

"She's doing this for us?" Amos bleated.

"*Jah*, for all of us."

"Seriously?" Aaron demanded. "No more dealing with leeches?"

Samuel nodded, his grin widening.

"When do we start?" They all asked in unison, then burst into laughter.

"Tomorrow morning early, after you take care of the animals," Samuel replied. "I will have to go into town today and get some equipment."

"Like a mini excavator?" Aaron replied, his eyes lighting up. "I know how to use one."

"*Was ist ein Bagger?*" replied Samuel.

"It's like a mini bulldozer," Aaron replied. "You can rent them."

"This would make the work quicker and easier?" Samuel asked.

All three boys nodded their heads.

Aaron replied, "We would still need to level the ground with hand shovels but it sure would help!"

Samuel rubbed his hands over his chin where his beard used to be. "Alright then, Aaron, since you have prior experience, you come with me into town to find a rental. The two of you can start preparing by drawing an outline marking the center of the pool where I show you. You'll need to have a rope that equals the 18' radius plus another six inches and make a circle. I'll provide further instructions later. I figure we'll also need sand for leveling, crushed limestone, and a lawn roller."

"We can find detailed instructions on YouTube and on-line for on each step as well as the directions that come with the pool." Abram added.

Samuel nodded. "Go get dressed and we'll head into town."

The boys elbowed each other aside, frantic to be the first into the *dawdi haus.*

Chapter Thirteen

"Moonlight and Magnolias"

Emma found Karen in their shared room, staring down at the floor with tears dripping from her cheeks. The sight made her pause with alarm. She had never seen Karen exhibit any sort of emotion in all the months she had been there.

She sat next to her on the bed and put an arm around her shoulders. She was rewarded when Karen responded by resting her head upon her shoulder in a rare show of affection.

"I'm so lonely," Karen whispered. "I have no friends!"

"You have me," Emma replied firmly, giving her a gentle squeeze.

"You're my friend?" Karen asked. "But there's such a humongous age gap; you're at least 8 years older than me."

"*Ach jah*, I'm just ancient!" Emma giggled, then added, "friendship has no age barriers. I've also come to think of you as a younger sister."

Karen dragged her arm across her nose. "Really? I always wanted a sister…"

"I also think Ruth, Annie and Naomi have grown rather fond of you too," Emma added. "We've all just been so busy, we haven't really had any time to get to know one another properly."

"Ya think?" Karen groused, "All I do is work, sleep, eat and repeat."

Emma chuckled despite herself, "*Jah*, I think it's time us girls had a little *girl time!*"

Karen visibly brightened at the prospect. "I would really, really like that. What could we do?"

"Well, I have some money saved, we could all go to lunch out in town somewhere, do a little shopping, maybe get our nails done…"

Karen sat straight up. "Could we do *all* of it?"

Emma shrugged, "Why not? I'll text the other girls and start making plans."

Karen threw her arms around Emma. "Oh, I'm so excited! Something to look forward to!" She hopped off the bed. "I've got some money saved from my eggs sales so I can pay for my own way!"

Emma stood up, smiling, happy that she had done something to make Karen feel a little better.

Karen bounded down the steps and found her mother in front of her computer. "Mom! Emma, Naomi, Ruth, Annie, and I are all going to go into town and have some girl time!" she announced happily.

Rachel looked up and smiled at her. "That's great, honey! Can I come too? I could use some girl time."

Karen instantly wilted. "It's just us *girls*," she replied, looking down and shuffling her feet. "No adults." She really didn't want her mom tagging along.

"Oh," Rachel's replied quietly, turning back to her computer. "Okay." Her mom visibly drooped.

Karen could tell that her words had really stung her mother and that she was struggling not to cry in front of her. *Why does she always have to get so emotional?*

Unsure of what to do next, she went outside in the blazing heat to the chicken coop to make sure her chickens had plenty of fresh water in the overhead dispensers and collect any newly laid eggs. She found Aaron inside, sweeping out the manure and scooping it into a wheelbarrow for spreading in the garden. Her nostrils were assaulted by the overwhelming smell as soon as she walked in; the oppressive heat making it so much worse.

She refilled all the water dispensers first then got her collecting basket. "Thanks for doing that," she said to Aaron, feeling a bit shy around him. "That's one chore I don't mind giving up."

He nodded and wiped his sweaty brow with his handkerchief then tucked it back inside his back pocket.

"*Bitte*[22]," he smiled gently at her, his dimples appearing. Tingles shot up her spine. Aaron was at least a full head taller than her, and very muscular with bronzed skin. They stared at one another for a full minute in pregnant silence, then he stepped forward and reached for her. Karen involuntarily hopped backwards, halting Aaron in his tracks. *Why did I do that?* She felt drawn to him, but her fearful reaction evoked a hurt look on his face.

She immediately regretted it.

"I'm sorry," he mumbled, turning back to his work. "I shouldn't have done that,"

Karen just stood there, not knowing what to say or do, fully aware she had offended him.

"No, I'm sorry." She replied, then hastily left the coop, leaving a very bewildered Aaron staring at her back as she fled.

Samuel entered the service porch. It was late afternoon and the temperature had climbed to unbearable levels. Despite the cooler air inside the Inn, he found Rachel slumped over the kitchen table with her face in her hands, her thin cotton t-shirt plastered to her back from sweat. It showed off every curve and he found himself imagining all sorts of things until he noticed the tears dripping onto the table.

---

[22] Please

He put a gentle hand on her shoulder. "*Was ist los?*" he asked gently.

Rachel looked up at him with red-rimmed, swollen eyes. "Karen and the girls are going to have a *girl's day* and I was explicitly *not* invited."

Samuel fell silent at the hurt in Rachel's eyes. He sat down and took her hands in his. Things had always been difficult between she and Karen, but he had expected better behavior out of Emma. He patted her hand then kissed it. "I will speak with Emma," he said, rising.

Rachel pulled him back down. "No, please don't. I don't want them to feel obligated to include me, it would be so uncomfortable! I just need to find some friends of my own somehow." She blew her nose on some Kleenex and tossed it onto the table that had become filled with them. "Ever since Ruth betrayed me; I've had no female friends."

"You have Janet and Rhonda," Samuel replied softly.

"Yes, but they are both hundreds of miles away and busy with their lives. I can call and talk to them on occasion, but I really need to make some local friends, I just don't know how. A woman needs her girlfriends, Samuel, at least one that she can lean on like a sister. The Amish are blessed that way, they have such a supportive community."

At that moment, Buddy whined, pawing at her leg, wanting to be picked up and cuddled. Rachel lifted him into her lap and snuggled him. He lifted his little chin and began licking her neck that was salty with tears. "You are just so precious," she sighed, offering Samuel a sad little smile.

He leaned closer and kissed her lips. "I have been neglectful of you," he admitted. "All work and no leisure ever since you got back."

"You have worked every bit as hard if not harder, Samuel." Rachel cupped his cheek. They both leaned forward and kissed longer this time until Buddy inserted himself and took turns licking them both while they kissed.

"Blah!" Samuel complained whipping his chin, but he caressed Buddy's head affectionately. He looked down at Rachel and made a decision. "Don't plan on making dinner here tomorrow," he said. "I have something else in mind."

Rachel's eyes lit up. "Do you mean we're actually going to go on a *date?*"

Samuel blinked at her. "*Was ist date?*"

"Sort of like a single night of *Rumspringa*. It usually involves going out to dinner, preferably someplace romantic, maybe a movie, or a picnic, baseball game; it all depends on what you like to do and usually ends up in heavy necking."

"Necking?"

Rachel stood up, set Buddy down then snaked her arms about his waist and pressed herself up against him, holding him close. She looked longingly into his eyes.

"You are irresistible," he murmured, pressing his mouth passionately upon hers. Heat suffused his entire body as she melted into him. After a very long and arduous kiss, he gently pushed her away.

"That is necking," she grinned at him, waving her hand before her flushed face.

Samuel shook his head although he was fighting a smile. "Necking will have to wait until our wedding night," he murmured. "A man can only take so much." He reluctantly released her and turned away. "I need a cold shower." With that he marched out of the Inn to the *Dawdi haus*, shut the door, marched into the bathroom, stripped, and stepped under the cool spray of the shower, lingering there for a good ten minutes until he felt it was safe. Then he turned on the hot water, lathered himself well, dried off, changed, and went in search of Emma for "date" ideas.

He found her on the service porch, loading a basket with freshly cleaned laundry.

"Emma," he greeted her.

"Hi Samuel," she smiled, hefting the basket onto her hip and walking out to the backyard to the clothesline.

"You aren't using the dryers?" he questioned as she began pinning the sheets to the line.

Emma shook her head, "*Nee*, it's so warm out I figure they'll dry in no time. They'll smell better and we'll save come electricity." She pinned the sheet and lifted another one to the line. "Is there anything you need?"

Samuel nodded; sorely tempted to bring up the subject of Rachel being excluded from her planned "girls' day" but respecting Rachel's wishes. "I need some advice," he said instead.

"Oh?" Emma paused, staring at him.

"I want to take Rachel out on a date and need suggestions to help me plan the date. I'm no good at romance,"

Emma stared back at him, then clapped her hand over her mouth to hide her smile. She cleared her throat, "Let me think while I finish pinning this load and I'll come find you when I've come up with some ideas. I think between the boys, Karen, and I, we can all come up with something very special."

Karen and Emma returned from their day out on the town loaded with both groceries and small packages from their shopping spree.

Karen spread out her loot on the island counter. "That was so much fun!" She admired her fingernails which had been painted in a pink ombre graduating color from light to dark. She held up the summer dress with daisies and spaghetti straps against herself. "You really like it?"

Emma nodded, "It looks really stunning with your dark hair."

They both began unpacking the groceries and storing the perishable items in the large commercial refrigerator.

Rachel entered the kitchen and Karen gawked at her. "Why are you so dolled up?" she demanded. Her mom was wearing a pink cotton summer dress with a sweetheart neckline, the pearl necklace her father had given her, matching earrings, and *make-up*. It made her uncomfortable.

Rachel smiled at them and twirled. "You like?"

Emma grinned at her and nodded enthusiastically. "*Ach*! You look *prächtig*[23]!"

"Thank you! I hope Samuel thinks so too!"

Karen's brow wrinkled. "What is *prächtig*?" she mispronounced, "it doesn't sound good."

"Gorgeous, honey." Rachel replied. "Samuel is taking me out on a mystery date!"

"Aren't you a little old for dates?" It was out of her mouth before she knew it.

Her mom gaped at her with an injured look then became serious. "…and aren't you old enough to have learned manners by now?" She turned on her heel, gathered up her purse and stalked out of house, letting the screen door slam shut behind her.

Karen could feel Emma's disapproving eyes on her. "Karen!" was all she said, shaking her head. "That was so unnecessary."

Karen bristled. "Well, don't you think she's too old to be acting like a teenager?"

Emma took Karen's hands in hers and looked deeply into her eyes, silently pleading. "Do you know what I would give to have a mother like yours?" Karen watched Emma's eyes fill up with tears. She could barely get the next words out. "I have no mother, no father…they disowned me. They can't talk to me or take anything from my hand. Do you have any idea how that feels?"

A lump rose in Karen's throat. "No," she squeaked.

Emma cupped Karen's cheek gently, her eyes imploring. "You almost lost your mother and yet you still treat her so shamefully. *Cherish her*, Karen! I know how you miss your *daed*, and how you have expressed regret over not letting him know how much he meant to you before he passed. *Don't make the same mistake with your mamm!*" She wiped the

---

[23] splendid

tears from her face and continued putting away the groceries while Karen stood there in silence watching her. Emma had not shamed her, but her words had made a deep impression.

"You're right," she finally admitted. "I don't know why I do and say things like that." She hung her head, remorse filling her.

Emma's arms went about her and embraced her. "She loves you, Karen, and she does her best. Don't take her love for granted like I did my *eltern* because someday you won't have her anymore."

Karen rested her face against Emma's chest and nodded. "Okay," she whispered.

Rachel knocked on the door of the *Dawdi haus*, her heart still stinging from Karen's words.

Abram answered it, the door swinging wide open with a bang.

He looked her up and down. "Wow!" he exclaimed appreciatively. Aaron and Amos crowded in behind him, admiring her and nodding in agreement.

Aaron pursed his lips and gifted her with a loud wolf-whistle, making her blush. "You look *niiiiiice!*"

"Well, thank you!" Rachel smiled, their reactions raising her flagging spirits a little. Samuel stepped into view then froze. The boys elbowed one another with grins as he gaped at her.

Rachel spread her arms and twirled. "Well?"

Samuel elbowed the boys aside and stepped out onto the front porch and took her hands in his. He took in every inch of her, starting at her feet and finishing with her hair that had been clipped up into a loose bun, the brown curls cascading against her long neck.

He swallowed, his Adam's apple bobbing, unable to express his feelings. Finally, he found his tongue. "You look like dessert!"

Warmth suffused Rachel's body as she read the admiration in his eyes. "Thank you," she smiled shyly. "I think that's just about the most flattering thing anyone has ever said to me."

Samuel reached for something and held it forth to her. "For you," he said. "I asked Karen to make it for me."

In his outstretched hand was a dainty corsage of pink and white rosebuds with lavender sprigs. "Karen said the lavender is a natural bug repellent."

Rachel burst into laughter. "Oh, she did, did she?" She held out her wrist, still giggling while Samuel slid it onto her wrist.

He exited the *Dawdi haus* with a handwave to the boys.

"You're a lucky man!" Amos called after him as the door closed.

Rachel felt Samuel's arm encircle her waist possessively and give her a gentle squeeze.

"Ouch!" she yelped loudly.

Samuel stepped away, guilt-ridden.

Rachel grabbed his arm and wrapped it back around her. "I was just kidding! Where are we going?" She did feel as giddy as a teenager out on her first date. It had been years since she had felt this way.

"*Ach*, it's a *geheim*[24]," he shook his head at her, laying a finger over his lips. He led her to where he had tethered Dodger to the hitching rail and helped her up.

The afternoon was waning, and the air was warm and balmy. The sound of crickets and cicadas filled the air, and the sky was ablaze with color. Rachel made room for Samuel as he climbed in then snuggled next to him, hooking her arm through his. He reached into his pocket and withdrew a clean bandana.

---

[24] secret

Rachel frowned at him. "That's going to ruin my eye make-up. I promise to keep my eyes shut."

"I have your solemn word?"

"Cross my heart and hope to die," Rachel said, as she did so. "Scouts honor!" she added for extra measure.

Samuel nodded. "*Gut*! You won't have to wait too long. Shut them now."

Rachel obeyed and temporarily lost her balance as the buggy surged forward. She kept her eyes shut as she promised, wondering where Samuel was taking her. She could tell when he drove down their long driveway and out onto the two-lane but after 10 minutes, she was hopelessly lost with all the turns he made.

"Are we there yet?" She couldn't resist.

"Just a few more minutes, keep your eyes shut!" he commanded her. The sounds of the two-lane faded behind her and Dodger's hooves were crunching on pea gravel. "Almost there," he said. The buggy pulled to a stop. "Now keep your eyes shut until I tell you," he warned. The buggy shifted up with his weight as he exited and came around to her side.

"Yessir!" Rachel giggled, becoming more nervous and excited by the moment. His familiar warm and calloused hands grasped both of hers and helped her out of the buggy. "I will guide you," came his warm breath in her ear. It sent delicious shivers coursing down her spine.

She stepped forward carefully, letting him lead her. Then she felt wood boards under her shoes. "Can I open my eyes yet?" she wanted to know.

"Not yet just wait right here and don't look or move until I tell you." She could hear the suppressed excitement in his voice which just made her expectations leap higher.

From somewhere above her the strains of romantic music filled the air, and she recognized her favorite song, *The Way You Look Tonight* by Steve Tyrell.

"Okay, now." Samuel whispered in her ear.

Rachel opened her eyes and could not believe what she was seeing. It was her barn but not how it had ever looked before. It was aglow with candlelight from dozens of clear Mason Jars scattered throughout the vast expanse as well as the light from the crystal chandelier. The interior has been cleared of all furniture except for a round table covered in a pristine, white tablecloth. On it was a vase of the most gorgeous pink rosebuds and blue hydrangeas. Her good bone China that she had brought all the way from California was laid out, glimmering in the soft candlelight. Floor vases surrounded the table, filled with flowers which had to have come from Karen's storehouse. She crept closer to inspect the table and found a small silver bowl filled with water for a single floating white gardenia that filled the area with a heavenly scent.

Overcome with emotion, she turned her face to Samuel, her eyes swimming. "You did all of this for me?" she whispered.

Samuel put his arms around her. "I had a lot of help… I'm rather clumsy in these matters. Emma, Karen, and the boys all contributed."

"Karen?" Rachel bleated in disbelief.

"*Jah,* who do you think did all the floral arrangements?" He picked up a tiny silver bell from the table and rang it, grinning at her.

She heard a flurry of excitement and out of the commercial kitchen came flying Aaron, Amos and Abram all decked out in their black and white serving clothes, with white cloths draped over their arms. Rachel stifled a giggle. "You three remind me of the Penguins in Mary Poppins!"

They stared at her, thoroughly confused.

She waved a hand at them. "It was way before your time, I'll show you the video sometime."

Aaron pulled out a chair for her. "Milady," he beckoned her to sit.

Amos filled their glasses with iced soda water and plopped in a slice of lime while Abram handed them each a menu.

Rachel covered her mouth, trying hard not to squeal with delight. "It was so very sweet of them to go through all this trouble for me." She looked it over and her eyes grew large. "All my favorites," she whispered. This time the tears spilled over. She dabbed at her eyes with the white napkin. "I should have worn water-proof mascara!" she bemoaned. "I'm going to look like a Racoon before the night is over!"

The music then changed to other standards from the Great American Playbook, featuring Frank Sinatra, Michael Bublé, Steve Tyrell, Nora Jones, and Diana Krall. The boys hurried off to the kitchen.

Rachel grasped Samuel's hand in both of hers. "Thank you," she whispered, fighting back her tears. "I can't tell you how much this means to me. Everything is just beautiful and the fact the boys, Emma and even Karen all helped to pull it off without my knowledge makes it just that much sweeter."

"We all wanted you to feel special tonight," Samuel said, taking her hands in his. "Shall we pray?"

Rachel nodded and bowed her head.

"*Der Herr, danki* for this wonderful woman who You have brought into my life and for all your goodness. We ask that you bless the food and the hands that prepared it and to be our honored guest."

"Amen," Rachel beamed at him.

Amos came out of the kitchen bearing the first course.

"Roasted beets, goat cheese, honey drizzle and candied pecans...*yum!*" Rachel grinned.

Samuel eyed the beets with a doubtful eye.

"Try it, you'll like it!" Rachel urged him.

He speared a golden beet with his fork and spread some goat cheese on it. As soon as the food entered his mouth, his face became wreathed in a smile. He nodded, again reminding her of Barry whenever he ate something he really liked. "This is *gut!*"

"I know these foods are not what you're used to, so I appreciate your indulging me," Rachel smiled, popping a mouthful into her own. Samuel dug in, his misapprehension disappearing along with the beets and goat cheese in record time.

The second course arrived, and Samuel stared at it, thoroughly bewildered.

"It's a bone with crackers?" He pointed his fork at it. "How do I eat this?"

Rachel stifled a giggle. "It's bone *marrow*," she corrected him. "The nectar of the gods! Here."

She took a small knife and scraped some of the sizzing fatty marrow from the bone and spread it over a cracker and handed it to him.

Reluctantly he popped it into his mouth. An enormous smile spread over his face as he chewed. "*So gut!*" He copied her and handed her a cracker with marrow on it.

Rachel nodded in bliss. "The only thing better is seared *foie gras*," she remarked.

Samuel shoved another into his mouth. "Next time!" He looked very dejected when the bone had offered only two helpings each.

Aaron appeared as Amos took away the bone marrow appetizer plate. "Your main course, honeyed lamb shanks with fruited couscous." He set the plates down.

"What is couscous?" Samuel asked eagerly.

Rachel was glad he was enjoying the food as much as she was. "It's like a tiny little pasta rolled by hand," she said. "I had this dish in a Moroccan restaurant and thought I had died and gone to gastronomical heaven." She cut off a bite of her own lamb and offered it to him.

He opened his mouth and as soon as it hit his tongue, she thought his eyes were going to roll back into his head in ecstasy. "*Mmmm!*" he nodded vigorously. He didn't speak another word until he had consumed every bite and wiped his plate clean with a pita bread triangle. He sat back and patted his stomach. "I can die happy now," he said then belched long and loudly.

Rachel burst into laughter and belched right after him. "I think I'm too full for dessert," she said, standing up. "Could we go for a walk?"

"*Jah*, but I have something better in mind," he pulled her chair out like a true gentleman and led her out to the area that had been created for dancing outdoors. The dance floor had been set up, the market lights all lit, and a full moon had risen in the cooling night air. The music floated out over the outdoor speakers.

"Samuel," Rachel gulped. "You truly thought of everything!"

He led her to the dance floor and put his arms around her. "Well, not everything. I have never danced and do not know how."

"I'm not very good either," Rachel murmured, looking up into his eyes. "We can just stand here and sway."

"As long as you're in my arms, I'm content," he whispered.

The music played on for another fifteen minutes while they slowly swayed on their feet, wrapped closely in each other's arms watching the full moon rise high into the night sky.

Samuel cupped Rachel's face in his hands and stared deeply into her eyes. "*Schön*[25]," he murmured, bending down to kiss her. At that moment they heard the little silver bell beckoning to them.

"Dessert!" Emma called out from the barn.

Samuel murmured against Rachel's lips. "I'm going to have to speak to her about what bad timing she has,"

Rachel giggled and rewarded him with a kiss. "Aw, they went to so much trouble for us, let's not ruin it."

---

[25] Beautiful

They walked hand-in-hand back to the barn and found a large serving plate. The moment Rachel clapped eyes on it, she exclaimed with joy. "The honeybee? Really?"

Samuel held her seat out for her. "*Was is* honeybee?"

"It's absolutely the best thing I ever ate," Rachel gushed. "I had it in Venice, Italy when Barry and I were on our honeymoon and never forgot it. I can't believe Emma even knew about it much more found the recipe! It's panna cotta frozen into the shape of a honeycomb, lavender ice-cream, and honey pearls." She scooped up a little bit of each onto her spoon and held it out for Samuel.

His mouth closed over it and for a moment Rachel thought he was going to cry. He nodded at her. "The best thing I have ever tasted!" he agreed. They polished it off then looked around the softly glowing barn.

"Best first date ever," Rachel smiled up at him. "How on earth are you going to ever top this?"

Chapter Fourteen

"Autumn Surprises"

It was mid-September; the weather had become a bit milder and events at Rachel's barn had resumed. She was fully booked every weekend for both the barn and the Inn except for the month of November which she had set aside for her wedding/family reunion/Thanksgiving.

It was early afternoon and her friend, Rhonda, had flown in for the weekend to make final adjustments for her last fitting.

Rachel lifted her arms. "I can't believe it's only two months away, *Oww!*"

"Sorry," Rhonda mumbled through the pins sticking out of her mouth. She was on her knees in Rachel's bedroom, pinning the hem and taking in the sides when she accidentally poked Rachel with a pin. Rachel felt uncomfortable with her friend kneeling on the floor and pinning her dress as though she were just a mere tailor instead of a world-famous fashion designer. She looked down at the muslin, wondering what Samuel would think when he saw her walking down the aisle for the first time.

She reminisced back to her wedding day to Barry. She had been near-sighted at the time but had refused to wear eyeglasses, so she had not been able to see his face from the other side of the church when he first beheld her. He had later told her that she had been the most beautiful thing he had ever seen. Since then, she had had Lasik done on her eyes (a gift from her late mother) so this time she was looking forward to seeing Samuel's face when he caught sight of her. Janet had given the videographer strict instructions to film both his reaction and her appearance at the same time with two cameras.

Rhonda stood back onto her feet and removed the remaining pins from her mouth. "Turn around slowly for me, please."

Rachel obeyed while Rhonda scrutinized her handiwork. "How does it feel? Lift your arms and let me know if the sleeves are too restrictive."

Rachel lifted her arms up and down. "Nope, feels good!"

"How about the waist and the length?"

"Both good!" Rachel replied. The hem came to just below her knees and she could take a deep breath easily.

"Okay, let me help you off with that, careful of the pins!"

Rachel lifted her arms over her head while Rhonda slipped the muslin off over her head.

"You're going to be a beautiful bride!" she assured her.

"I hope Samuel will think so," Rachel replied. "To be honest, the closer the wedding gets, the more nervous I become."

"Why is that?" Rhonda wanted to know, carefully packing away the muslin.

"Well, you know…" Rachel replied, embarrassed to even bring the subject up.

Rhonda blinked at her, completely confused. "No, I don't know what."

Rachel sighed and covered her face with her hands, her next words coming out muffled. "I have never been with another man other than Barry. He was my first boyfriend and even though we dated a few years, we waited until our wedding night…for…well…you know."

Rhonda burst into laughter. "Sweetheart…it's just like riding a bicycle! You just hop right back on after you fall off and make sure you wear white at night!"

Rachel moaned, "You're no help! That's exactly what Barry would have told me."

The days were growing shorter. Wedding invitations had all been sent out weeks before and responses received. Over fifty family members and friends were coming into town to celebrate and meet Samuel for the first time. The air was charged with excitement and anticipation. The countdown to their nuptials had begun.

It was late afternoon. Rachel stood over the hot stove, stirring a large pot of chili for the evening's meal, her mind in turmoil. Trays of cornbread were cooling on the counter while she went through a mental checklist of all she needed to get done before the big day. Emma was slicing the last of the vegetables for a fresh salad and had already canned and pickled enough produce from their garden in the past few weeks to last the winter months. Everyone had lent a hand in the canning, even the boys, and now the pantry was fully stocked. The special wedding day celery was almost ready for harvest, an Amish tradition that Rachel was more than happy to give to Samuel as one of his wedding gifts.

The wedding was to be a week-long affair to include a family reunion celebrating Thanksgiving together for the first time since Barry's death, followed by their wedding on the Sunday after. Everyone was getting increasingly excited as the days counted down, except, she noticed, for Samuel, who was becoming quieter and more distant with each passing day, and it was making her paranoid. She was feeling very uneasy around him, much like she had when Ruth Beiler had tried to torpedo their relationship but this time, she had no idea what was bothering him, and Samuel wasn't talking.

Maybe he doesn't want to marry me anymore? She fretted for the 100th time that day. He had hardly touched her in the past several weeks and was avoiding eye contact. No one else seemed to take notice but it was driving her crazy. She had confided in Rhonda and Janet but since they were both out of town until their arrival date, they could do no more than make blind guesses as to why he was acting so strangely.

An acrid smell filled the air.

"Oh no!" she yelped. She grabbed the oven mitts and opened the oven door. A cloud of smoke billowed out. She had completely forgotten about the apple cider donuts she had been baking in the oven. She retrieved two pans of small black, incinerated donuts and dumped the smoking pans on the counter in dismay, shutting the oven door with her shoe. "Great, just great!" she grumbled, surveying the damage. "More baked goods ruined." She had hoped she had overcome her baking handicap for good, but she hadn't been paying attention to either the smell or the small kitchen timer, too distracted and worried about Samuel. Tears of frustration welled up in her eyes.

"And another one bites the dust!" Karen announced to no one in particular, entering the kitchen. "What did you cremate this time?"

"The apple cider donuts," Rachel grumbled.

"Bummer," Karen replied. She lifted the lid off the chili and took in a deep whiff. "Is this Genesis Chili?" she asked. Genesis Chili had come from her cousin and was a family favorite. It was hearty and both spicy and sweet at the same time because of the red pepper flakes and honey that was added to the mixture.

"Yes," mumbled Rachel.

Karen looked at her. "What's eating you?"

"Nothing,"

"Doesn't look like nothing," Karen replied, crossing her arms.

"Honestly, Karen, I'm not sure what it is. Maybe I'm just paranoid...but I think Samuel is getting cold feet..." *Oops,* she hadn't wanted to say that.

Emma stopped chopping and stared at her with concern. "Cold feet? As in not wanting to get married, cold feet?"

Rachel nodded, misery descending on her like a wet blanket.

"Has he said anything?"

She shook her head, "No, that's just it. He hardly talks to me at all, won't look at me…" The concern in Emma's eyes was both gratifying and frightening.

"I just left him in the barn milking the cows," Karen said. "You should go talk to him."

Rachel shook her head. "I'm afraid to," she squeaked, a tear sliding down her cheek.

Karen rolled her eyes. "Mom, get a grip! You need to go talk to him!"

"Karen is right," Emma agreed, giving Rachel a much-needed hug. "*Honesty is like a straight line; it may not be the shortest way, but it is the best way and most reliable path,*" she quoted. "Go and clear the air, I'll watch the chili and make another batch of donuts."

"Oh, alright," Rachel hung up her apron on a peg and grabbed a sweatshirt. She went out the service porch and crossed the pea gravel lot to the barn. She glanced at her vegetable garden, now barren except for the wedding celery, the remainder of the dirt rows laying fallow for the winter. It looked as sad as she felt. She hugged the sweatshirt closer to her body, her teeth starting to chatter from the cold and entered the barn. The smell of hay, manure and animals greeted her nostrils.

"Samuel?" she called, nervous as could be.

"Here," came his voice from one of the stanchions.

She threaded her way through and found him on his milk stool.

"Hi," she said shyly.

"*Hallo,*" he replied, still focused on his milking.

Rachel shuffled her feet. "It's been a while since we talked, Samuel."

"*Jah?*"

"*Jah*…I mean, yes. You haven't spoken to me, won't touch me, won't look me in the eye…is there anything bothering you?"

His hands paused on the udders and there was a long silence. "*Jah*," he replied softly, still refusing to look at her.

Rachel's heart was hammering, fear gripped her. "Do, do…do you not want to marry me anymore?" It came out as a pathetic squeak.

Samuel's head jerked up, his eyes going wide with surprise. "*Nee*, why would you think something like that?"

"Well, why wouldn't I think something like that?" she retorted. "I've been imagining all sorts of horrible things because you won't tell me what's wrong." She kicked a clod of dirt on the floor. "Maybe you just aren't attracted to me anymore…"

Samuel sprung to his feet, his stool and pail of milk falling over with a clatter. He advanced on her, caught her in his arms and pressed her up against the wall behind her, catching her completely off guard. His arms tightened about her possessively.

His sudden ferocity completely discombobulated her. She felt his lips a mere breath away from her right ear, his breathing labored. "Don't even think such things," his husky voice rasped, pressing himself against her to make his point. If he hadn't been holding her up, she would have collapsed with relief. His physical proximity was making her weak at the knees. His eyes searched hers and his rough calloused hands cradled her head. "*Das Warten auf dich war eine Tortur*[26]."

"Really?" she asked.

In answer, his bent his mouth upon hers and kissed her until she couldn't think straight. When they broke apart, they were both breathing heavily.

"I'm so confused," Rachel said, laying her head against his chest. "If marrying me isn't the problem then what is?"

---

[26] Waiting for you has been torture

Samuel's words came out muffled against her shoulder where he had smothered his face.

"What?" Rachel asked. "I didn't understand you."

He lifted his face and looked her tenderly in the eyes. "I desire to marry you more than anything, *mein liebling*[27]," he finally whispered. "It's just suddenly hit me that I will have no family, no pastor, no one to stand up for me…my side of the sanctuary will be empty…and it *hurts*."

Rachel's guts twisted in pain for him and the look of hurt in his eyes tore her heart out. "Oh, Samuel," she whispered, "I'm so sorry."

Of course he's mourning the loss of his family, friends and community, she berated herself for not realizing this sooner. *He gave up everything for me.*

"What can I do?" she whispered, cupping his face. "How can I make this better?"

"Just love me, Rachel" Samuel whispered back, tears seeping from his eyes.

Rachel snaked her arms about his muscled body and held him close. "Forever," she promised, then an idea popped into her head. "I think I know what we can do."

A flicker of hope appeared in his blue eyes, "*Jah*?"

"*Jah*…I mean yes." She wiggled out of his embrace but planted a kiss on his cheek as reassurance. "Just give me some time," She looked down at the milk spreading across the floor. "What a mess,"

"I'll take care of it." Samuel replied.

Rachel ran back to the house, removing her milk-sodden shoes outside and made a beeline to her computer.

She brought up Facebook and the Ex-Amish/Mennonite Group she had used to obtain labor for the event barn and typed furiously. She read over her post several times before submitting, hoping there would be a speedy response.

Within minutes her phone was blowing up with gratifying texts and phone calls in response. She was beside herself with joy and just hoped that her last-minute effort would

---

[27] splendid

somehow make it up to Samuel for all he had sacrificed for her.

Samuel, Rachel, Karen, Emma and the boys were all seated around the dinner table when a knock sounded upon the door, interrupting the blessing.

"Were you expecting guests this week?" Samuel asked Rachel.

She shook her head. "No, the entire month of November was cleared just for us, I have no idea who would be knocking this time of night."

The knock came again, a bit louder.

Samuel stood onto his feet and went to the front door, the boys right behind him. He opened the door and peered out.

Emma, Karen, and Rachel leaned forward, trying to catch the conversation. They could hear a male voice on the other side of the door but couldn't make out the conversation. They watched in surprise as Samuel opened the door all the way and invited a thirty-something-aged man into the room.

"Rachel," Samuel beckoned. "This is Josef Eicher, he said he came in response to your invitation.

Josef came into view. He was very tall, blonde, and dressed modestly. His face was clean shaven.

He smiled and held out his hand, "Mrs. Winston, I came in response to your invitation earlier today."

Rachel stood up, momentarily blanking on what he meant by her invitation. "Oh! You mean the Facebook group post?" She walked over to him and shook his hand, giving him a friendly smile. "I wasn't expecting a personal visit and so soon!"

Josef backed towards the door. "I'm intruding, please forgive me…"

"No, no, no it's quite alright!" Rachel caught his arm and beckoned to the table. "Would you like to come in and join us for supper? We were just about to eat."

"I don't wish to inconvenience you," he said, but his eyes and grumbling stomach said otherwise.

Rachel felt immediate compassion for him. "When's the last time you had a home-cooked meal, Josef?"

"Not for quite a while," he replied. "I eat at Amish run restaurants quite bit, but it can be uncomfortable and expensive."

"Sit," Rachel commanded, pulling an extra chair to the table. "We have plenty."

Samuel and the boys scooted their chairs over for him and gave him encouraging smiles.

"We are all outcasts here," Aaron explained, retaking his seat.

Josef sat down and looked around the table at the welcoming smiles and seemed to relax a little bit.

"Let us pray," Samuel said.

They all bowed their heads.

Samuel cleared his throat, then began "*Der Herr, You show mercy to us in times of affliction, and You give us comfort. I pray for all at this table, that You would be gracious and merciful to us. Thank You, Der Herr, because in Christ we are secured, accepted, and loved. In Christ, we find eternal life and forgiveness from our sins. We have joy in Christ that no one, even the thief, can ever steal from us. I pray that You will bless this food, be in our midst and bless our conversation. Lead and guide us, in Jesus' name, I pray. Amen.*"

Emma popped up and collected a clean plate, bowl, drinking glass, and cutlery, and placed them before Josef.

"*Danki,*" he said, giving Rachel a look that made her throat tighten in compassion for him. "I did not expect to find such a welcome from strangers."

Rachel ladled a healthy helping of chili into his bowl. Samuel passed the platter of cornbread and soon they were all tucking into their meal. Rachel noticed that everyone pretended not to notice the way Josef attacked his food as only a famished man could. There wasn't much conversation until he had finished his third helping.

"Forgive me," he murmured, a bit chagrined by his ravenous behavior. "It's been at least a day and a half since my last meal." He wiped his mouth with the napkin and took a long drink of milk. He sat back in his chair and looked around the table.

"I recognize a few of you," he said, looking at Aaron, Abram and Amos. "I helped a little at the barn raising a few months ago, it brought back fond memories."

Rachel leaned forward, "You said you came in response to my post?"

Josef nodded. "*Jah*, you mentioned that you could use a pastor in that Facebook group."

"You're a pastor?" Samuel asked, shooting a questioning glance at Rachel.

"*Jah*," Josef nodded. "I felt called by *Der Herr* from an early age, but my parents believed it was out of pride and so discouraged it. They wanted me to marry and perhaps later become an elder or bishop in the community, but I felt called to go to seminary and lead a celibate life devoted to *Der Herr*."

"Are you catholic?" Rachel inquired, noting the absence of a clerical collar or other raiment.

Josef shook his head. "*Nee*, I did go to seminary, but it was Protestant and against their wishes."

"Where did you attend?" Emma asked.

"Lancaster Bible College, not too far from here," Josef replied. "I graduated last May with a master's in divinity and ministry but have been unable to find a position so I have been taking odd jobs where I could find them, such as your barn raising, and staying on friend's couches but I am worried that I am wearing out my welcome. I saw your post today and got a ride here hoping it was a sign from *Der Herr*.

Your Inn is aptly named, I also could use a second chance," he smiled, and Rachel's heart went out to him.

"We have been hoping and praying for a shepherd to pastor this flock," Samuel continued. "I just didn't expect one to come knocking on our door!" He gave Josef a smile. "You are welcome to stay the night in the dawdi haus for tonight. We will also need to pray and seek *Der Herr's* will in this matter."

...and run a background check, Rachel thought to herself. "Would anyone like some coffee and dessert? We have apple cider donuts tonight."

"Yes!" everyone chorused enthusiastically.

While Emma busied herself with the preparations, Rachel excused herself to her office and got on the computer. First, she looked up Josef on the Facebook group and found his profile. So far, everything looked "kosher". Next, she went onto the Lancaster Bible College site and searched for the list of recent graduates and verified he was one of them. "Check, check!" she smiled to herself. Next was a Lexus/Nexus search which would run a thorough background check on both public and private records. She got available public domain information, none of it concerning. As far as she could tell, he had never even gotten a traffic ticket, but a more detailed report would take at least a week. She returned to the kitchen where everyone was enjoying the donuts and coffee. Josef was sitting in his chair but was obviously having a hard time staying awake, his head kept drooping only to wake up with a jerk.

Rachel beckoned to Samuel. "His story checks out so far," she whispered into his ear. "Poor man looks ready to fall over, let's get him to his room."

"*Jah,*" Samuel agreed. He laid a gentle hand on Josef's shoulder. "Did you bring any luggage with you?"

Josef stood up. "I have just the one bag with some clothes and my books," he replied. "I left them on the front porch."

Rachel watched as they walked together out the front door. Despite the unusual circumstances, she felt at peace about welcoming Josef for the night, just as she had with Emma and the boys. Time, of course, would tell but for the time being, they would give Josef his second chance and a place of refuge.

Chapter Fifteen

"A Shepherd for the Flock"

It was the first week of November. The days were noticeably shorter and finally becoming much colder. Samuel was making fires in the hearth every night and the cast iron stove was fed constantly with wood to warm the house instead of using the expensive heating system. Rachel was fully recovered and able to resume most of her tasks, which now consisted mainly of coordinating the travel of her friends and family to the Inn and getting their rooms ready. She also got to indulge again in her love of cooking and threw herself into making hearty, rib-sticking meals, featuring beef barley, split pea, and bean soups, savory roasts with roasted root vegetables, roast chicken, as well as freshly baked breads and canned fruits. The air was filled with anticipation both for their first church service in the new barn and their combination wedding/family reunion/Thanksgiving as well.

Josef's *bona fides* had all checked out and they had all grown very fond of him, especially, and most obviously, Emma. He was humble and meek as a mouse but also diligent, always willing to lend a hand in the barn and around the Inn if Samuel and the boys were otherwise engaged. He had turned out to be quite the handyman as well, saving Rachel from an expensive plumbing bill after her kitchen sink spouted a small leak.

A knock came upon Rachel's office door the week prior to their first church service.

Emma poked her head in. "Rachel, there is a great deal of preparation that normally goes into Sunday services on an Amish farm,"

"Oh?" Rachel straightened up from her computer. "Like what? Come on in and sit for a bit."

"Well, a thorough cleaning for sure," Emma began. "*There is nothing that cleans a house, or barn like company coming,*" she quoted. "It usually takes weeks to prepare but since the barn is new and built for events, it just needs a thorough once over with mops on the ceiling, walls and floor."

Rachel's eyes widened, incredulous. "You *mop* the ceiling *and* the walls?"

Emma nodded, "*Jah,* also we power-wash the picket fences, mulch the flower beds, polish all the furniture and make sure the water trough for the horses is free of dirt and the water not frozen."

Rachel's head was spinning. "Anything else?"

Emma thought aloud, "Well, you won't need a bench wagon for seating because you already have your own for the barn events."

"Bench wagon?"

"*Jah,* there is one for each district. It's an enclosed cargo carrier that comes a few days before church driven by a team of horses carrying long wooden church benches. You won't be needing it which is gut because they wouldn't let you use one."

"Well, can you organize Ruth, Naomi, Annie and Karen to do all the other things?" Rachel asked, then added with a roll of her eyes, "I can just hear Karen now when she's told to mop down the walls…"

"There's also the food to consider," Emma added. "You will want to have the women here to help prepare the food to feed everyone a few days ahead of time."

"I'm almost afraid to ask, but what is normally served? A fatted calf?" She giggled at her poor attempt at humor.

Emma smiled, "*Nee*, it's usually two different soft spreads, plenty of bread to make sandwiches with them, pickled beets and cucumbers, butter, homemade jelly, pretzels, Snitz and Shoofly pies…"

"*Snitz pie?*" Rachel replied. "I have not heard of that one before, it doesn't sound appetizing at all…"

"It's apple butter and applesauce baked into a pie shell," Emma explained.

"Do you know how to make it?" Rachel replied.

"*Jah…*"

"Good, then I'll let you handle those. Can I supplement with recipes of my own?"

"Not if this were a traditional church gathering," Emma replied. "Changes are usually frowned upon but since this isn't, what were you thinking of?"

"Well, it's been pretty cold out, so I was thinking beef and barley soup, maybe some home-made baked beans." Rachel replied, then lapsed into an Irish lilt. "Something to warm the cockles of their heart."

Emma nodded, "I'll get the girls organized; they were super excited about having church again."

"Me too, it's been too long," Rachel agreed. "This past year I've had to content myself with online Bible studies, streaming services from my old church, and the Maranatha Praise Singers station on Pandora to make up for not going to church, but it's high time we had Christian fellowship, and the members of that group seem to be very hungry for it. Josef has been holed up in the *dawdi haus* all week working on his sermon. Do we have to do this every week like English churches?"

Emma shook her head, "*Nee,* every other week and the families usually take turns hosting in each community, so they are not overly burdened. It's a lot to take on."

"Well, I don't plan on mopping down the ceiling and walls of the event barn and Inn every other week, that's for sure or I'll have a revolt on my hands." Rachel replied. "Once a quarter should be sufficient."

Karen was bundled up with wool beanie, neck scarf, mittens, and down jacket, collecting eggs when she heard familiar footsteps. Her heartbeat picked up a little, anticipating who it might be. Aaron rounded the corner and gave her a smile. He was bundled up as much as she was.

"*Guten Morgen*[28]," he said, his dimples showing, his breath coming out in smoky billows.

"Morning," Karen replied softly. She turned back to her task, keenly aware that Aaron was watching her as he swept out the droppings. They had fallen into a daily routine of "bumping into one another" on a regular basis. In the mornings it was at the chicken coop and at various other times of day. He always found an excuse to be near her. She found it to be both unnerving and exciting at the same time.

"Are you looking forward to having church services?" he asked, dumping a shovel full of chicken droppings into a wheelbarrow.

"Not really," Karen admitted. "It just meant more extra work...I mean mopping the walls, polishing the furniture? Give me a break! I'm exhausted!"

Aaron grinned and nodded "*Jah,* it always entailed two weeks of preparation at our house when we hosted,"

Karen carefully retrieved an egg from under a squawking chicken. "How long was the service?" she asked, just to be conversational.

"It could go on for a good four hours," Aaron replied.

---

[28] Good morning

"What?!" she screeched, dropping the egg; it smashed open onto the floor. "Dang and dang it!!" she grouched.

Aaron set aside the shovel and squatted next to her as they both cleaned up the mess.

"Four hours?" Karen bemoaned. "I'm going to go out of my mind with boredom! Why does it take so long? Is that why you left the Amish? What are Amish services like?" It was the most she had said to him in all the months since he had come to the Inn.

He grinned at her. "*Nee,* that's not why I left. I enjoyed our services. We start out singing…"

"Did you play an instrument?" Karen interrupted.

"I wasn't allowed to," Aaron replied. "I loved to play guitar and had to hide it and practice secretly. Musical instruments are not allowed, just our voices singing hymns," he replied patiently. "Like our singings, it's a *capella.*"

"Then what?"

"Then the sermon which can last about an hour followed by more singing."

"I like to sing," Karen murmured, reaching for another egg.

"*Jah,* I've heard you singing to the chickens, you have a gut voice," Aaron responded.

Karen could feel her face growing hot with embarrassment; he had heard her singing *Lady Gaga to the chickens!* "Well, what if you need to use the bathroom sometime during those four hours? Do you just have to hold it?"

"*Nee,* we are permitted to take bathroom breaks as needed," Aaron replied, clearly enjoying Karen's sudden interest.

"What do Amish preachers talk about?"

Aaron leaned in close, his face mere inches from hers. It both thrilled and intimidated her.

"You're about to find out," he grinned.

It was the Saturday night before the first church service in their event barn. Rachel was stirring a large pot of baked beans she had made for the following day. She glanced over her shoulder at Karen who was doing her homework at the counter. "Almost done with your history assignment, honey?"

"Yes," Karen mumbled, tapping away at her laptop. The assignment was due to be uploaded by midnight and as usual, she had waited until the last minute to get it done.

"How come Amish kids only to have go to school until the end of junior high?"

"You already asked Samuel that," Rachel replied, trying not to lose her patience. It was a sore subject and one that Karen constantly brought up every time she procrastinated on a hated homework assignment. "They learn their trades from either their families or apprentice with other Amish businesses where their skills and interests lie. They learn a trade from which they can support a family."

"Well, why can't I do that?" Karen whined. "I really hate being homeschooled. I would much rather go to school and have a social life and make friends my own age or be a full-time florist apprentice."

Rachel turned away from the stove and pointed out the window. The outside temperature was averaging 46 degrees Fahrenheit for the high during the day. For transplants from California, it was absolutely freezing, and they had had to invest in a lot of long underwear and other cold weather clothing that wasn't available in their home state. "So let me get this straight, you would actually prefer to get up at 4:00 am when it's 22 degrees out, so you can complete all your morning chores in order to catch the school bus in both frigid and sweltering weather, stay chained to a desk in a classroom for seven hours and then come home to do all of your afternoon chores plus homework instead of the three solid hours of home study you have here each day where you get to roll out of bed at 6:00 am?"

Karen just stared back at her, refusing to answer. It was a constant source of friction between them.

Rachel crossed her arms and called her bluff, "Just say the word, Karen, and I'll have you enrolled in Pequea Valley High School for your senior year."

Karen shook her head. "Well, what would be the point, then, if it's only for one year? Everyone would already be in their little cliques, and I would be the odd one out."

Rachel turned back to the beans and added more boiling water before she put the heavy Le Creuset pot back into the oven to slow cook. "So, you just wanted to gripe, then?"

Karen did not respond but worked, silently fuming until she finally got the assignment finished and uploaded to the Homeschool site. "There, happy now?"

Rachel bit back the snarky come-back she so wanted to hurl at her daughter because Josef entered the room at that moment. It would not do to be a snot to her daughter in front of the new pastor.

"What smells so *gut?*" he wondered aloud, favoring both Rachel and Karen with a shy smile. "I smell both bacon and maple!"

"I'm making Saturday Night baked beans for after church service tomorrow," Rachel replied. "How's the sermon going?"

"I believe I finally have it finished the way *Der Herr* would want it," he replied. He went to the kitchen sink and turned the faucet on. "No more leaks?" he wanted to confirm.

"No," Rachel smiled. "You did excellent repair work. Did you apprentice as a plumber before you went to seminary?"

At that moment, Emma entered the kitchen, her arms laden with mason jars of pickled vegetables and canned peaches she had collected from the root cellar.

Josef rushed forward to help, "Let me help you with those," he rescued four jars and placed them on the counter.

Emma's face turned beet red, "*Danki,*" she squeaked.

Rachel and Karen exchanged knowing glances.

It was patently obvious to both how besotted Emma had become with Josef. She lit up like a firefly whenever he came near and behaved in a very flustered and awkward manner in his presence. Although he had made it very clear to all when he first arrived (and many times after that) that he felt called to a life of celibacy, it only fueled Emma's growing infatuation with him that much more (because as every woman knows, the more she can't have something, the worse she wants it). It worried Rachel not only about Emma's feelings but also for the tranquility of the Inn and all those she had taken in. The last thing she wanted was a heartbroken Emma and a guilt-ridden pastor. It was a future train wreck waiting to happen, but she had no idea how to circumvent it.

An invisible television announcer began narrating an introduction for an Amish soap opera spoof inside her head…

Next on Trouble in Paradise, will Emma win the elusive Pastor Josef over with her winsome ways, or will she be doomed to pine for a man she can never have?

Rachel mentally slapped herself back into reality. "Emma, could you call the boys in for supper? We have a lot to do still, before service tomorrow."

"*Jah,*" Emma nodded, reluctantly leaving the kitchen, her eyes lingering upon Josef for a moment.

Karen leaned forward, "She's got it bad," she whispered.

Rachel nodded. I *know* she mouthed, so Josef wouldn't pick up on their conversation.

Karen stood up, closing her laptop, and unplugging it from the outlet. "I'll just put this away before I set the table," she announced loudly for Josef's benefit.

"Okay." Rachel replied, *sotto* voce. She turned back to Josef who was smiling at her, completely clueless as to the drama that was going on around him. "Hope you like roast beef and noodle kugel,"

"Everything you make in *wunderbar*," he smiled, patting his tummy. "I think I'm putting on weight from all the gut cooking."

"You and Samuel, both," Rachel replied. "He has filled out quite a bit since I came here a year and a half ago after he had gone through all of his canned goods, but he always says *A round wife and a full barn are the signs of good success*, so I assume that applies to men as well."

"*Jah*, I have been lately rethinking my vow of celibacy in favor of marriage," he admitted.

Rachel's eyebrows climbed high into her hairline, her hopes rekindling. "Oh?" she encouraged.

"*Jah*, because of how expensive and abysmal I find fast food and prepared foods, it would probably be healthier to have a wife."

Rachel's heart soared with renewed hope for Emma, but his next words sent her hopes crashing back to earth.

"But now that *Der Herr* has provided me with such gut food and regular meals here, I see no need to renounce my vow." He smiled at her as if he thought his words would be welcomed. It had the exact opposite effect.

"Oh," was all Rachel could manage, her hopes crashing and burning. The cogs began to churn in her head. If all it took for Josef to reconsider his vow of celibacy was the lack of regular, home-cooked meals then by gosh, for Emma's sake, she would find a way to make him reconsider.

Operation Emma Nuptials here we come!

Rachel was up early that Sunday, both excited and nervous for the Inn's first church service. She had received over fifty responses and was expecting a full house. Because the barn was so relatively new and constructed to hold people instead of animals, preparations were relatively easy. She already had sufficient seating and tables upon which they could serve food, and the commercial kitchen was more than adequate to meet the demands of such a gathering.

The grass was covered in frost and her breath coming out in billows of smoke as she hurried to the barn to check on the set up. Samuel exited the *dawdi haus* followed by the boys as well as Josef Eicher.

Samuel grasped Rachel's hand and despite the numbing cold his hands were warm. They entered the barn and shut the large sliding door behind them to keep out the cold. In addition to the existing wooden benches (with backs for comfort} there were also numerous high-quality, Amish made, wooden folding chairs with cushions for those who were elderly, infirm, or pregnant. Tables stood on one side of the barn near the entrance to the kitchen to hold the vast amounts of food they had been preparing all week.

"It all looks *gut*," Josef nodded, bouncing up and down on his heels nervously.

"Are you nervous?" Rachel asked him.

The look he gave her spoke volumes. "It's my very first sermon since I graduated. I hope it will be received well and please *Der Herr*."

Rachel grasped his hand and reached for Samuel's who, in turn, took the hand of Aaron until all of them stood in a small circle, clasping hands. "Samuel, would you pray over our shepherd?" she asked.

They all bowed their heads.

"*Der Herr*, we come to thee humbly and give thee thanks for sending Josef to us in response to our prayers. We ask thy blessing upon him and that you would fill his heart and mouth with thy words. We pray that thy holy spirit would fill this place and touch the hearts of all who come as it pleases thee, amen."

A knock sounded on the barn door. Samuel slid it to one side and a small host of women entered, among them, Ruth, Emma, Naomi and Annie, clutching their woolen cloaks about them.

"It's absolutely freezing out there! Hallo, Rachel! We're ready to get everything prepped!" Emma smiled. She walked by Josef and favored him with an encouraging smile that drew Rachel's attention.

Poor Emma, she thought. *Why are all the good ones, 'bachelor's till the rapture?*

"Ach, so nice and toasty in here!" she added, with a wink in Josef's direction, something that would have earned her the ire of traditional Amish folk who frowned upon flirting. They made a beeline for the kitchen, hanging up their cloaks and donning aprons as they swept through the swinging service door one by one. The sounds of singing, talking and laughter floated through the door as the men made their final preparations and more women arrived to help with the food and socialize a bit before the 8:00 am service.

"Almost show time!" Rachel announced as Josef nervously paced from one side of the barn to the other. She opened the barn door and was gratified to find so many people waiting outside of both genders and all ages. The older men and women entered first, men taking their seats on the left and the women on the right from long-ingrained custom, even though there were no such restrictions in place.

"Old habits die hard," one of them grinned at Rachel, shuffling to the front.

Rachel peered out the barn door and gasped. A line of cars was filling her long driveway, waiting patiently to park in the area usually reserved for barn events. Soon her parking lot was filled with the rest of the vehicles having no choice but to park on the shoulder of the driveway.

Samuel joined her, marveling at the response to their invitation.

"I hope the Fire Marshall doesn't decide to inspect us this morning," she whispered to him. "I'm not sure we'd pass."

"*Jah,* which is a concern we should take into account before the next meeting." He nodded.

In short order the barn was filled with former Amish/Mennonite attendees. There were hugs all around and animated chatter.

Rachel and Samuel let them socialize for the good part of half an hour then she gave a nod to Josef to begin.

He stood before the simple wooden podium. "Welcome to all of you," he greeted them, his voice an octave higher than normal due to his nerves. He cleared his throat. "Welcome," he repeated in a more normal tone of voice. He was greeted with warm smiles and a few giggles. Rachel stole a glance at Emma who was seated near the back, her blue eyes fixated on Josef. "Welcome to all of you to…to…" He paused for a moment, casting about for the right word, then smiled sheepishly. "Church." He finished. "I am Josef Eicher, we will begin with *Das Loblied*, hymn of praise."

The congregants stood, all familiar with the age-old Amish hymn:

> *O Lord Father, we bless thy name,*
> *Thy love and thy goodness praise;*
> *That thou, O Lord, so graciously*
> *Have been to us always.*
> *Thou hast brought us together, O Lord,*
> *To be admonished through thy word.*
> *Bestow on us thy grace.*
> *O may thy servant be endowed*
> *With wisdom from on high,*
> *To preach thy word with truth and power,*
> *Thy name to glorify.*
> *Which needful is to they own praise,*
> *Give hunger for thy word always,*
> *This should be our desire.*

Rachel had ordered and distributed copies of the traditional *Ausbund* on the benches as well as handbooks of Maranatha Worship that were used in her former church. As the voices lifted in simple, vocal praise, she closed her eyes in rapture, transported to another place by the simple beauty of the *acapella* singing. She was unfamiliar with the tune so was content to just listen, amazed by the beautiful harmonies.

Next, Aaron stepped up front, an acoustic guitar slung over his shoulder. "This is the main reason why I wasn't baptized into the Amish community," he admitted to all of them, tuning the guitar as he spoke. "I played in secret and loved to create music."

Several people nodded in silent understanding.

"Next we will be singing Psalm 134, verses 1-3," he announced. He strummed the guitar and led everyone in song, encouraging them to echo back at him to learn the words:

Behold bless ye the Lord
All ye servants of the Lord
Lift up your hands in the sanctuary
And bless, bless ye the Lord
Behold bless ye the Lord
All ye servants of the Lord
Lift up your hands in the sanctuary
And bless, bless ye the Lord
Behold bless ye the Lord
All ye servants of the Lord
Lift up your hands in the sanctuary
And bless, bless ye the Lord
Behold bless ye the Lord
All ye servants of the Lord
Lift up your hands in the sanctuary
And bless, bless ye the Lord

For the next fifteen minutes, they took turns singing from both the Ausbund as well as new worship songs. Finally, Aaron put his guitar in its stand then sat down next to Karen on the bench, something that would have been strictly forbidden in a real Amish church meeting.

"You play, really good," Rachel heard her whisper in an aside to him.

"*Danki,*" he whispered back, taking her hand in his.

Here we go *again,* Rachel thought to herself, easily recognizing the early signs of infatuation.

Josef came back up to the podium and nervously cleared his throat. "I prayed long and hard about what the Lord may want me to teach on in my very first sermon," he began. "He led me to the parable of the prodigal son, something to which all of us can relate, I'm sure."

A general murmur and chuckles came from many members of the congregation.

He opened his Bible. "Let us pray first." He bowed his head and closed his eyes. "*Der Herr,* I ask for You to fill my heart, mind and mouth with thy words and to bless all who hear it today, amen."

"Amen," repeated the congregation.

For the next hour Josef spoke simply yet eloquently of the father's love and pain for his prodigal son, expertly weaving in a profound message from both a human and divine perspective. When he was done, there was not a dry eye in the room. Rachel dabbed at her eyes with a Kleenex and exhaled. She turned to look at Samuel who was looking down at the floor, tears dripping from his eyes.

Everyone was frozen in their seats, visibly and deeply moved. The long awkward silence that ensued made Josef shift nervously back and forth on his feet, wondering if he had done something wrong or was misreading their reactions. Somewhere in the back, someone blew their nose very loudly.

"Wow," Karen whispered.

Rachel turned to look at her daughter. Karen who rarely, if ever, shed a tear and who had them visibly welling up in her eyes.

"I agree, to hear this from the father's point of view instead of the prodigal son's was a real eye opener," Rachel whispered back.

Aaron stood up and went to the front to play a final worship song, wiping his own tears away as he lifted the guitar and slung the strap over his shoulder.

"Thank you, Pastor Eicher," he said and began strumming a tune that Rachel recognized as the featured song for alter calls at the local Harvest Crusade. "If anyone needs to come up for prayer, please feel free to do so," he added.

Rachel watched in awe and amazement as a couple dozen of people stood up, weeping, to make their way to the front in response as Aaron sang:

Come just as you are
Hear the spirit call
Come just as you are
Come and see
Come receive
Come and live forever
Come just as you are
Hear the spirit call
Come just as you are
Come and see[29]

One by one, Josef prayed with each one and exchanged hugs until all who had come up had been taken care of while the congregation sat respectfully in their seats.

Rachel leaned over and whispered to Samuel. "Josef really set the bar high for himself, how is he ever going to top that?"

Samuel stared into her eyes and shook his head. "*Gut* question," he whispered.

---

[29] *Come just as you are - Lyrics by Crystal Lewis*

Chapter Sixteen

"Healing"

Rachel joined her staff in helping to set out the food as the hungry congregants milled around Josef, thanking him for the message and asking for prayers.

Samuel came to her side and slid an arm about her waist.

"Hi," she smiled up at him.

"Hallo," he returned her smile. His aquamarine eyes twinkled down at her.

"Is it typical for the Amish, or in this case, ex-Amish to become so emotional after a sermon?"

Samuel shook his head. "Nee, this was an exception. Josef's sermon struck a lot of nerves…in a good way," he murmured, "myself included. I have never considered how it breaks the heart of our heavenly *vater* [30] when we are led astray by going our own ways. It also put me in mind of my *schwester*, Sarah, *bruder-in-law*, Mark, and my nieces and nephews. I miss them."

Rachel looked up at him, her heart aching for him. "You could go back, Samuel," she whispered, terrified that he might do so. "I never wanted to take you away from your family,"

He looked down upon her uplifted face and cupped her cheek. "I didn't leave them, they forsook me," he replied. "I could no more leave you than shed my own skin! I wish it could be different, but the *Ordnung* is clear on these matters. There's no going back."

---

[30] father

Emma bustled over, laden with several covered bowls.

Rachel removed the lids and sniffed. "What is this?"

"Sandwich spreads," Emma replied.

"What's in it?" Rachel asked.

"Velveeta cheese folded into hot milk and the other is peanut butter whipped with marshmallow fluff and corn syrup."

Rachel grimaced. "*Yuck.*"

"Don't knock it until you try it," Samuel rebuffed her. "It's *gut!*"

"I guess you'd have to have grown up with it," Rachel replied. "Me, I'm a peanut butter and honey or baloney and mayo girl." She helped Emma to lay out the last of the food and when everything was ready, Josef offered a blessing.

They all sat down to eat, and the air was filled with lively chatter, laughter, and *bonhomie.* It wasn't until quite late in the waning afternoon that the last parishioner finally left the property with promises of returning in two weeks.

Emma, Rachel, Karen, Annie, Ruth, and Naomi made a beeline into the commercial kitchen, working together to gather up and wash and dry all the serving platters, bowls and dishes while the men put away the benches, chairs and tables.

"Wasn't Josef's sermon just amazing?" gushed Emma. "I don't think I have ever been so moved."

Ruth and Naomi exchanged bemused looks.

"Emma," Karen nudged her. "You've been washing the same bowl for the past ten minutes, are you okay?"

Rachel examined Emma whose frequent sighs and giggles displayed all the earmarks of being thoroughly besotted.

"Careful, Emma, Josef did say he felt called of God to lead a celibate life..." Karen continued.

"Ach, I know," she nodded, a bit too agreeably. "I just greatly admire him, that's all."

Karen suddenly turned around and pointed. "There's Josef!"

"Where?" Emma turned, looking about and dropping a bowl. It broke into a dozen pieces.

"Hah! Got you!" Karen grinned. "You totally have a crush on the new pastor."

Emma's brows knit together in a combination of disappointment and hurt. "Why would you do something like that, Karen?"

"Karen, that really wasn't very nice," Rachel chided her, mortified by her behavior.

Karen looked at Emma and then back to Rachel who was scowling at her.

She flung down her dishtowel, defensive. "Well, I'm *soreeeee*, I didn't mean anything by it!" She turned and stalked off, abandoning her work while the others looked on in shock.

Rachel regarded Emma with sympathy, who stood looking as if someone had slapped her in the face. "I apologize for Karen's behavior," she said, putting an arm around her shoulders. "She has no filter and unfortunately no empathy when it comes to other's feelings."

Emma nodded, fighting back her tears. Compassion swept over Rachel. She wrapped her arms about Emma and held her close. "Just be careful with your heart, honey," she whispered in her ear. "I don't want to see it get broken."

"*Jah*," Emma nodded, her voice muffled against Rachel's shoulder.

"Come on, Emma, don't take it to heart." Naomi coaxed her.

Emma returned to her tasks, but the mood had soured considerably. They finished the cleanup in moody silence and then all returned to their respective homes.

Rachel was furious with Karen. Once back in the house, she marched up the steps and found her glowering on the bed in the room she shared with Emma. She shut the door behind her and confronted her. "What were you thinking?" she demanded.

Karen was defensive. "I was only kidding!"

"No one thought it was the least bit funny," Rachel retorted. "Least of all, Emma! She thinks of you as a little sister, and you go and embarrass her in front of everyone like that with no thought for her feelings?!"

"I said I was sorry," Karen mumbled, refusing to look Rachel in the eyes.

"Words with no substance behind them, no one believed you. Do you really want to alienate everyone else just as you've done with me?"

"No," Karen pouted.

"Just because I've had to put up with your lack of empathy all these years as your mother doesn't mean anyone else will, Karen. You'd do well to think of other's feelings before opening your big mouth again!" Not waiting for anything further, Rachel turned heel and stomped out, slamming the door behind her. She abruptly came face-to-face with Emma.

"Ummm, you heard all that?"

Emma nodded, looking at Rachel with wide eyes. "I have never heard you raise your voice like that before," she replied. "It was…"

"Scary?" Rachel finished for her.

Emma nodded.

"I have my father's German temper and Karen knows just which buttons to press to bring it out. It's one thing to have her smart off to me but quite another to hurt you like that and I wasn't going to stand by and let her get away with such thoughtless behavior."

Emma nodded again; her arms wrapped tightly around her slender figure as if to comfort herself. "I just came up to get my things, may I use one of the guest rooms until your family arrives?"

"Of course," Rachel said softly, wishing so badly she could make Emma's hurt go away. The injured look on her face made Rachel want to cry.

Emma hung her head, "I miss my *mutter*," she whispered, tears plopping from her cheeks onto the floorboards.

A huge lump formed in Rachel's throat. Without thinking, she took Emma into her arms and embraced her in silence. There was a moment's hesitation then Emma wrapped her arms about Rachel and allowed herself to weep. After a few moments, Rachel drew back and cupped the sorrowful girl's chin in her hands.

"Can I make you some tea?"

Emma nodded, "I'd like that."

They walked arm in arm down the steps and into the kitchen. Rachel filled the kettle with water and put it on the already hot stove while Emma took a seat at the island, staring vacantly at the butcher block counter.

"I'm all ears if you need to talk, sweetheart." Rachel offered, clasping her hands.

"I wouldn't know where to start," Emma replied, her eyes refilling. "I feel as lost as the prodigal son, only I can't go back to my *vater's* house and be welcomed unless I repent and go back to living under the *Ordnung*."

"It's a very difficult life," Rachel agreed. "I entertained the idea of becoming Amish just for Samuel's sake but it's too hard to change that drastically later in life unless it's something you really want for yourself; otherwise, you just end up resenting the person for whom you did it all for."

"You considered becoming Amish?" Emma asked, shocked.

Rachel nodded and pulled her hair back into a temporary bun. "Can you imagine me in a prayer kapp?"

"No," Emma admitted, a smile ghosting her lips.

"I even tried to participate in a quilting bee to see if I could fit in,"

"And?"

"…and I bled all over the quilt. I was humiliated. Just too many obstacles and hurdles for me to overcome as well as long-ingrained habits. I like listening to music, and slow dancing with Samuel and so many other things that would be frowned upon."

"I grew up with it, but the older I got, the more I wanted freedom to just be me," Emma replied. "Individualism is frowned upon, the good of the community comes first."

The tea kettle began to whistle loudly. Rachel took it off the heat with mitts and poured the hot water into a teapot filled with loose, chamomile tea to let it steep. "So, what was it like for you when you first went out into the *English* world?"

"At first it was thrilling and amazing, so many things to see, do, and experience." Emma's face took on a far-off look. "But just like the prodigal son, when the money ran out, it turned ugly, mean, and dangerous. People who I thought were my friends just wanted to use me for their own sick purposes and I was frightened for my life. I left just in time with barely enough money to make it back home only to have my parent's shut the door in my face and reject me." Emma collapsed onto the counter with pent up grief, laying her face on her arms and sobbing. "My *daed* and I used to be so close…I just adored him! It was like a knife in my heart when he said he had no *dochder*[31]!"

"Not much like the father in the Prodigal son, story, huh?" Rachel commiserated, her heart aching for Emma.

"*Nee*, not at all. I either publicly repent, get baptized, and live under the *Ordnung* or I remain outcast and shunned."

"It's a heavy price to pay," Rachel agreed. "Samuel gave up everything for me, I can never make up for what he lost, and it hurts."

"He did it out of love for you," Emma replied. "I did it out of a desire to live differently." She looked around the Inn. "I don't know what I would have done if *Der Herr* had not led me here." She grasped Rachel's hands in hers. "I may have

---

[31] daughter

helped you with all the chores, but you gave me a *home and a family* with all its ups and downs." She offered a weepy smile. "Karen and I will get this worked out, but I need a few days away to myself."

Rachel filled Emma's cup with hot tea and raised her own mug in salute. "Here's to family," she toasted with a wry grin. "The good, the bad and ugly…warts and all."

After finishing her tea and calming down, Emma returned upstairs and knocked on the bedroom door she had shared with Karen.

"Come in," said Karen.

Emma opened the door and found Karen on the bed. Her eyes were swollen and her face red from crying.

"I'm sorry," Karen said, unable to meet Emma's eyes. "I totally blew it; it was wrong to tease you like that."

"I forgive you," Emma replied, gathering up her personal belongings.

Karen watched her, surprised and hurt that she was moving out. "Wait, you're not going to share the room anymore with me? I thought you forgave me?"

Emma paused, her pillow and clothes bundled up in her arms. "I do forgive you, but I need a few days to myself. Your behavior really hurt me, Karen, and despite my forgiveness, your actions have consequences." She put her bundle down and laid a gentle hand on Karen's shoulder. "We'll get through this, but I need some time alone, can you understand?"

Karen nodded, her eyes refilling with tears. "I'm sorry," she whimpered and this time there was genuine remorse in her voice.

Emma nodded. "I believe you." She gathered her things to take them to one of the other vacant rooms, shutting the door quietly behind her.

Supper that night was a muted affair. Everyone was tired after all the work they had done to prepare for their first church service. There were plenty of leftovers, so the meal was a hodge-podge of baked beans, meatloaf, some chicken and pickled vegetables with freshly baked popovers from the oven. Josef, Samuel, and Rachel lingered at the table over hot mugs of decaffeinated coffee with fresh cream. A cozy fire was blazing in the hearth.

"Josef," began Samuel, "Now that you are our official shepherd, would you do us the honor of performing our wedding ceremony?"

"Yes! That's a wonderful idea!" Rachel nodded, surprised she hadn't thought of it first.

"I would consider it a privilege," Josef smiled. "Yours will be my first wedding; I couldn't think of a better couple to do it for." He took a sip of his coffee. "Have you also given any thought as to who would stand up for you?"

"Well, Emma and my friends, Janet and Rhonda and my daughter will be bridesmaids," Rachel replied. She looked at Samuel who had become pensive.

"Normally I would have had my bruder-in-law, Mark, and other friends stand up for me, but that is not possible anymore," he replied.

"We'll do it!!" a voice said from the service porch.

They all turned around to find Aaron, Amos and Abram standing there, grinning at them.

"*Jungs, seid ihr sicher*[32]?" Samuel asked.

Taking that as an invitation to join in on the conversation, the three of them entered the room.

"Of course," Aaron exclaimed. "It's the least we can do! You have given us all a home, a second chance, and a new family; we would be hurt not to stand up for you!"

Abram and Amos nodded enthusiastically. "That's right!" they agreed.

---

[32] Guys are you sure?

"Well, that settles that," Rachel smiled, happy for Samuel. Her brow wrinkled, "It's too late to order tuxedos, what do the men traditionally wear at an Amish wedding?"

"We wear black suits with coats and vests that fasten with hooks and eyes, not buttons." Samuel replied.

"Also, white shirts and black, high-topped shoes with black stockings." Aaron added.

"Don't forget the black hat with a three-and-a-half-inch brim!" Amos said, wagging his finger.

"Where are we going to get those in such short order?" Rachel wondered. There's only 2 weeks left!"

"I still have mine," Samuel replied.

"Us too, but they need to be cleaned." Abram said.

"I'll take care of the cleaning," Rachel smiled at them, touched by their offer to stand up for Samuel. "I guess all that is left is the cake, flowers, and mountains of food we have to prepare."

Samuel grasped Rachel's hands in his in front of everyone. "And our guests," he added.

Chapter Seventeen

"Family Reunion"

The countdown to Thanksgiving and their wedding had officially begun. Rhonda and Janet were the first to arrive with their husbands and were put up in the Inns' guest rooms. Rhonda still had her final fittings to do for herself, Rachel, and Janet, and had secreted the gowns in large, black garment bags that prying eyes could not see through, into her room.

Due to the lingering heat of a longer summer season, fall arrived later than usual and as a result, the trees surrounding the property were ablaze with fall colors in mid-November. The air was cold and crisp and often the air was filled with the smell of maple trees weeping sap from the surrounding trees.

Rachel loved the fall and threw herself into preparations for activities that she thought her family might enjoy like pressing apples for cider, roasting chestnuts, and making pies and tamales together, a family tradition on Barry's side.

After a week away, Emma moved back into her shared room with Karen, having finally reconciled. Rachel often found the two of them whispering and giggling, conspiring together over something only to abruptly hush up when she entered the same room.

No doubt they are up to something, she thought, but was happy to see them reunited.

Rachel was at the kitchen island, chopping vegetables and peeling potatoes for the pot roast that was to feed her staff and Inn guests when Karen popped into the kitchen.

"Mom,"

"Yes, honey?"

"I have a favor,"

"No." Rachel replied automatically then burst into laughter. It was an old game.

"Mom, I'm serious!"

Rachel dumped the vegetables into the humongous Le Creuset pot alongside the meat, covered it with the lid and set it inside the oven to slow cook. She straightened and regarded her daughter. "Sorry, okay what?"

"I need you to stay away from the wedding barn and rose arbor until the day of your wedding, okay?"

"That may prove difficult," Rachel replied.

"Well, you're just going to have to find a way to do it, no questions asked." Karen replied. "Emma and I are working on something special, and we want it to be a surprise."

Rachel crossed her arms. "Didn't you just now let the cat out of the bag?"

Karen blinked at her stupidly for a moment, then shook her head. "Not really, just promise me you'll stay away, okay?"

Rachel crossed her chest and held up her fingers. "Cross my heart and scouts honor." She replied. "If I need anything done that might endanger your surprise, I'll send someone else to do it, sound good?"

Karen nodded. "Yup!" She scampered off, practically skipping out the front door.

Rhonda, Janet, and their respective husbands came downstairs for the afternoon's charcutier nibbles. Emma had laid out a board with various cheeses, dried fruits, nuts, and cured meats with crackers. The men began piling their plates with goodies and catching up with each other.

Rhonda grasped ahold of Rachel's arm and steered her towards the stairs. "No food for us until I get the final fittings done!"

"Why don't you start with Rachel while I check on the preparations in the barn and then you can do mine," Janet suggested.

"That's a fabulous idea!" Rhonda grinned, hauling Rachel after her back up the stairs.

"Okay, okay! Not so fast!" Rachel giggled, stumbling as Rhonda dragged her upstairs.

Rhonda pushed her into the room she shared with Charles and locked the door behind them. She snatched up a black silk kerchief and held it up. "Close your eyes!" she commanded.

"Wait, what? I'm going to try on the dress blind-folded?" Rachel protested.

"Yes! I don't want you to see it until the day of your wedding!"

"But what if I start crying the day of my wedding because I love it so much?" Rachel shot back with a grin.

Rhonda forcibly turned her about and tied the kerchief over her eyes and knotted it. "Wear water-proof mascara!" she replied. "Now, step out of your outer clothes and hold your arms straight up."

Rachel sighed and commenced disrobing. First off was the thick, cable-knit oatmeal sweater, followed by a long-sleeved shirt, followed by her jeans and silk underwear. Her teeth began to chatter. "H-h-hurry I'm–m *fre-fre-freezing!*"

She felt a heavy, satiny dress slip over her and with Rhonda's help got her arms through.

Rhonda zipped up the back then proceeded to button all the tiny, covered buttons that lay over it. "There, how does that feel?"

"G-g-good," Rachel replied. "But I'm going to freeze my patooties off outside during the ceremony!"

"Not to worry, Janet told me she's renting space heaters." Rhonda said. "Now, lift your arms and rotate in small circles."

Rachel complied.

"Do you have freedom of movement or is it too tight?"

"It's per-per-perfect." Rachel replied. "But don't you think my Ugg boots will spoil the look?" She was kidding and only said it to get a rise out of Rhonda, who took everything so seriously.

She fell for it, hook, line, and sinker. "Absolutely not! *You.are.not.wearing.Uggs.with.my.masterpiece!*"

Rachel felt her tug the seam at the waist, still huffing and puffing. "I covered pumps in the same fabric as your dress so you're wearing those!"

"Well, I hope they don't have spikey heels, or I'll be aerating my lawn!" Rachel joked.

"Of course not," Rhonda sniffed. "I took everything into consideration. You have a nice, chunky, 2" heel."

"Are we good now? Can I get dressed?" Rachel pleaded. Her entire body was covered in gooseflesh. She was going to have to wear some silk undergarments under the dress or she wouldn't get through her vows without her teeth chattering. *Lucky Samuel and the boys, getting to wear warm, black woolen suits...*

"Oh, I almost forgot," Rhonda said, lifting the dress off her and zipping it back into the garment bag. "Now you may look."

Rachel removed the blindfold. "What?"

Rhonda reached into her suitcase and brought out a custom-made-for-the-dress, smokey blue silk body suit and a pair of heavy silk stockings that were flesh colored. "Can't have you ruining my design with ugly, off-the-rack winter wear," she grinned.

Rachel gratefully pulled back on her clothes. "You really do think of everything!" she grinned back at her.

"I do, indeed." Rhonda agreed, completely serious.

Rachel checked her watch for the millionth time, anxiously pacing from the kitchen and back again to the front porch windows.

"Where are they?" she muttered to Karen, marching back into the kitchen. "They should have been here a half hour ago!"

Karen shrugged, focusing on the last of her homework assignments and mumbled something incoherent in response.

"What?" Rachel asked her.

"I said you need to be more patient, mom!" Karen repeated louder. "It's your worst personality trait: no patience!"

Rachel folded her arms. "Well, if it wasn't for us 'inpatient people' nothing would ever get done!" She turned back to the front windows. "They're here!!! They're here!!" She grabbed her heavy coat off the peg and raced out the front door, Karen, and Buddy on her heels as two small minibuses pulled up in front of the house. Buddy barked and pranced with excitement. Rachel scooped him up into her arms and waited as the doors opened. First to exit was Barry's older brother, Greg, followed by his wife, Monique, and their teenaged son, Noah.

"Hey Rachel, so good to see you again!" Greg smiled, catching her in a big embrace, followed by Monique.

"Who's this?" Monique smiled, petting Buddy's head.

"This is Buddy," Rachel replied. "He just showed up one day out of the blue in the barn about a year ago."

Monique caressed Buddy's silky ears. "He's adorable!" she cooed. "Can I hold him?"

Next came Steve, Barry's younger brother, and his wife, Julie and their three children, Matt, Will, and Sarah, all in their teens.

Karen ran forward with her arms held out. "Oh my gosh I missed you all so much!" she screeched, hugging her cousins each in turn.

"Hello, hello, hello!" Julie sung out, opening her arms wide for a hug to Rachel.

Rachel deposited Buddy into Monique's waiting arms so she could embrace the others. "I'm so glad you're all here!" she said, tearfully. "I've missed you all so much!"

"How are you feeling, Rachel?" Julie asked, looking her up and down. "Are you fully recovered? We were all so worried about you!"

"I'm fine now, but it was a pretty bad buggy accident," Rachel replied. "They had to shock my heart three times, and several ribs were cracked."

Several more people exited, Debbie and Craig, Barry's older sister and her husband as well as Rachel's older sister, Susan, and her husband, Herb, whom she hadn't seen in years.

The other minibus dislodged its passengers and Rachel was soon surrounded by her older cousins, Florence, Birdie, Jack, Sandy, Wendy, Cheri and Jim, all of whom surrounded her with happy smiles. They all exchanged hugs and kisses.

"This is absolutely beautiful!" Florence commented, taking in the red barn and Farmhouse Inn."

Last out of the minibus was Mary and AJ.

Rachel ran forward to greet them. "I'm so glad you could make it!!"

"Oh, I wouldn't have missed this for the world," Mary enthused, her face wreathed in smiles. "We got to know your family a little on the ride over. Are Rhonda and Janet here yet?"

Rachel nodded, "Oh, yes, they arrived a day or so ago. "You'll be staying at the Inn with them, and my immediate family will take up the entire loft area in the new barn. The rest are staying at a local hotel or Airbnb's.

Samuel and the boys joined the throng, "*Willkommen!*" He smiled and stuck out his hand. "I'm Samuel, and this is Aaron, Amos, and Abram," he introduced. "We'll be glad to help you all with your luggage,"

"The three stooges," Karen joked, giving Aaron a flirtatious wink.

"Which one of us is Curly?" he wanted to know. "I want to be Curly!"

Herb was the first to shake Samuel's hand, smiling broadly. "Nice to meet you, Samuel, I'm Herb!" he grinned. "We've heard a lot about you from Rachel. So, we hear you're Amish?"

Samuel shifted uncomfortably on his feet. "It's a long story, best kept for later," he replied politely. "Let me show you all to your rooms," he walked over to the side of the first bus where the driver was removing large suitcases from the storage compartment under the seats. "The boys and I will help to carry your luggage upstairs."

Monique turned to Rachel, "Are you coming?" she asked.

Rachel shook her head. "I'm under strict orders not to go anywhere near the event barn or rose arbor until the day of the wedding."

"Is that why your clothesline is full of sheets? To block your view of everything?" Julie chuckled.

Rachel nodded, "Yes, partially, also because it saves money on gas and electricity to hang them outside. Even in frigid weather they still smell better than from the dryer; however, once the temps go below 35 degrees during the day, I'm switching over to my heavy-duty, front-loading dryers! Even I have my limits!"

Rachel gave Debbie a hug. "I'm so glad you came! How did Craig get you on a plane?"

"Lots of heavy-duty prescription drugs," Debbie smiled abashedly. "I think I slept the entire 12 hours from Hawaii."

"Well, I appreciate you taking on your phobia of flying just for me," Rachel said. "I know it wasn't easy."

She turned to give Debbie's daughter, Holly, and her husband, Genesis, a welcoming hug. "I'm so glad you both came!"

"Okay, everyone, please follow us!" Amos said, both arms laden with two suitcases each. Everyone gathered up the remaining luggage and followed him beyond the clothesline to the event barn and the accommodations that had been prepared for them in the loft.

"Dinner is at 5:00 pm!" Rachel called after them and led Mary and AJ back into the warm Inn with Buddy at her heels.

"Your rooms are all ready," Rachel beamed at them. "I'll let you get settled before we catch up."

Samuel led Rachel's family up the stairs to the loft area and set down his share of the luggage. Everyone else followed suit and looked around, admiring the high vaulted ceiling with the exposed, heavy wooden beams and trusses. Light poured in from the windows that ran around the entire perimeter.

The loft had hardwood floors overlaid with plush area rugs for comfort and the walls were all painted a creamy beige where Rachel had hung bed-sized, jewel-toned Amish quilts as artwork between the large windows.

"Let me show you around," he said, leading them first to the communal area. He gestured to the over-stuffed couches, recliners and the stand-alone fireplace which had a fire crackling inside of it. "This is the great room," he said. "The cabinets over there have board games and this table here can be flipped over to become a ping-pong table. There is also a wooden swing suspended from the ceiling on the opposite side and a dart board over there."

"Dibbs on the swing!" Sarah piped up.

"There's also one in the red barn," Karen said. "It's not as 'tame' as this one here."

"Oh, I'm totally up for that!" Noah grinned, looking to his male cousins. "Who else is with me?"

Will and Matt both raised their hands. "Us!"

Samuel led them a little further in and pointed to Amish-made bookshelves that were stuffed with books of all types. "Please help yourself to any of the books you see."

"Did she buy them just for the guest's use?" Birdie asked.

"*Nee*, Rachel is a voracious reader, these are all hers." Samuel replied. He went around the corner and stood in front of the kitchenette and elaborate coffee station. He opened all the cabinets so they could see the contents. "The pantry is stocked with nonperishable snacks, whole bean regular and decaffeinated coffee, and the refrigerator with bottled water, juices and canned fruits from our garden. The plates, mugs and cutlery are all here." He indicated the cabinets and drawers.

Cheri and Jim made a beeline for the coffee station, admiring the high-end espresso machine, Nespresso capsule coffee maker, coffee grinder and French press. "You thought of everything!" Cheri exclaimed. "What about coffee creamer? I really like the flavored ones."

Samuel opened the refrigerator and proudly held up a glass milk jug with a label that said *Second Chance Inn Creamery* on it. "Fresh milk and cream from our very own cows, Daisy, Bessy, Dolly, and Buttermilk, none of that 'floor wax' stuff they call creamer, that stuff will kill you." He quipped, putting the jug back into the refrigerator. "Next are the bathroom facilities," he went over to a window and pointed outside, fighting back a mischievous grin. Everyone crowded around the window and looked down at the original outhouse that Rachel and Karen had been forced to use until the indoor plumbing had been installed. "You will have to take turns, one at a time and make sure to wear your long underwear as it can be quite cold," he said.

Silence descended upon everyone. It took Samuel every ounce of discipline he possessed not to smile or bust up laughing at the horrified looks on all their faces. If he had been one of the *English* and carried one of those smart phones, he would have snapped a photo. The only one who didn't buy it was Herb.

He slapped Samuel on the back and laughed out loud. "That's a good one, Samuel!" he chortled. He turned around and addressed the rest of the family members. "He's pulling your legs!"

"Thank God," Susan added.

Samuel grinned and nodded at them in confirmation. He was greeted with nervous laughter and a collective sigh of relief. "*Ach*, not really. There is indoor plumbing…it's just there in case of emergencies, you know, like frozen pipes, backed up plumbing…" Again, there was a long, awkward pause as everyone tried to figure out if he was still kidding or serious.

"Um, how often do your pipes freeze?" Florence wanted to know.

"Flo – he's still joking," Susan explained to her with a roll of her eyes.

"Oh," Florence replied, then giggled. "I'm glad to hear it."

"This way," Samuel gestured and led them around the entire perimeter which had been partitioned off into several different types of bedrooms with adjoining bathrooms that contained both a shower and/or bathtub combination and water closet. "There is a common wash station here for everyone, but the showers and water closets are all private," he pointed.

A large, five foot long, vintage, beautiful white porcelain wash basin stood before them. Twin mirrors on either side extended the length of the sink with four individual faucets on either side along with soap dispensers and toothbrush holders mounted beneath the mirror. Below the sink was a polished nickel rail holding white hand towels.

"Just put your soiled towels in that basket there," he pointed. "You may put your laundry in the hampers provided inside each of your rooms." He walked over to the first bedroom and opened the door which had a small black chalk-board label on it with two names scrawled in white chalk that said: *Susan and Herb.* Inside was a king-sized, black iron farmhouse bed with Amish quilts upon it and a cedar chest at the foot holding more quilts and extra pillows. On either side of the bed were Amish-made wooden nightstands with a drawer and compartment below with both electrical plugs. On each nightstand was a glass water carafe that had Psalm 42:1 etched onto it and a small vase of cut lavender stalks to promote sleep. Plush terry cloth robes hung from hooks near the bathroom door.

"Susan and Herb, this will be your room for the duration of your stay," Samuel said, bringing their suitcases inside.

"Nice!" Susan smiled, admiring the beautiful Amish quilt. She sat on the bed and bounced a little. Her husband, Herb, went to investigate the adjoining bathroom. It was a wet room. The entire ceiling and four walls were covered in plain white subway tiles. The floor was comprised of smooth pebble stones on a tile mesh so there was no chance of slipping. A large rain shower head hung from the ceiling at the far end of the bathroom and in the wall was a niche that held Amish hand-made soaps, shampoos and lotions. A tall white cabinet stocked with luxurious white Egyptian cotton plush bath towels and other toiletries stood nearest the door.

"Are all the bathrooms just like this?" Herb asked Samuel.

"*Nee,* some of them have bathtubs so little ones can be bathed," he replied. "I'll show you the rest of the rooms so you can get settled in. I understand the rest of you are staying at a hotel or Airbnb's?"

One by one, he showed Rachel's immediate family to their rooms which were all furnished simply with high-quality Amish furniture and goods.

When Monique and Greg saw their room, Monique went straight to the bed and laid on it to test out the firmness of the mattress. "Oh, this is just lovely," she said, closing her eyes in bliss. "I'm ready for a nap right now."

Samuel led them all back to the common room where the rest of their luggage sat and held up a Tupperware container. "Before I go, there is one more thing," he said. "This is an Amish-style Inn which means no technology except in cases of emergency. I will need to collect all your cell phones and iPads. If you have need of anything, there is a direct phone line from this barn to the Inn for your use." He pointed to an old-fashioned landline hanging on the wall near the kitchen.

Everyone looked around at each other for a moment, hesitant to give up their technology. Then to no one's surprise, Herb shrugged and was first to put his phone in the container. "Fine with me," he grinned. "It'll be nice not to be glued to that little screen every waking moment."

Everyone else reluctantly followed suit, except for Rachel's older sister, Susan, who didn't look the least bit happy. "How am I going to play solitaire if I don't have my phone or iPad?" she asked.

Samuel nodded. "Ah, yes..." he said, fishing around in his back pocket for something. He took it out and laid two small packets of Bicycle playing cards into her hands. "Rachel forewarned me of your addi...I mean particular passion," he smiled.

"Really?" Susan drawled sarcastically, staring down at the cards with irritation. "What else did she have to say?"

Samuel thought a moment then brightened. "That you would have to play Solitaire using *analog* instead of *digital* cards while you were here, whatever that means."

"*Harumph!*" Susan snorted. Herb chuckled and gave Susan an affectionate squeeze.

"It's only a week, Susan, I'm sure you'll survive. Plenty to see and do here, you won't miss it at all."

Susan muttered something unintelligible and handed her phone over to Samuel with a grimace.

Rachel greeted Samuel at the door. "How'd my sister take it?" she grinned at him.

Samuel held up the iPad. "I had to pry it out of her cold, dead hands," he dead panned.

Rachel stared at him for a moment in shock then busted up laughing. "You're funny!" She took the container full of electronic gadgets and put it into the safe, locking the door. "We're going to keep them so busy; they'll never miss them!" she added.

Samuel sniffed the air. "Something smells *gut*,"

"It's your favorite, pot roast," Rachel replied.

Samuel slid his arms about her and pulled her close against him. He nuzzled her earlobe sending waves of delicious chills down her body. "I'm hungry for more than just food," he whispered against her neck. "Just one more week, *Mein Liebling*, and you're all mine!"

Rachel melted into him and lifted her face to his so his lips could claim hers. He kissed her long and thoroughly then stepped back. Rachel pouted at him.

"That's all that I can take for now," he said, holding her at arm's length. He cleared his throat. "I have to go into town for some last-minute errands, I'll be back in time for supper."

"Can't you send one of the boys to pick up the feed?" she asked.

Samel nodded. "I could, but I need some time to myself, to think," he replied gently.

Rachel regarded him in silence for a moment, her brows crinkling with worry. "Pre-nuptial jitters?" she asked, giving him an out.

Samuel nodded, "Something like that," he smiled gently, patting her cheek.

"Okay," Rachel said, reluctantly releasing him. She fished around in her apron pocket. "Would you mind picking up a few things for me too?" She handed him a short grocery list.

Samuel tucked it into his pocket. "Of course," he smiled down at her and then kissed the corner of her mouth."

"I'll see you later," he promised. He left Rachel standing alone in the living room and exited out the service porch door.

Chapter Eighteen

"Complications"

Samuel hitched Molly up to the buggy and guided her out to the two-lane highway, his mind pre-occupied. A car horn blared a warning at him, startling his horse. Molly neighed loudly and reared up as the car passed, still honking at him in outrage. Samuel applied the brake and got out.

"Shush, there now," he said in a comforting voice, patting her neck. It took a few minutes to calm her down before he could continue. He got back into the buggy and flicked the reins. Molly took off at a brisk clip, her ears still flattened to her head, clearly nervous.

Samuel tried to concentrate on his driving but the arrival of Rachel's entire family, although expected and welcomed, had also accentuated his isolation and separation from his family and the community he had grown up with his entire life. He was finding it difficult not to feel resentful at the fact that Rachel's side of the barn would be filled with family and friends while his would be virtually empty. He thought back to his wedding day to his wife, Rachel, in his youth, remembering all the families that had come to bear witness to their betrothal, how happy he had been; innocent of how very fragile life and happiness were. Before the tragedy that had taken everything away from him that he had held most dear. Before he buried his *ehefrau*[33] and *kinner*[34] in the cold ground.

---

[33] wife
[34] children

Der Herr has given me a second chance at love, he chided himself, not liking where his private thoughts were leading him. *He brought love and purpose back into my life; I should be grateful not resentful...*

Another car horn blared at him, warning him that he was veering into oncoming traffic. Startled, he corrected his steering. *Pay attention to what you're doing!* He admonished himself and refused to think about anything other than driving until he reached his destination.

He pulled up to the local feed store and tethered Molly to the hitching post, paying no mind to the other buggies parked alongside his.

He entered the store and froze; coming face-to-face with his *schwester*, Sarah, and *bruder-in-law*, Mark, who were exiting at the same time. They all stood and stared at one another in astonishment for a long awkward moment.
Samuel recovered first, and stepped to one-side, avoiding eye-contact. "*Entschuldigung*[35]" he mumbled, feeling instant shame, and hating himself for it. What happened next, he didn't expect.

"Samuel?" Mark whispered, as if not quite sure it was him.

Samuel nodded, afraid to say anything. Instead of stepping around him and taking Sarah with him, Mark and his sister both continued to stand there and stare at him, looking at him up and down. It made him acutely aware that he no longer had his beard, straw hat, or traditional Amish clothes and for the first time he felt shame at his appearance. He was wearing blue jeans, and a heavy denim jacket lined with shearling. A hand lightly touched his arm. He involuntarily jerked and looked up to find Sarah looking at him, her eyes welling up with tears.

"You look...well," she finally whispered, her eyes darting around to see if any of their community was watching them.

The fact that she had spoken to him, touched him, caused his heart to start pounding wildly in his chest. They should

---

[35] Excuse me

not be speaking to him, touching him, or even acknowledging his existence. They were violating the *Ordnung!*

He turned to leave but Mark's hand caught his arm. "Samuel…can we find somewhere to talk? Away from prying eyes?"

Samuel stared back at him, completely at a loss as to what to do or say.

"*Bitte*," Sarah added, her eyes pleading.

When they continued to stand there and wait for his answer, he finally nodded, wracking his brain for a safe venue where he was sure they couldn't run into any Amish. Restaurants? *No, too risky…maybe a bar?* He searched the bars on his smartphone, acutely aware of Mark and Sarah's mortified looks that he owned such a device. "I'll meet you at the Altana Rooftop Lounge." He said, "It's on King Street in Lancaster."

"When?" Mark asked.

"Two hours, I have to pick up some things for the Inn and the wedding."

"Whose wedding?" Sarah asked, her brows knitting together in suspicion.

Samuel looked down at his feet as if confessing to a crime. "Mine. To Rachel."

"You're getting married?!" she hissed loudly, unable to help herself.

"Sarah – we'll discuss this later." Mark interjected, taking her arm. He looked at Samuel one last time. "Two hours, Altana Rooftop Lounge."

Samuel nodded and stepped around them, casting furtive glances about the feedstore to see if anyone had seen them as Mark and Sarah exited behind him, then chided himself. *Why am I nervous? I've already been excommunicated!*

He got the horse and chicken feed he came for as quickly as possible then drove to the market to pick up the few items on Rachel's list. He felt anxious, nervous, excited and full of dread, all at the same time. Samuel sat in the buggy, arguing with himself as he steered Molly back onto the two-lane. Half hour to go. *Maybe I should just go straight back home and pretend I'd never run into them; no one would be the wiser...*

He flicked the reins and set Molly off at a brisk pace. When it came time to turn right for home, he turned left instead, heading for the meeting place. What are you doing? He thought to himself.

I miss them, we're just going to talk. He argued back. *After all, they reached out to me not the other way around!*

You still have time, here's a good place to turn Molly around... go back home.

He ignored the voice, his curiosity getting the better of him and continued to carefully guide Molly through a more congested part of town that rarely, if ever, saw Amish buggies on the streets.

He found the building and circled it, looking for a suitable place where he could park and found nothing. A part of him sighed with relief, ready to return home, until he found himself back in front of the building entrance again where the lobby was and saw another buggy that had been parked next to a valet parking sign. It was Mark and Sarah's buggy. He could still go home; they hadn't seen him yet...

"Samuel!" A voice cried out. Mark and Sarah were waiting for him beside the buggy, waving him over. His heart sank.

Reluctantly, Samuel guided Molly to an open space behind Mark's buggy and got out, a strange feeling of dread enveloping him.

A valet came up and gave him a paper ticket. "First time I ever parked an Amish buggy here and today I get two!" he said with a grin. "I'll make sure your horses have water."

"Thanks," Samuel mumbled, taking the ticket.

The valet handed Mark his ticket. "The lounge will validate your tickets up there," he pointed straight up. "Just take the elevator to the top floor; you won't need a reservation this time of day."

Samuel followed Mark and Sarah through the lobby and into the elevator, no one saying a word as they passed one floor after another. After an interminable silence, the elevator dinged, and the doors swished open to reveal a swanky-looking bar with retro, sputnik light fixtures and a rooftop bar that overlooked the city below.

The hostess greeted them. "Three," Samuel said, holding up three fingers.

She collected their menus. "This way, please." She led them out to the bar which was comfortably warm with all the space heaters running and led them to a table at the far end which overlooked the street below. "Your waiter will be with you shortly,"

Samuel waited as Mark and Sarah took their seats first, Sarah visibly uncomfortable in such a setting, her gaze constantly flitting to the scant number of other patrons like a scared rabbit. Samuel took his seat last and waited, wondering what they wanted to talk to him about.

Mark cleared his throat. "We've been worried about you, Samuel," he began. "Except for your recent barn raising, which was common gossip, we've had no word of you."

Samuel was unable to keep the bitter tone out of his voice. "That was your doing, not mine…and the elders." He stood up abruptly, ready to leave.

"You gave them no choice in the matter," Mark replied softly, grasping Samuel's hand. "*Bitte*, sit."

Samuel sat back down, glowering at a speck on the otherwise gleaming table. A young woman approached them at that moment.

"May I take your order please?" Her little notepad and pencil poised in readiness. They all looked up at her.

"*Ummm*," Sarah hastily scanned the menu. "I'll have sweet tea and some fries," she said.

"Same," Mark repeated, handing her the menus.

"Nothing for me," Samuel added; his stomach was twisting with knots.

"Okay, thank you," she said; disappointed they hadn't ordered any alcoholic beverages or a real meal. She flounced off.

Mark captured his gaze. "We all miss you, Samuel; especially my *kinner*. They constantly ask why they can't see their *onkle* Samuel anymore despite knowing the rules of shunning. Sarah especially has missed you."

Sarah reached for his hand, her own were trembling. "You're my only *bruder*, Samuel. You have always been there for me; especially after *unsere eltern*[36] died."

"She hasn't slept well since you were excommunicated," Mark explained. "We were actually talking about you this morning over breakfast so when we saw you at the feed store, we took it as a sign from *Der Herr* that perhaps it was time."

Samuel blinked at him, thoroughly confused. "Time for what?"

"Restoring you back into our community." Mark whispered, then added, "Reconciliation, repentance..."

Samuel couldn't believe his ears. "On what basis?"

"Be honest with me," Mark replied. "Are you happier now, even after losing your entire family and community? Has your love for this *English* woman made up for all you have lost? We all supported you in your darkest hours and did our best to take care of you until she came along."

"Her name is Rachel," Samuel gritted out, not answering Mark's question. He should have said: *YES!* Why was he hesitating?

Mark took his nonresponse as encouragement to continue. "Samuel, we have been discussing it ever since we ran into you earlier today, so if...if you ever wanted to return... the *Dawdi haus* would be all yours. We would all take care of you. You see, my parents passed...and..."

"Leroy and Miriam passed?" It hit him like a ton of bricks. He had loved them very much. *So much has happened in this past year that I've known nothing about...*

---

[36] Our parents

"I know you have feelings for this woman,"

"Rachel," Samuel corrected him. "Rachel…I love her, Mark." He stood to go.

Sarah's hand covered his, tears sliding down her cheeks. "More than us? More than our *kinner?*"

Samuel grew defensive. "I never said that!"

"We know you didn't." Mark interjected, always the peacemaker. "*Bitte*…please sit down and hear me out."

Samuel sat down.

At that moment, their tea and a large basket of fries arrived. "Bon appetite!" smiled the waitress, "will there be anything else?"

They all shook their heads 'no'.

She peeled off the check and set it on the table. "I'll take that up when you're ready," she added and walked away.

"I've spoken many times to the bishop and elders since you left," Mark continued, causing Samuel's eyebrows to climb into his hairline. "Like me, they all believe you made a hasty decision based solely upon desperate and very emotional circumstances."

Samuel opened his mouth to protest, but Mark held up his hand. "Let me continue." He cleared his throat. "You don't have to answer to either of us, you're a grown man… but…and I emphasize, but: if you ever find that you have any regrets at all about your decision and desire to find a way to return, I just want to let you know that the door may be open. As long as you have committed no sin with this woman and still hold to your faith, it's not too late."

"The wedding is in four days," Samuel shook his head. "I couldn't do that to her."

Sarah leaned forward and grasped his hands, her eyes beseeching him. "But is it what you truly want for yourself, Sammy?" she asked, using his childhood pet name.

An enormous lump formed in Samuel's throat as he struggled with his warring emotions.

He stood up. "I need to get back," he said, leaving cash on the table although he had ordered nothing. He turned and left Mark and Sarah sitting there, refusing to look behind him, his heart in turmoil.

Once safely inside the elevator he rested his hands on his knees, hyperventilating, trying to calm down.

The doors opened and he exited, almost barreling into a small party of young women out for a late afternoon drink.

"Excuse me," he gasped, hurtling for his buggy. He found the valet ticket and shoved it at the waiting young man.

"You forgot to get it validated," he opined. "Normally it's cost you $20 but since I can't legally drive and park a buggy, I'll let you off with just a tip." He grinned and held out his hand. Samuel peeled off a five-dollar bill and slapped it onto his palm, climbed into his buggy and shook the reins.

"*Giddyap!*"

Molly jolted forward and skittishly maneuvered around the other parked cars and out onto the street. Once he got out into the country, he urged her into a fast canter to make up for the time he been away.

He arrived home way past dinner time and found Rachel waiting for him on the front porch, wrapped in a quilt on one of the rocking chairs. It was much later than he thought. Only a dim light shone in the living room from the glowing fireplace. She stood up the moment he entered the property and ran half the distance to meet him.

"I've been worried sick about you!" she wailed. "I texted and called over and over and you never responded!"

Samuel got out of the buggy and unhitched Molly, leading her into the barn while Rachel followed him, her voice shrill from a combination of anger and relief.

"Why didn't you answer or at least let me know you were okay?"

"I lost track of time," Samuel replied lamely, a bit irritated at her upbraiding. "I'm sorry."

"My entire family was looking forward to getting to know you better! Do you have any idea how embarrassing it was to admit I had no idea where you were or why you didn't make it home for our first dinner with them?"

Samuel covered Molly with a blanket and gave her oats.

"Well, do you?" Rachel demanded when he didn't answer her.

Samuel turned on her, bristling with anger. "Why do we have to have so many people here?"

Rachel blinked at him. "Huh?"

"Why has this become such a production? Why couldn't we have kept it simple with just a few people? Now it's an entire week of entertaining, hunting, parties, Thanksgiving; it's turned into a big circus like most *Englisch* weddings!" He spat.

Rachel stared at him in horror, completely blind-sided. Then her infamous temper kicked in. "Why on earth are you bringing this up *NOW*? You've had months to speak your peace and tell me what you really wanted, but you said *ab.so.lute.ly nothing* so I assumed you were okay with it! Well…*stupid* me. You knew all of this was being planned by our friends and family just because they love us and wanted to do something nice, but *now* it's become a *huge headache for you?*" Her voice rose to a strident level he had never heard come out of her before. Never had his own Rachel ever spoken to him so disrespectfully. The horses nickered nervously in the barn, unused to human shouting.

"What happened to you in the past four hours?" Rachel demanded.

"I ran into Mark and Sarah," he muttered.

"What?!"

"*My bruder in law and schwester.*"

"I know who they are, Samuel, what did they want?"

He refused to look her in the eyes. "They asked me if I had any regrets and wanted to return."

Rachel stared at him in stunned silence. "Well, *do you?*" she finally asked, her voice accusatory.

Samuel nodded. "If I am to be honest with you, yes, I have some regrets. I miss them and my nieces and nephews. I also miss my brethren, so I'm sorry." He repeated.

Rachel crossed her arms. "That's it? Just: *I'm sorry?* What am I supposed to do with what you just told me? How am I supposed to feel about our wedding now, knowing you resent 'the big production' it's become!? How long have you felt this way?"

"I didn't realize I did until I ran into them," Samuel replied.

Rachel crossed her arms. "So, are you seriously considering it?"

"What?"

She rolled her eyes in frustration. "Are you seriously considering going back?"

She spoke to him as if to a child and he didn't like it one bit. He just returned her glare, too angry and afraid of what might come out of his mouth.

"Fine," Rachel spat, brushing angry tears from her eyes. "Just fine!"

She turned and stalked off back to the Inn, slamming the door shut behind herself.

Samuel marched to the *dawdi haus* and flung open the door. He refused to look at the boys as he stomped past them until he was in the relative safety of his own room then slammed his own door in a fury.

"What was that all about?" he heard one of them say through the closed door.

He threw himself face first onto his bed, smashed his face into the pillow and pounded the mattress.

Rachel stumbled into the living room and finally succumbed to her tears. She felt as though she had just been slapped in the face. She didn't recognize this Samuel from the affectionate, kind and gentle one that had left her hours earlier. This Samuel had turned as frosty cold as the weather.

She clutched the quilt closely about her and made her way to the service porch, her tears so blinding her that she didn't see Josef until she ran straight into him. "Oh! I'm so sorry!"

He caught her as she lost both her balance and the quilt. He picked it up and placed it back around her shoulders.

"Rachel, are you okay?" His voice was filled with concern. "I just came to check on you and see if Samuel had returned yet."

"*Nooooooooo!*" she replied, her voice rising a full octave. "No, I am not okay." She dropped the quilt again and covered her face with her hands and began to bawl. This felt too much like the moment she had discovered Ruth in Samuel's arms, only this time there wasn't a Ruth Beiler around to blame.

"Come with me," Josef began to lead her to the *dawdi haus* where he stayed with the other men.

"No!" Rachel dug in her heels. "Not there!" She didn't want to be confronted by Samuel again.

"How about here, then?" he suggested.

Rachel shook her head. "No privacy here, everyone could overhear us." She thought a moment. "My office might be better."

"Isn't your office part of your bedroom?" Josef wanted to clarify.

"Yes,"

"That would be most inappropriate," Josef said. "Isn't there anywhere else?"

Rachel thought for a moment, regretting that she had ever run into him. "No, that's all I can think of. It's okay, let's just forget it."

Josef thought for a moment. "You don't seem okay, Rachel, I'd like to help if you need to talk."

Rachel shook her head, feeling suddenly very exhausted and defeated. "I think I just want to go to bed now," she said wearily. "But there is one thing you can do,"

"Anything!" Josef said earnestly.

Rachel grasped his hands before fleeing to the comfort of her bedroom. "Pray for both of us."

Chapter Nineteen

"Decisions"

Rachel opened her eyes the next morning and stared up at the ceiling, wishing she could go back to sleep and never wake up. She had cried herself to sleep the night before, aching for Samuel but feeling like she could no longer go to him. An enormous wedge now existed between them. All motivation and excitement to host her family and friends after months of waiting and planning had completely evaporated.

How can I fake a happy face in front of them all when I feel like the bottom has just dropped out of my world? She turned over and found Buddy nestled beside her. I should have stuck to dogs. Buddy rolled over onto his back for a belly rub and whined.

Rachel gently rubbed his belly and chest area while he enjoyed her attention in blissful silence, his eyes closed with pleasure.

From the kitchen came the jarring ring of the iron triangle and Karen's voice splitting the morning silence.

"Wakey, wakey! Rise and shine!"

Rachel continued to caress Buddy. *Maybe I can just hide out here until next year...*

A loud knock on the door was followed by Karen poking her head in. "Mom, I've got chores to do, you need to get up and start breakfast for everyone!"

Rachel got up and tied on her robe. "Where's Emma?"

"She in the commercial kitchen working on your wedding cake,"

"Oh," Rachel mumbled, not happy with the reminder.

Karen pushed the door open farther. "What's eating you?" She scowled.

Rachel wasn't about to bare her heart to Karen who was notorious for having no empathy for anyone. "Nothing, I'll be in as soon as I get dressed."

Karen shut the door and left, her bedroom door shutting behind her with a bang. Rachel hurriedly went to the bathroom and got dressed, putting on a beige sweat suit and her Uggs.

She clipped her hair up into a sloppy bun and entered the kitchen. Craig and Greg were sitting at the kitchen counter, catching up, already fully dressed.

"Morning!" Greg greeted her.

"Hey Rachel!" added Craig.

"How did you all sleep last night?" Rachel asked politely, heating up several cast iron skillets on top of the already warm stove. She added some fuel and stoked the embers until she had a good fire going.

"Great!" smiled Greg. "Hey, that coffee set up you have in the loft is great! I've already had two cups! What's for breakfast? Do you need any help?"

"The usual heart attack on a plate," Rachel smiled at him. "Sausage, bacon, scrambled eggs, biscuits, and canned fruit. You can set the table if you like." She pointed to the stacks of white plates, cups, and saucers on the open shelving. "I think we have about fifteen total, so I need some folding tables and chairs set up too."

Craig laughed. "You sure you got enough eggs to feed all of us?"

Rachel went to the service porch and opened the commercial refrigerator and pointed to the dozens of filled egg cartons. "Got my own chickens so I think we're good,"

Craig peered in and whistled. "You aren't kidding!" he replied good naturedly.

Rachel stacked four egg cartons into her arms and took them to the kitchen. At that moment, Samuel entered with the boys and some of her family members. He was dressed in camouflage gear.

Craig's face lit up. "Are we going hunting?" he asked, also an avid hunter.

Samuel nodded, avoiding Rachel's eyes. "Jah, but we'll need to leave early. I've already packed some food for us." He indicated the large wicker hamper at his feet.

"I want to come!" Noah announced, Greg's only son. "Can I, dad?"

"I have spare camouflage enough for two more besides me," Samuel replied.

Rachel stared at him with rising irritation, silently daring him to look at her while he steadfastly refused to do so as though he were a guilty child. "I was just about to make breakfast for everyone," she announced, forcing a smile. "Can't it wait until after breakfast?"

"I can wait to eat," Craig replied, clueless to the undercurrent of hostility flowing between them. "I haven't been hunting since we moved to Hawaii." He clapped Samuel on the back. "Just, let me get my things." He raced out of the Inn and back to the loft. "You coming, Noah?"

"Yup!" Noah did not need a second invitation and raced after him. That left her, Greg, and Samuel. She was keenly aware that Greg, the clinical psychologist, was silently evaluating the tension between them but thankfully saying nothing.

"I'll meet them at the barn with the clothing," Samuel announced and left. No hug. No smile and no kiss, not even on the cheek.

Rachel felt devastated. Fighting back angry tears, she placed the egg cartons on the counter and began cracking eggs two at a time (one in each hand) into a large ceramic bowl. Mercifully, Greg was kind enough to pretend that he noticed nothing amiss. Instead, he went to the refrigerator, found the sausage and bacon himself and laid them out onto the hot pan, resulting in a satisfying sizzle. Once Rachel was done cracking all the eggs, she retrieved the biscuit dough she had prepared the night before and rolled it out onto the marble section of her counter with her rolling pin; cutting out discs and laying them on a sheet overlaid with a Silpat. They worked in companionable silence as the other members of her family slowly filed in.

Monique came up next to her and gave her a big hug. The affection was enough to instantly trigger her tears. "Excuse me," she said, sliding the sheet pans into the oven.

"Are you okay?" Monique whispered, staring at her with concern.

Rachel hated to lie but she just couldn't lose it now in front of everyone like this. "I'll tell you later," she whispered. "Right now, I need you to run interference for me and distract everyone while I get breakfast ready."

"Consider it done," she smiled.

"Hey everyone, let's help out and get the tables set up," Monique said loudly.

"Oh yeah, I forgot," Greg said, turning over the two pans filled with slices of bacon and sausage."

While Monique, Julie, and Debbie helped to set out three more folding tables and Steve set up the chairs, Rachel began scrambling the eggs, snipping in dried Rosemary as well as minced garlic. She dropped a large hunk of creamery butter into the hot pan. It swirled about and melted with a satisfying sizzle. She poured in the contents of the bowl and began to slowly stir, adding in cheddar cheese and scallions.

"The table is all set," Julie announced.

"Great! There's cream, milk, and a jug of orange juice in the commercial frig if you'd like to set those out." Rachel replied. She washed out the ceramic bowl, swiftly dried it with a paper towel then began to scoop the steaming scrambled eggs into it.

Monique came up next to her and took an appreciative sniff. "Smells yummy!"

Rachel handed her the bowl. "Go ahead and put that on the table, I need to check on the biscuits before I burn them to a crisp." The image of Samuel's teasing smile while knocking a rock-hard bread roll on the tabletop came rushing back unwanted to her mind's eye. She choked down her pain, retrieved the sheet pans from the oven and laid them atop heavy-duty trivets to cool.

Julie returned with the beverages as well as several jars of canned peaches. "Did you can these all yourself?" she asked. Julie had done her own fair share of canning in the past and recognized homemade preserves instantly.

Rachel nodded and gave her a thumbs up; afraid to open her mouth and start crying. Before she exploded, she made a beeline to her bedroom and shut the door behind her, taking deep breaths and trying to calm herself. Monique was right on her heels. She entered the room and stared at Rachel with great concern.

"Something is definitely wrong," she surmised. "You can't talk about it yet?"

Rachel shook her head. "Please let me just get through breakfast without making a scene, especially in front of Rhonda and Janet. If they see me, especially Rhonda, I'll be getting both the third degree and inquisition until I yell uncle." She grabbed a Kleenex and blew her nose, wiping her eyes. "Samuel left for an errand yesterday and came back a completely different person. It was totally like the invasion of the body snatchers!"

"Have you talked to him?" Monique pressed, going into Rachel's bathroom, and coming out with a cold washcloth. She pressed it to Rachel's face.

"Oh, that really helps," Rachel sighed. She wiped her entire face and then the back of her neck. It calmed her greatly. "We had some words last night, none of it good."

"Is he getting cold feet?"

Monique's shrewd guess was almost enough to wreck her. "I just can't talk about it now," Rachel choked, hiding her face in the washcloth.

"Well, you better clear the air and soon." Monique muttered. "Take a minute to collect yourself, I'll meet you out in the dining room. I'll try to keep Rhonda and Janet distracted."

"Thank you!" Rachel said. Monique closed the door behind her. Rachel spent a few more moments looking at herself in the mirror. *He doesn't want to marry me anymore,* came the thought. *He just proposed out of guilt and now that the wedding date has arrived and reality has set in, he wants out.*

The famous, age-old adage popped into her mind:

IF YOU LOVE SOMEONE, SET THEM FREE.
IF THEY COME BACK, THEY'RE YOURS;
IF THEY DON'T, THEY NEVER WERE.

Maybe that's what I should do, Rachel thought to herself and the thought, now realized, made all her hopes and dreams crumble into ash. *Maybe I should just set him free and let him know he's not obligated to marry me if he really doesn't want to.*

Tears flooded her eyes. She had never seen this coming or in a million years would have imagined that Samuel would entertain second thoughts. Not after the many ways he had told her he loved her and couldn't wait to marry her for the past year. Not four days before they were supposed to take their vows. She was completely devastated.

It must be done.

It would be the hardest thing she ever did. She was scared to death, but deep within she knew it needed to be said and lovingly offered without spite or anger. In the meantime, she would pray and cling to the fragile hope that he would turn her offer down.

Samuel sat miserably in the blind, debating silently with himself, rehashing over and over everything that Mark had said to him. He was thankful that Noah and Craig were completely distracted by their hunting. They had bagged one turkey each so far while Samuel had merely sat there and reloaded their rifles while they remained oblivious to his inner turmoil. Mark and Sarah's words had haunted his every waking moment as he tossed and turned all night; unable to sleep. He didn't know what to do and hated himself because of it; especially after seeing the hurt in Rachel's eyes at his harsh response. Truth be told, he did miss his family and community much more than he had cared to admit. He missed the camaraderie and the fellowship of his family and other the men he had known all his life. He missed his nieces and nephews, especially. The arrival of the boys at the Inn had managed to suppress much of his pain until it smacked him right in the face the moment he saw Mark. It had been made abundantly clear. If he was willing to swallow his pride, repent and come back honestly penitent, his community would welcome him back with open arms. He would have a place he could call his own, want for nothing and would get to see his nieces and nephews, whom he loved like his own *kinner*, and watch them grow up. He closed his eyes and Rachel's face filled his mind. He just couldn't hurt her like that. He truly loved her, but he also loved his family. He had just never realized how much until now. He felt absolutely torn in two.

"I think we're bagged enough, Sam." Craig said, holding his Tom Turkey upside down from the hocks. "There should be plenty for all of us."

Samuel nodded. "Ready to go then?" He led them back on the trail from the large pond to where his buggy was parked.

Noah and Craig clambered in back, putting the turkeys into the large cooler filled with ice for the journey home. They peppered him with questions about other hunting opportunities to which he merely nodded, grunted or shook his head. Finally realizing he wasn't in a talkative mood; they fell silent until they reached the Inn. It was approaching noon. They had been gone for almost six hours.

"I'll take care of the turkeys if you too want to get cleaned up for lunch." He offered, lifting the cooler out of the buggy.

"Thanks!" Craig and Noah smiled, heading to their rooms above the event barn.

Samuel carried the cooler onto the service porch and found Rachel there waiting for him.

Her face was red, and her eyes swollen from crying. "Can we talk somewhere private?" she asked quietly, her voice quavering.

He set the cooler down and nodded, an ominous feeling coming over him. "In the *dawdi haus*," he said, leading the way. They walked in silence, Rachel right behind him. He opened the door and checked all the rooms.

"We are alone," he said, shutting the door.

Rachel studied her feet, wringing her hands nervously. Samuel watched her, feeling as though they were a million miles apart though they only stood two feet away from one another. She cleared her throat and finally looked at him.

"I release you," she said and expelled a long shuddering sigh.

Samuel blinked. "What?"

"I release you," Rachel repeated, struggling not to cry.

"Release me?"

She nodded, fighting to keep her emotions under control. She cleared her throat again. "Look, I totally understand how you miss your family…no…let me finish what I came to say." She held up her hand as he attempted to protest. "I love you, Samuel, more than I could ever express and I know you love me too, but I also know that loving me forced you to give up your entire family and the only life you have ever known. Maybe you proposed in haste, not really thinking through all the consequences, and maybe you totally meant it at the time, not realizing how you might regret it later… at any rate, I don't want to marry you if you feel this torn in two. I don't want you resenting me for the rest of your life."

Samuel wilted inside, her words piercing his heart like arrows as though she had read all his thoughts for the past 24 hours.

"I can't go through with this wedding feeling like you are having second thoughts or will harbor regrets, so…I release you from your promise."

"What about your family and all the plans you've made?" he whispered and with those words he knew he had just confirmed all of her worst suspicions." He crumpled inside at the heartbroken look on her face.

She shook her head, opened her mouth then closed it again without speaking, overcome with hurt. She turned away and walked out of the *dawdi haus* leaving him there to wish that the earth would just swallow him up and put an end to his misery. The door clicked shut.

Samuel stood rooted to the floor, unable to believe what had just happened between them. It was like a waking nightmare.

The door reopened and for a moment his heart leapt, thinking Rachel might have reconsidered and come back. Instead, Josef Eicher entered the room.

"I just passed Rachel," he said, his face and voice both alarmed. "I tried to speak with her, but she just ran to the house, sobbing uncontrollably. What is going on with you two, Samuel?"

"I've made a terrible mistake, Josef," Samuel exclaimed, cradling his head in his hands. "*Der Herr*, forgive me! *Der Herr forgive me*! I've lost her, I've lost Rachel." He beat his chest with his fist, dropped onto his knees and laid his forehead on the floor, dissolving into violent sobs.

Josef shut and locked the door then knelt beside him and put his arms about his shoulders, but Samuel could not be comforted. He sobbed harder and harder, snot dripping onto the floor along with his tears. He wept and wept and wept until he could weep no more. After fifteen minutes and utterly exhausted, he rolled prone onto his back and stared at the ceiling as though hoping his gaze might somehow pierce all the way into heaven.

Josef sat beside him and just waited until Samuel finally quieted. "Tell me everything and leave nothing out." He said in a voice that brooked no argument.

Samuel took a long, shuddering breath and for the next hour recounted everything that had transpired while weeping tears of remorse and regret. Josef listened without interrupting until there was a long silence, indicating that Samuel was finished.

"So," he said, choosing his words carefully. "Rachel offered to release you from your obligation before you had the chance to say it first, is that correct?" he finally surmised.

Samuel nodded miserably.

"She gave you the freedom to make a choice of your own free will whether to love her and truly renounce your old life willingly or go back to your family and lose the unconditional love of a very good woman?"

Samuel nodded, unable to suppress the tears that seeped from his eyes.

"Sounds familiar, *jah*?" Josef concluded gently.

Samuel gasped, instantly grasping his meaning. He moaned and covered his face with his hands and began to weep again. "I am not worthy of her. I am not worthy of her. I don't blame her for rejecting me!"

Josef stirred. "That is not what you told me, you said she 'released' you. That doesn't sound like rejection."

Samuel turned his head to look at him, a tiny glimmer of hope igniting in his heart. "Do you think there's still hope, then?"

Josef held out his hand and helped Samuel back onto his feet.

"I'm not the one you should be asking that question," he replied gently.

Chapter Twenty

"Confrontation"

Rachel ran blindly into the Inn and almost bowled Rhonda and Janet over. They were instantly alarmed.

"Whoa, what's wrong?" Janet demanded.

"Did you and Samuel have a fight?" asked Rhonda, ready to do battle on behalf of her friend.

"Yes and no…I can't talk about it now!" Rachel replied and fled to her room, shutting the door.

Janet looked at Rhonda. "*Ruh roh!*" she said, mimicking Scooby-Doo.

"This is no laughing matter," Rhonda growled at her. "I'm going to find Samuel and find out what happened!"

"There's no need," said a male voice behind her.

They both turned and found Samuel standing there, looking every bit as miserable as Rachel. Rhonda's remonstrations died in her throat. "You look awful," she observed.

Janet gestured to a chair. "Would you like some tea?"

He shook his head. "I need to speak to Rachel," he replied, looking at her closed door. They could all hear her weeping inside.

Rhonda shook her head at him. "I don't think now is a good time,"

"But…"

"I agree with Rhonda," Janet added gently. She took Samuel by the arm and tried to steer him back to the door, but he refused to budge. Janet dropped his arm. "Just let her cry herself out and you can both hash it out in the morning after you've both slept on whatever it is," she sighed.

"You think I could honestly sleep after what I've done?" Samuel replied. "I've made a terrible mistake.""

Rhonda and Janet exchanged glances.

"Wait, what?" Janet replied.

Rhonda's hackles went up. "What did you say to her?"

Samuel blinked stupidly at them for a moment, trying to recall. "I actually said nothing," he finally realized. "She figured out that I was torn between returning to my family and marrying her without my saying anything!"

"And was she right?" Janet asked, shocked.

Samuel dropped his head in shame and nodded. "I came to beg her forgiveness."

Rhonda gasped audibly. "Are you kidding me?!"

"I wish I were," Samuel mumbled.

Janet glanced at Rachel's bedroom door. Her sobs had subsided. *She's listening,* she mouthed, pointing to the door. As if on cue, Rachel's door opened. She stood in the doorway, her eyes riveted upon Samuel.

Janet grabbed Rhonda's arm and hauled her away. "Let's go," she commanded.

"But…" Rhonda protested.

"*Now,* Rhonda." Janet insisted, pulling her out of the Inn. The door shut behind them. Rachel and Samuel were alone.

He stood before her and waited, his heart drowning in remorse. He reached out for her, his eyes pleading. "Forgive me," he whispered.

The guarded look remained upon Rachel's face; unwilling to trust and be hurt again. "Forgive you for what, exactly?" she asked.

Samuel paused and thought about it. He dropped to his knees. "Forgive me for being a horribly flawed, weak man." He reached for her hand, but she refused to take it.

"Samuel," she finally said, her voice coming from a place of deep weariness. "Stand up. I want you to go back to the *dawdi haus* and really think about what it is you truly want."

"But I do know," he pleaded. "I want you."

"Yesterday you were prepared to leave me and everything else behind until I beat you to the punch," Rachel replied gently and without anger. "I don't want you to marry me out of a sense of guilt or obligation or panic. I want you to pray and really weigh all the pros and cons and come to a rational decision you can live with for the rest of your life." Her voice broke at this point as she struggled to finish, tears streaming down her cheeks. "Because I can't bear to live with a man whose heart is so torn in two. You would just end up resenting me for the rest of your life and I couldn't bear that! I won't have you marry me unless it's what you truly want...for *yourself.* You can take all day today and tonight to think hard about it and give me your answer tomorrow. Whatever you decide, I will still love you. If returning to your community is what you really want, I will release you." She returned to her bedroom and shut the door in his bewildered face.

Rachel sat at her computer desk, tears sliding down her cheeks. *Might as well get it over with.* She picked up her cell phone and dialed the number for Emma's bakery. After five rings, Emma picked up.

"Hallo, Rachel!"

"I need to see you,"

"Okay, I'm right in the middle making sugar flowers for your cake, can it wait for a few hours?"

"No," Rachel replied, her voice heavy with sadness. "It can't wait."

There was a long pause. "This doesn't sound gut," Emma finally said. "Okay, I'll be over in a few minutes."

Rachel hung up and buried her face in her hands. Her entire world was falling apart again, only this time it was in front of her entire extended family and friends. *How am I going to tell them all that the wedding is cancelled? How am I going to tell them my entire life is cancelled?*

Her primary worry was Janet and Rhonda and all the time and personal expense they had put into planning her wedding. Then it hit her like a ton of bricks. *How am I going to live here without Samuel? How could I possibly go on and run the Inn and event barn without him?* The entire life she had rebuilt after losing Barry was teetering on a very thin razor's edge. By the time she heard Emma knocking on her door, she had plummeted into the depths of despair.

"Come in," she said, "and shut the door behind you."

Emma stepped in, shut the door and turned to look at her. Her hands flew to her face. "*Oh mein Gott* [37], what has happened?"

Rachel shook her head, struggling for composure. "I want you to stop working on the wedding cake for now," she said.

Emma stared back at her, horrified. "Why?"

"I just need you to stop just until tomorrow."

"What happens tomorrow?"

"The beginning of a happy new chapter or the end of my life as I knew it."

Emma just stared at her in horror. "Rachel, is there anything I can do to help you? Anything at all?"

Rachel nodded her head and offered her a joyless smile. "Pray and please don't breathe a word of this to anyone else."

Emma nodded. "I won't."

"*Especially* Karen."

Emma nodded again.

Rachel sighed. "Okay, that's it for now. I must face my entire family for the Tamale party I scheduled for later today."

Emma left the room, leaving Rachel alone for a moment.

---

[37] Oh my God

Showtime, she said morosely to herself.

Samuel headed to the barn, harnessed Molly, then hitched her to the buggy. Soon he was cantering as fast as he could go to Mark and Sarah's home ten miles down the road. He arrived within the hour, Molly breathing hard, her breath coming out in plumes of smoke from her nostrils. He covered her with a blanket near the water trough and marched up the steps to the house, bursting in without knocking.

"*Onkle* Samuel!" squealed Isaac, running to meet him. Samuel caught him as he jumped up into his arms.

Hearing their younger brother, Mary and Martha came running to the living room. They jumped up and down, clapping their hands with joy. They threw their arms around his waist. "Oh, we've missed you!" they cried.

Sarah entered the room, her eyes wide with surprise, her apron covered in flour as usual. "Samuel! You came!" She peered out through the window. "Did anyone see you?"

Samuel put Isaac down and gently extricated himself from his nieces embrace. "*Nee,*" he replied. "Is Mark here?"

"He's in the barn, I'll have Isaac fetch him."

Isaac needed no urging. He ran out the front door, leaving it wide open. Sarah hastily shut it and beckoned him into the kitchen. Samuel followed her, a niece clinging happily to each arm.

Sarah wiped her hands on her apron. "Girls, your *daed* and I need to speak with Samuel alone for a while."

"No," Samuel interrupted her. "Let them stay. I want to visit with them; I've missed them."

"Are you sure?" Sarah replied, her question pregnant with hidden meaning.

Samuel nodded then stood up when Mark entered the room. Mark opened his arms and gave Samuel a big bear hug. "I'm so glad you came," Mark whispered into his ear.

Samuel stepped away, nodding but also dreading what he had come to say. It would have to wait for a bit. For now, he just wanted to do what Rachel had suggested and count the cost before he made his final decision.

Mark gestured to the kitchen table. "Can you join us for lunch?"

Mary, Isaac, and Martha jumped up and down. "Please stay, *onkle* Samuel, *pleeeeaaase!*"

"*Jah*, okay," he smiled at them, unable to refuse such unapologetic affection. Out of the corner of his eye he could see Mark and Sarah exchanging hopeful glances.

The girls set an extra place for him, and the rest of their children soon gathered for the midday meal, among them, Willis.

"*Onkel* Samuel!" he said, his eyes growing large with surprise. "Are you supposed to be here?"

"Willis, hush. This is a special circumstance," Sarah chided her son, shooting Samuel a happy smile.

"Oh," Willis replied. "Umm, how's Karen?"

"She's well," Samuel replied, aware of what had happened between them. Willis just stared at him blankly for a moment, obviously wanting to know more but not brave enough to ask. They all washed up then took their seats, bowing their heads in silent prayer. Samuel also bowed his head, praying fervently to *Der Herr* that He would receive some kind of sign from heaven as to what to do.

"Help yourself, Samuel," Sarah handed him a platter of cold roast beef sandwiches on homemade bread.

Samuel took two halves and laid them on his plate.

Little Mary came over and wiggled onto his lap, resting her head against his chest with a happy sigh. "*Mamm*, may I eat here instead?" Her little arms stretched over her head so she could clasp them behind Samuel's neck. His heart melted.

Sarah nodded, if it's okay with your *onkle*."

"I would be happy to be your chair," Samuel smiled down upon her, kissing her pink, chubby cheek.

She giggled then stared at his bare chin. "*Onkle* Samuel, where did your beard go?"

Silence descended upon all at the table. Sarah and Mark exchanged glances. Their children all turned questioning eyes onto Samuel. Mary had unknowingly exposed the elephant in the room.

There was no avoiding it now. Samuel cleared his throat. "It's a long story, would you like to hear it?"

Several heads bobbed up and down. They had been told little if anything other than their beloved uncle had been excommunicated.

Sarah leaned over and whispered into his ear. "Are you sure this is a *gut* idea?"

"It must be done," Samuel whispered back, then addressed the entire family in a louder voice. "As you all know, I lost Rachel and your cousins over a year ago..." he began, then launched into all that had happened since, leaving in only the details he felt were essential to their understanding. They listened in rapt attention, barely eating until an entire hour had passed then sat quietly, thinking upon all he had told them.

"I like your new Rachel," piped up little Mary to her mother's obvious displeasure. "She's nice!"

Samuel nodded, touched by her innocent response. Mary twisted her head up and around to look him in the eyes, her little face becoming serious. "If you really, really love her, *onkle* Samuel, I will understand."

Tears sprang into Samuel's eyes he stared back into her large blue ones. There was no guile, she had spoken from her heart.

"*Danki*," he whispered, and held her for a moment in a tight embrace. "*Danki*." He had received his sign.

The Inn's entire kitchen and living room had been transformed into a large, tamale-making factory for that evening's dinner. Her entire family had all been outfitted with aprons, hairnets, and food prep gloves, talking animatedly amongst themselves as they worked.

Rachel's large farmhouse sink had been scrubbed clean, filled with hot water, and was soaking the 100+ dried cornhusks in it. Julie and Monique were on masa duty, mixing the masa, cumin, broth, and lard in two enormous bowls until it became a smooth dough. Debbie, Karen, and Holly stood by, ready to spread the masa onto the corn husks followed by either a choice of fillings: beans and cheese, carnitas, or shredded chicken.

Greg, Steve, Charles, Ben, and Craig had the messy task of folding the tamales together and standing them up in large steamer pots until they were crammed full.

Rachel stood at the stove, stirring a large pot of pinto beans, glad they were all too distracted to notice her misery. *At least they will all have one more night of carefree fun before I spoil everything.*

An hour later, three large pots containing over thirty tamales each were steaming on her large cast iron stove. Her friends and family had dumped their soiled aprons into one of the hampers on the service porch and gone to their respective rooms to clean up for supper. Rachel hadn't seen or heard from Samuel since he left earlier that day; each passing minute just confirming that her worst fears were about to be realized. The tamales were almost ready, and her family was gathering in her kitchen for supper.

Chapter Twenty-One

"A Fateful Decision"

"Should we wait just a little longer?" Mary asked Rachel, checking her watch for the umpteenth time. Her husband, AJ nodded. "I don't mind waiting a little longer," he added.

Everyone was seated at the folding tables for supper as they had been for the past half hour while the food grew cold. The only person missing was Samuel and she wasn't sure he was even coming. Rachel looked at his empty seat at the head of the table and shook her head, her emotions roiling with abject terror. She took Julie's hand and that of Debbie's to her right and bowed her head, signaling that the blessing should be given.

Everyone bowed their heads.

"Lord, we give thee thanks," began Josef.

He was interrupted by the front door opening.

Everyone looked up.

Samuel stood there in his Amish clothes; his eyes laser focused on her face; his expression unreadable. Rachel's heart dropped. *He's going to do this now, in front of everyone?!* She shook her head at him in desperation, her heart pounding wildly. He ignored her and strode forward.

"Rachel," he said, his eyes pleading.

"Please…don't…not here with everyone looking," she begged, her tears spilling over.

You could have heard a pin drop when Samuel dropped to one knee before her and pulled out a tiny black box from his pocket.

Gasps erupted from around the table.

"What are you doing?" she hissed, thoroughly confused.

"Proposing to you properly as I should have done long ago," he replied and opened the lid of the box to reveal a diamond engagement ring. "Rachel Elizabeth Winston, will you do me the profound honor of becoming my wife?"

Rachel sat frozen, staring at him in shock. She had been preparing for the worst all day and he had just blind-sided her with a public proposal she hadn't seen coming. The vise around her heart melted and her emotional dam burst. She nodded, bursting into tears while everyone whooped and clapped in joy.

Samuel stood to his feet and took her into his arms. He slid the ring upon her finger and kissed her between the eyes. "Much better than an Inn sign, *jah*?" he smiled. "Can you ever forgive me?"

Rachel wrapped her arms around his neck and nodded. "Just shut up and kiss me properly!"

Samuel grabbed her face and brought his lips down upon hers, his arms encircling her in a vise, little caring that everyone was watching him commit a public display of affection. Finally, he broke away. "I love you," he said. He leaned forward and brought his lips close to her ear. "And I can't wait to marry you."

Rachel caught Emma's face beaming at her, tears of happiness glistening in her eyes. "You can finish the cake now, Em," she told her.

Karen looked at Emma then at Rachel. "Did I miss something? Why did Emma have to stop work on the cake?" she demanded. "And why wasn't I informed to stop working on the flowers? What is going on around here?"

"That information is on a need-to-know basis," Emma replied on behalf of Rachel. "And *you* didn't need to know."

"Argh!" growled Karen. "No one around here tells me anything!"

Samuel took his empty place at the head of the table and nodded to Josef. "I apologize for interrupting grace," he said.

Josef smiled at him and winked. "Let us pray," he said. They all bowed their heads as he said grace.

The awkwardness that had hovered over the dining room the entire day and evening dissolved into unrestrained joy. When he wasn't passing bowls of tamales, salsa, guacamole, salad and refried beans around, Samuel was insistent on holding her hand, making it a bit difficult for both to eat. She gently disengaged his hand after giving him an affectionate squeeze and reassuring smile. "It's okay, I'm good now."

Greg stood up and clinked his fork against his glass to get everyone's attention, lifting his glass of diet coke high. "A toast to the happy couple," he grinned, favoring Rachel with a look that told her he had known all along that something wasn't right and was now glad it had been resolved.

Everyone stood and raised their glasses of soda, sparkling cider, water, cerveza, or lemonade.

"Congratulations!" Everyone cheered and clinked glasses.

"Mazel tov," came Josef's voice above the din.

"MAZEL TOV!" they all echoed.

Rachel and Samuel sat cuddled together on the porch swing despite the freezing cold weather, a large blanket insulating them from the frigid night air. The sky was clear and ablaze with thousands of stars.

"When I saw you in your Amish clothes tonight, I practically had a heart attack," Rachel admitted. "I thought for sure you were going to say goodbye."

"I'm so sorry," Samuel replied, wrapping his arms about her tighter. "I'd gone to Mark and Sarah's for the day and didn't want to seem conspicuous, so I dressed Amish. "I went straight from there to a local jeweler to purchase your ring and came straight home without changing."

"What happened there that made you decide to give it all up?" Rachel was dying to know.

Samuel smiled as he remembered the cherubic face of his young niece smiling at him. "*Out of the mouths of babes and suckling's,*" he quoted. "*Thou hast perfected praise,* or in my case…good advice."

Rachel sat up and stared at him. "*Your niece told you to marry me?*"

"Yes, in her own innocent way," Samuel replied.

Rachel gave him an affectionate but frustrated smack on the chest. "Samuel Miller, are you going to tell me what she said or what?"

In response, Samuel bent down and kissed her thoroughly on the lips. "She said she wouldn't mind," he repeated.

"She wouldn't mind what?"

"If I married you."

"That's it?!" Rachel couldn't believe her ears.

"You had to be there," Samuel tried to explain. "I had gone there as you suggested and spent the entire day with my family so I could make a rational decision about what I truly wanted. I was still struggling terribly when little Mary climbed onto my lap and said she wouldn't mind if I married you because she liked you." He smiled down upon her. "I had asked *Der Herr* for a sign, and He gave me one. Suddenly my indecision just miraculously evaporated, and I knew what I wanted more than anything," he concluded, wiping a tear from her eye. "And that was you."

"So, what gave you the idea to propose to me in front of everyone like that? I know for a fact that Amish men don't typically do that."

At this Samuel fell silent, then "I'm embarrassed to admit it," he confessed.

"Admit to what?"

"I searched YouTube for ideas on how to propose."

"*You searched YouTube?*" Rachel was incredulous.

"Most of the top results were ridicules. One man enlisted the entire wedding party, guests, a film crew and even a drone to film a five-minute-long musical parade through his town to propose." Samuel snorted with derision. "I finally just decided to make it simple and propose in front of your entire family so you would know I meant it."

"Well, it certainly worked!" Rachel replied then gasped, pointing to the sky above them. "Look!" she cried.

Samuel turned his head just in time to see the falling star arching across the night sky.

"Another sign," he grinned at her.

The next day was Thanksgiving, and everyone had gathered in the kitchen after breakfast to help Rachel with the preparations except for Rhonda who was holed up in her room with her sewing machine making last minute alterations to their dresses and Janet who was directing all the vendor deliveries that began to arrive for the wedding.

Emma was busy in the commercial kitchen assembling the wedding cake while also preparing the three large turkeys for Thanksgiving dinner since they wouldn't fit into the vintage iron stove in the Inn. They had been dry brining for the past two days and were now ready to roast. She had her cell phone propped up onto the counter in speaker mode so she could hear Rachel's instructions.

"Talk louder!" she yelled over the noise coming from the event barn which had become a flurry of activity.

"Make sure to rinse off all of the brining spices well, pat them dry and fill the cavities with the aromatics I told you about." Rachel yelled. "Spread the butter all over the outside and under the skin and season with everything *except for salt. NO SALT."*

"*Jah*! No salt!" Emma repeated.

"Right! Then put them in the browning bags per the directions and in a 350 oven no more than three hours before supper time, about noon."

Emma frowned. Her mamm used to put in their bird at 6:00 am and baste it every hour, all day, for a good seven hours at a much lower temperature. "Are you sure?"

"Trust me!" Rachel yelled. "No more than two and a half hours of cooking time; the meat will be falling off the bone and they will be super moist! I've done it this way at least half a dozen times; it's fail-safe!"

"Okay," Emma said, still doubtful. "I'll have the boys carry them over to rest as soon as they come out of the oven."

"It's such a pain in the neck for me not to be able to work in that commercial kitchen!" Rachel griped for the millionth time that day. "It would have been so much easier to have everyone gather for meals together in the event barn instead of eating off folding tables in the Inn!"

"It's just for one more day, Rachel, so suck it up!" Emma grinned. "You don't want to ruin the surprise Karen has been working so hard on!"

"It'd better be a doozey after all this inconvenience!" Rachel retorted good naturedly, then hung up.

Everything was ready. Rachel looked at her kitchen island, overflowing with three golden-roasted turkeys, cornbread stuffing, green bean casserole, Praline sweet potatoes (her specialty), garlic mashed potatoes with sauteed onions and bacon, homemade potato bread rolls and a large green salad. The folding tables had all been covered with clean white tablecloths and table runners and decorated with baby pumpkins and autumn leaves mingled with mason jar candles. Each place setting featured her Thanksgiving

Johnson Brothers porcelain wear. Amber-hued tumblers and ruby red goblets were set at each place and on the stove she had hot mulled cider and mulled wine simmering in her large Le Creuset pots. The house smelled amazing.

Everyone began filtering into the house, shedding their heavy coats and hanging them up on the wall pegs.

"It smells heavenly!" Monique commented, opening her arms to give Rachel a hug. "What am I smelling beside turkey?"

"Mulled wine and cider," Rachel replied.

"Ooowww I want to try some of that cider!" enthused Mary.

"I'll have the wine!" added AJ.

"Just help yourselves, there's mugs over there and ladles." Rachel pointed.

Monique bent down and whispered in her ear. "Everything good now?"

Rachel's smile lit up her face. "Couldn't be better."

"Smells great, *Ratzli*!" Debbie said, admiring all the food. Debbie really appreciated home cooked meals since she didn't cook and just served prepared meals from Costco.

Everyone but her immediate family stared at Debbie, confused.

"Thanks, *Debula*" Rachel responded in her best Dracula voice. "It's my pet name, she gives one to everyone she loves," she explained to everyone else.

Karen rang the iron triangle. "Everyone, please go to your seats!" she yelled.

Rachel covered her ears and gave Karen a look. She had been standing right next to it.

They needed no urging and stood behind their chairs.

Samuel opened his arms in welcome. "Thank you all for coming such a long way to share not only in our first real Thanksgiving in this blessed place but also to witness our marriage." He nodded to Josef. "Would you honor us by leading grace?"

Everyone quieted and in the flickering glow of candle-light, Josef closed his eyes and lifted his arms to heaven. *"Good and Gracious God, we thank thee for gathering us here today and for all the gifts that you've given us in the year that's past. We welcome the new addition(s) to this table, grateful for their presence, and bless all those responsible for the food we are about to eat, both near and far, amen."*

"Amen!" Everyone repeated.

"It's buffet style, everyone!" Rachel announced. "Just take your plates and feel free to load up, there's plenty to go around!"

Unlike in traditional Amish homes, the men deferred to the women who had prepared the food, allowing them to line up first, beginning with Rachel as the host, followed by Emma, Annie, Naomi, and Ruth and after that Karen and the rest of the family in no particular order.

Rachel sat down and was soon joined by Samuel who had piled his plate so high she was afraid all his food would go sliding off onto the floor. She leaned over and whispered in his ear. "Hungry much?"

He lifted the turkey leg to his mouth and tore off a hunk in response with his teeth. His eyes rolled back into his head with pleasure. "So *gut!*" he exclaimed despite his full mouth. "The flavor goes all the way through!"

Rachel nodded. "By the way, us women cook, you men get to clean!"

Samuel looked askance at her. "Is that so?"

Rachel nodded, enjoying how they were back to teasing each other.

Samuel swallowed and gave her a rakish smile. "You don't want it to just be the two of us, at the sink?" His double meaning was clear. He had often joined her for the evening meal clean up so he could seize the opportunity to nuzzle her neck and ears, effectively driving her crazy.

Rachel knew exactly what he was referring to. "I think I could be persuaded to kick everyone out and have just us do the dishes," She gave him a long, seductive look.

The drumstick slipped out of his fingers and plopped onto his plate.

Rachel busted up laughing, causing everyone to turn around to look at them and wonder what was so funny. Samuel caught the turkey before it could drop off the table into the waiting jaws of little Buddy.

He *harumphed* with frustration and left, stationing himself under Aaron's chair who was sure to pass him table scraps when no one was looking.

Samuel sat back in his chair and groaned with discomfort, followed by most every else at the table.

OMG I'm never eating again!" Karen announced. An enormously long and obnoxious belch erupted from her mouth. She dissolved into giggles. "Sorry! Too much sparkling cider!" she apologized.

Samuel waved off her apology. "In Amish homes, it is how we show our heartfelt thanks for a *gut* meal!" He explained, "otherwise, the cook would feel insulted." To emphasize his point, he followed up with a belch that rivaled Karen's who burst out laughing again.

"Well, I think it's kind of rude," Julie said.

Genesis elbowed her in the ribs. "Hey, me and Holly belch all the time at home!" He sat straight up and belched louder and longer than Samuel.

Karen stood onto her feet and threw her hands in the air. "BELCHING CONTEST!" She announced to everyone with a huge laugh.

Soon all the men were belching as loudly and as long as they could until the women became consumed with laughter and started belching right along with them, albeit with their mouths covered. After half an hour of the most obnoxious belching and laughing session imaginable, they quieted down.

"That was so much fun!" Karen observed, still giggling.

Rachel nodded. "Yes, you all made me feel incredibly appreciated!" Then she let out the biggest belch of any of them.

Karen applauded. "Mom wins!"

After pie, coffee and hot cocoa everyone made their way back to the event barn and nearby accommodations for a good night's sleep, the tryptophan hitting hard. Sunday was the big day and there was still much to do.

Rachel and Samuel stood at the sink, attending to the mountain of platters, pots and pans to wash as her two dishwashers cleaned the plates, tumblers, and cutlery.

Rachel sighed, resting her head upon Samuel's chest as she attempted to wash the large Le Creuset. She kept getting distracted by his hands which seemed to have a mind of their own. She could hear his heart hammering in his chest, his breath becoming ragged in her ear as he caressed her hands, her arms and nibbled on her ear lobe while murmuring endearments in Pennsylvania Dutch.

She turned around to face him, and he pressed himself up against her. "Samuel…"

His mouth closed over hers, rendering her mute and her knees weak. Her soapy hands and arms encircled his neck, and she kissed him back with abandon, making up for the last few days of feeling estranged. Samuel groaned and then to her surprise, he lifted her up onto the kitchen counter, so her face was level with his and continued to passionately kiss her. Her legs wrapped around his waist. He pressed against her. She slipped back, her behind slipping into the sink full of soapy water.

"Stop!" she yelped and dissolved into helpless laughter. "I'm getting all wet!"

Samuel flinched and let go upon which her bottom sank to the bottom forcing her short legs to be jacked upright. Water sloshed over the sink and onto the floor. Samuel slipped, lost his footing, and crashed onto the floor. They both burst into hysterics.

"Help! Help!" Rachel choked, flailing about, trying to get some leverage to lift herself out. Water sloshed out and onto Samuel's head. He fell back, helpless with laughter.

Karen chose that moment to enter the kitchen and just stared at them, her mouth gaping open. "What is going on?"

Neither one could answer her; they were laughing too hard.

Samuel was absolutely soaked to the skin and Rachel was stuck with her entire bottom in the sink, her legs sticking straight up. Karen dragged Samuel out of the puddle, threw her towel onto the floor to absorb the water and reached for her mom's arms. "On the count of three: one…two…" She pulled with all her might and dragged Rachel up and out so her feet could land on the floor. Her sodden shoes slipped and down she went next to Samuel laughing and clutching her middle.

"I give up, goodnight!" Karen exclaimed, stomping upstairs to her room. "Try to keep it quiet down there!" she added from upstairs. *"I still have to get up at four fricken o'clock!!!"*

Rachel collapsed on top of Samuel and laid there until they laughed themselves out. It was close to 9:00 pm and they still had the pots and pans to do.

"I don't think I have ever laughed that hard in my life," Samuel grinned at her.

"Well, I definitely haven't," Rachel replied, glad that he couldn't see her red face in the dim light. "We're going to have to drain the sink and put in fresh water."

Samuel sat up on one elbow, his eyebrows climbing. "Oh? Why?"

Rachel covered her face with her hands and tried not to scream with laughter. "I peed myself in the sink!" she shrieked and collapsed on the floor again.

Samuel exploded with laughter despite Karen's warning. "I have a better idea," he choked out. "Let's leave it for someone else to deal with!

"Yeah," Rachel drawled. "We're on vacation!"

Chapter Twenty-Two

"The Big Day"

Rachel stared at the ceiling, listening to her clock tick away the hours while she tossed and turned. She went to the kitchen and drank a huge glass of milk, went back to her bed and waited. Then she tried some left-over mulled wine. Nothing was working. She threw off the covers at 2:00 am and went into the kitchen where all the dirty pots and pans still lay piled up.

She drained the sink, rinsed everything down well then refilled it with hot sudsy water and began to wash. Buddy padded out of her room and snuggled into his little bed next to the island to keep her company.

She had left all the wedding arrangements to Janet, Emma, Rhonda, and Karen to deal with and kept wondering what the 'big surprise' was. Knowing Janet as well as she did, she had no worries about anything being missed but then a new thought jumped into her mind that would not let her rest until she investigated it. She dried her hands and went to her computer to conduct a search. Buddy came back into the room and curled up under her desk on his pillow.

How and where do the Amish typically honeymoon? She typed. The results that came up made her jaw drop. "What!?" she screeched, reading aloud under her breath. "No honeymoon? No wedding night? They stay in their parent's home

230

and help to clean up from the reception?!!! "*Well @#$&** that!*" She clapped a hand over her mouth.

No wonder Samuel had mentioned nothing about going somewhere for a honeymoon! She had assumed he had been secretly planning something for them all along and would surprise her. It had never occurred to her that the word 'honeymoon' wasn't part of the Amish vernacular. That's what the *Englisch* did; usually the groom or his family. Now it was too late! She slumped, ready to cry again. They were going to have to go to a local Motel 6! Rachel stomped back into the kitchen, a confused and tired Buddy trailing behind her. She looked down at him and he clearly looked back at her as if to say *make up your mind*.

She finished washing the pots and pans while muttering under her breath and put them all away until *four fricken am* then climbed into bed exhausted and disappointed.

A hand shook her awake. "Rachel! Time to get up!"

Rachel cracked open one eye to find Rhonda's face hovering over hers, her brows furrowed in concern. "You have bags under your eyes! Didn't you sleep last night?"

Rachel shook her pounding head. "Couldn't sleep so I washed up," she mumbled, her mouth as dry as dust. She reached for her water bottle. It was empty. "I need coffee!"

"Stay there, I'll be right back." Rhonda hurried out of the room.

Rachel fell back and instantly began snoring.

Rhonda returned with her To Go mug and nudged her awake again. "Here, drink this," she commanded.

Rachel put the drink to her lips with her eyes still closed and sipped. "What time is it?"

"Nine am. The stylist is here to do your hair."

Rachel took another gulp. "I need to shower first," she said, rising to her feet. "Give me twenty minutes."

"Okay, I'll have her work on us first," Rhonda agreed.

At that moment, Janet entered the room. "The makeup artist just arrived," she announced and examined Rachel with concern. "You have bags under your eyes."

Rachel nodded. "Yeah, so I've heard; plus, it's all over the news so I think we're covered."

"You look awful!" Janet added. "But nothing that a good makeup artist can't fix."

Rachel shook her head. "No makeup. The Amish don't wear makeup."

"You're not Amish," Janet replied. "Just some foundation to hide the bluish bags, blush and natural lip tint."

"Promise? No false eye lashes, mascara, eye liner and eye shadow?" Rachel confirmed, gulping her coffee and scalding her throat. She erupted into a coughing fit and fell onto her bed. "Can this day get any worse?" she muttered into her pillow.

Janet pulled her up into a sitting position. "Okay, spill the beans, what now?"

"You're going to think I'm being petty," Rachel pouted.

"Just spit it out!" Rhonda demanded, losing her patience.

"No honeymoon," Rachel whined, her exhaustion and disappointment making her weep.

"Oh no you don't, snap out of it, Rach!" Jane spat. "We can't fix swollen eyes in the space of two hours if you start crying and what do you mean by no honeymoon?"

"The Amish don't have them," Rachel replied, wiping her eyes. "So obviously, Samuel never thought to plan for one and make reservations."

"Oh, that will never do!" Rhonda said, aghast.

Janet rolled her eyes. "You so underestimate me!" She lifted Rachel onto her feet and pushed her into the bathroom. "I've taken care of everything; you have nothing to worry about, now cheer up and get into the shower!"

Rachel lifted her head, a smile wreathing her face. "Really?"

"Really!" Janet assured her. "When you're out of the shower we'll put some tea bags under your eyes." She turned to Rhonda, all business. "You're up first for hair and makeup, they're waiting for you in your bedroom."

"See you later!" Rhonda called over her shoulder.

Rachel felt like a new person after her shower and lay on the bed with the ice-cold tea bags over her eyes. A banana, coffee and an Ibuprofen got rid of her headache and the shower had removed her weariness and brain fog for the time being. She just hoped the lack of sleep would not result in a migraine later.

She heard Janet enter the room. "Can I get up now?" She asked.

Janet lifted the tea bags off her eyes and nodded with approval. "All gone!" She smiled.

Rachel did a double take, looking her best friend up and down. "Wow." She ogled, "you look amazing!"

Janet modeled the icy, sage green, tailored, silk shantung suit dress Rhonda had created. "You like?" She spun around. "I have to say, Rhonda is a genius at design. I wouldn't mind wearing this again out to dinner or to a special event, unlike most hideous bridesmaid dresses."

Rachel nodded. "I can't imagine mine being more gorgeous than that!"

"Just wait!" Janet winked at her.

A brief knock sounded upon the door and Rhonda entered, her hair coiffed, wearing a matching dress to Janet's. She carried in the garment bag containing Rachel's gown that she had jealously guarded all week from prying eyes. Following her came the hair stylist and makeup artist.

"Sit here," Janet said, pushing Rachel's office chair into the middle of the room.

Rachel padded over in her robe and slippers and sat down. "When do I get to see the dress?"

"Not until your hair and make-up are done." Rhonda replied, hanging the garment bag from a hook over the closet door.

The women set to work with Rhonda and Janet watching and supervising. The stylist used product that brought more of the curl out of Rachel's hair and used beautiful, jeweled combs on each side to sweep it away from her ears. The makeup artist had been prepared in advance by Janet and went light on the makeup as she had requested so that it enhanced her natural beauty.

"Okay, now," Rhonda said, retrieving the garment bag. "Close your eyes, remove your robe and lift your arms."

Rachel stood, quivering with excitement, not knowing what to expect. She felt a silky garment slip over her arms.

"Just a moment while I fasten you," Rhonda said, doing up all the tiny buttons in the back. She led Rachel over to where her full-length mirror was. "Okay now."

Rachel opened her eyes. She blinked and looked closer. "Oh....*myyyyyyyyyy,*" she breathed. She didn't recognize herself in the mirror. She was twinkling!

"I was inspired by your fireflies at twilight," Rhonda said. "Well?"

Rachel gulped, fighting down her tears. "It is the most beautiful thing I have ever laid eyes on," she whispered. The gown was in a smokey blue hombre that went from light at the bosom to midnight blue at the bottom and overlaid with matching lace. The neckline scooped in a modest oval above her breast and the fitted bodice accentuated her tiny waistline, flowing out into a full A-line at the hips that came to just below her knees. Scattered throughout like tiny stars were aurora borealis Swarovski crystals that reminded her exactly of the fireflies that had so enchanted all of them on their property.

In the mirror she could see everyone in the room staring at her, their collective mouths hanging open in awe.

"*Dang!*" The makeup artist finally said.

They all nodded in agreement.

"How does it feel?" Rhonda asked, pleased with their reaction.

"Amazing!" Rachel replied, unable to tear her eyes away from the dress.

"Oh, I almost forgot the cap and the shoes!" Rhonda rummaged into a small suitcase and brought out what resembled an Amish prayer kapp except that it was in the same dark smokey blue lace as the dress. She set it upon Rachel's curls and secured it with bobby pins. She placed the matching pumps on the floor and Rachel stepped into them. Overwhelmed, she embraced her friend. "Rhonda, I can't thank you enough! I feel like…like…Cinderella at the ball!"

Another knock came upon the door and Karen entered, carrying three bouquets in her arms. She was also dressed in a beautiful, midnight blue dress. Karen froze the instant she laid eyes on her mom. "Dang!" she exclaimed. "You look absolutely amazing, mom!" She held out the largest bouquet.

"Oh sweetheart, it's just beautiful!" Rachel cooed, admiring her daughter's handiwork. "It reminds me of a blazing fall sunset!" The bouquet had roses in a combination of blazing coral, reds, and yellows, fuchsia Gerber daisies and sunflowers with ivy trailing down. Janet and Rhonda's bouquets were smaller versions of the same.

Everyone paused as the sound of a string quartet playing music drifted into the room. Rachel looked out the window and saw a huge white tent surrounding the rose arbor. "How did you manage that without my seeing it?" She asked Janet in amazement.

"Magic." Janet grinned at her mysteriously. She checked her watch. "It's time!"

"Now?" Rachel bleated, checking herself in the mirror one last time.

"Now."

"Everyone is in the tent and waiting for you." Rhonda confirmed.

"Will all three of you walk me down the aisle?" Rachel asked. "It would mean a lot to me."

"Of course!" Janet replied, hugging her. "But three might look awkward, how about if Karen goes first like your flower girl and us on either side?"

"I think that's better, mom." Karen agreed, nodding.

Rachel took a deep breath, unable to believe that the moment had finally come. She had survived death, injury, and the potential loss of Samuel all in the space of one year and now that the day of her wedding was here, it felt surreal.

"Okay, I'm ready," she whispered.

She followed Karen out of the room and was followed by Janet and Rhonda. The makeup artist and hair stylist both were misty-eyed.

"I so want Rhonda James to design my wedding dress!" the makeup artist said, blowing her nose into a handkerchief.

"You can't afford her," replied the stylist.

A blast of frigid air hit Rachel as soon as she stepped outside. She paused, tempted to turn around and get her winter coat out of the closet.

Janet grabbed her right arm and Rhonda her left, preventing her from making the side trip.

"Don't worry, mom, it's toasty warm in the tent!" Karen whispered over her shoulder. They hurried through the front yard and entered what was the back of the tent into a small entry space that hid them from the guest's view.

"Much better!" Rachel nodded.

Janet looked through the plastic window and gave a thumbs up to Josef who was standing at the front of the tent under the rose arbor. He nodded to the musicians and the sound of Beethoven's *Ode to Joy* wafted across the tent. A chill went up Rachel's spine which wasn't from the cold air. Janet watched for a moment until she saw Samuel, Aaron, Amos, and Abram take their places at the front then she nodded at Katie and Miriam who stood on the other side of the tent flaps to open them up.

Karen walked down the aisle first, her gaze fixated on Aaron who looked dashing in his black suit, white shirt, and midnight blue bowtie.

Josef nodded at them. "Please rise," he told all the guests. They all stood and turned to look at Rachel and a hush fell over them.

The moment Samuel laid eyes on Rachel, tears sprang into his eyes; momentarily blinding him. He dashed them away repeatedly so he wouldn't miss a moment of her walking down the aisle to him. Everything else around him faded away except for the music and Rachel's shy smile as she approached him in the most amazing gown he had ever seen. In a nod to his culture, she also wore a kapp in dark blue that twinkled fitfully in the candlelight. A sob of joy erupted from his throat as she came closer with eyes only for him. His knees went weak. Josef reached out and grasped his elbow to steady him to ensure he didn't collapse.

Samuel felt his heart pounding in his chest, unable to believe this dazzling creature would soon be all his.

Rachel saw nothing but Samuel, standing tall and broad shouldered before her in his black suit, white shirt and traditional black hat, tears streaming down his clean-shaven cheeks.

She stopped before him then glanced at Josef who gave her a wink.

"Who gives this woman in holy matrimony?" he asked loud enough for everyone to hear.

"I do," said Karen.

"We do," chimed in Janet and Rhonda.

Samuel offered Rachel his arm and they stood together before Josef as he opened his Bible to the last chapter of Proverbs and recited the verses about a woman of noble character. It was then, for the first time, that Rachel allowed herself to notice her surroundings. The rose arbor was garlanded with flowers that matched her bouquet, arching over the wedding podium and extending down either side of the front. Out of the corner of her eye she spied crystal chandeliers glittering fitfully on candelabra stands and beneath her feet was a carpet of rose petals.

"*AHEM.*" Josef cleared his throat loudly.

Rachel's attention snapped back to him.

Josef looked at Samuel. "Samuel, do you promise… that if Rachel is afflicted with bodily weakness sickness or some other circumstance that you will care for her as is fitting as a Christian husband?"

"I do promise," Samuel responded, his gaze fixated upon her face.

Josef continued with the traditional Amish vows, "And do you also solemnly promise that you will love her, bear and be patient with each other and shall not separate from each other until dear God shall part you from each other through death?"

"I do so pledge," Samuel said, then added. "I have something else to add, if I may?"

Josef nodded.

Samuel reached for both of her hands. Rachel handed her bouquet to Janet and took his warm hands in her own, staring up into his cerulean eyes. He gazed down upon her with a look of ineffable sweetness. He cleared his throat nervously several times, his Adams apple bobbing beneath his skin. He withdrew a simple gold wedding band from his pocket and slipped it onto her finger.

"Rachel, with this ring I thee wed; with my body I thee worship, and with all my worldly goods I thee endow. I pledge to love you as Christ loves His church, and..." He paused for a moment, fighting back a smile. "I also promise not to regrow the scraggly beard that you hated..."

A ripple of laughter swept over the room. Rachel suppressed a giggle.

"...in the name of the Father, and of the Son, and of the Holy Ghost, amen," he finished.

Now it was her turn. "I Rachel Elizabeth Winston, do also solemnly promise that I will love and honor you, bear and be patient with you and will not separate from you until dear God parts me from you through death," she promised.

They both turned and looked at Josef expectantly.

"By the power invested in me by *Der Herr* and the State of Pennsylvania, I now pronounce you husband and wife."

Rachel grinned at Samuel, waiting for Josef's next words. An awkward silence ensued, and she looked back at him then at Samuel whose shoulders were shaking with laughter.

"What happened to *you may kiss the bride?!*" she finally demanded loud enough for everyone to hear. The entire tent erupted in laughter. Out of the corner of her eye she could see Janet giving Rhonda a warning glare not to start laughing.

Josef regarded her with wide eyes, the picture of innocence. "Amish do not exchange kisses during the wedding ceremony!" He replied with a straight face.

Rachel was aghast. "*Well, the heck with that!*" she finally cried, grabbed Samuel's face and planted a big one on him. "I'm not Amish!"

This time Rhonda couldn't contain herself and her screams of laughter filled the air until everyone was in hysterics.

"Rachel!" Samuel said in a voice that would brook no argument, interrupting the gaiety.

Rachel's attention snapped back to him. She was tempted to salute. "Yes?"

He crooked a finger at her and beckoned. "Come here," and not waiting for her to comply, he swept her into his arms, bent her over backwards in a dip and kissed her thoroughly to the whoops and cheers of all in the tent.

When she was back upright, she felt giddy and lightheaded, swaying unsteadily on her feet. Samuel's arm went about her waist as Josef concluded the ceremony.

"Ladies and gentlemen, I now present to you Samuel and Rachel Miller."

Rachel and Samuel turned to face their family.

"Is this your doing?" Samuel whispered into her ear, indicating his side of the aisle that was filled with the all the men and women who had been instrumental in building the event barn months earlier.

Rachel looked up at him and nodded. "My wedding gift to you," she whispered.

At that moment, Karen signaled to several people stationed around the tent and yelled out "*Now!*"

There was a moment's pause then suddenly the air was filled with thousands of butterflies descending, floating, and flitting throughout the entire space.

The air filled with *oohs* and *aahs*, hands reaching up and cries of delight as the butterflies alighted on them. The musicians lifted their instruments and played The Blue Danube Waltz by Johann Strauss as the butterflies danced about the room above their heads.

"This is absolutely *magical...*" breathed Rachel, giggling as one alighted upon her nose.

Karen was Johnny on the spot and snapped a picture of a Monarch fluttering its wings on Rachel's face with her ever present iPhone. She got the photo just in time before it fluttered away.

Rachel grabbed Karen and gave her a hug. "Honey, was this your big surprise?"

Karen nodded. "Uh huh, I've been working on it for months," she grinned. "I had to buy the caterpillars way in advance and time it just right so the chrysalides would emerge from their cocoons in time for the wedding. I had Butterfly habitats all over the event barn and had to keep the temperature at 78 degrees inside so they wouldn't die. You're going to have an enormous electric bill...sorry...not sorry," she grinned.

Rachel kissed her daughter on the forehead. "Worth every penny!" she whispered and meant it.

Samuel recaptured her attention. "Shall we?"

"Let's!" Rachel smiled up at him, tucking her arm through his and retrieving her bouquet from Janet.

Chapter Twenty-Three

"Celebration"

Rachel and Samuel entered the event barn first and paused to take it all in. The rustic 8' long wooden tables were lined end to end and were decorated with dozens of ball jars containing tea lights. Down the center of the tables were autumn leaves in every color imaginable that Karen had gathered from the property as well as miniature pumpkins and gourds. The centerpiece of each table was a white Cinderella pumpkin containing flowers that matched Rachel's bouquet.

"This is just amazing!" Rhonda exclaimed, gazing all around her.

"Karen did an incredible job!" Janet agreed.

They walked further in and up to the table for the bride and groom which stood at the head of the room. Next to that table was the wedding cake that Emma had been working on for over a week.

"Oh Emma!" Rached cried, wrapping her in an embrace. "It matches my dress!!!"

Emma returned her hug. "You like it, really?"

Rachel nodded, admiring her handiwork. "It looks like twilight on the farm, you even included fireflies!"

"Rhonda had some left-over crystals from your dress, so I used them on your cake." She pointed to both the fresh and sugar flowers cascading down the blue hombre cake in a spiral.

"Emma, it's a work of art!" Samuel said, remembering his very plain sheet cake from his first wedding.

"*Will everyone please take your seats?*" came Josef's voice over the loudspeakers.

Their family and friends all made their way to their seats and sat down, quieting themselves.

"*Let us pray.*"

Everyone bowed their heads.

"*Der Herr, we give thee thanks and praise for this day which Thou has made. We ask that you bless this food and the hands which prepared it. In thy holy name we pray. Amen.*"

"AMEN!" everyone said in unison.

"The bride and groom will go first then the rest of you may line up table by table at the buffet line." Josef instructed them.

Samuel took Rachel by the hand and led her to the buffet where the silver lids of the steamers were rolled back to reveal the contents. He pointed at the first one. "Is that creamed celery?" he asked, incredulously.

Rachel nodded. "I got the recipe, and the girls made a huge batch of it for us. I honestly don't get what the deal is with celery at weddings, but I knew you would appreciate it, so…"

Samuel leaned over and kissed her on the cheek. "*Danki!*" he whispered, deeply touched. He plopped a healthy scoop of creamed celery onto his plate then moved onto the next steamer. "I'm going to need two, maybe 3 plates," he whispered to Rachel, ogling all the food.

Rachel nodded, her eyes wide at the vast selection of entrees and sides.

There were several roast turkeys, a carving station containing an entire side of beef, poached salmon with lemon dill sauce, garlic mashed potatoes, roasted potatoes, a huge selection of homemade rolls, creamed corn, roasted Brussel sprouts and butternut squash with bacon bits and craisens tossed in a maple glaze, fresh green salad, a vast array of pickled vegetables and canned fruit.

Samuel was juggling two plates that were piled high with food.

"Something is missing," he told Rachel as they made their way back to their table.

"What on earth could be missing?" Rachel replied.

"Your artichoke dip," he teased, recalling how he had been the only one to eat her offering at a Quilting.

"Did someone say artichoke dip?" Janet grinned, taking a seat near their table with her husband Ben.

Rachel nodded. "We forgot the artichoke dip."

"Total bummer," Janet smiled. "I guess I didn't think of everything." Rachel's artichoke dip was Janet's favorite.

Ben sat down next to her. "Quite a spread!" he exclaimed. He reached over and shook Samuel's hand. "Congratulations!" he said.

"*Danki!*" Samuel smiled.

The air was filled with the murmur of happy voices and soft background music. Once Samuel and Rachel had eaten, they made their way to every table, greeting everyone in person and accepting their well wishes.

"Everything is so lovely!" Monique gushed, giving Rachel a hug. "And your dress! Where did you find it?"

"My friend Rhonda made it," Rachel smiled, glancing down to admire her dress. "I had no idea she was a famous fashion designer."

"Really?" Monique, also a devoted seamstress, admired the handiwork more closely. "Turn around and let me see the back."

Rachel turned.

"Did you realize that each of these tiny buttons in back were individually hand covered in your fabric, also in an hombre pattern to match?" she marveled.

Rachel shook her head. "She wanted to start a line of wedding apparel, and this is the first one," she replied.

"Well, hang onto it, because it's probably going to increase in value; especially if it's the first and only one of its kind!"

"It is absolutely stunning!" Julie agreed. "But why blue and not white or pale pink?"

"Amish brides wear blue or lavender," Rachel replied so I wanted to honor their traditions for Samuel."

"I love it!" Debbie smiled.

"Hey Rachel," said her husband, Craig, lifting a spoon full of creamed celery. "What this? It's great!"

"Creamed celery, another tradition." Rachel smiled at him.

"Don't look at me!" Debbie chided Craig. "I don't cook!"

Emma approached them. "Samuel and Rachel, it's time to cut the cake."

"Duty calls!" Rachel grinned at her sisters-in-law, following Emma over to the cake table with Samuel.

Josef Eicher took up the microphone. "The bride and groom will now cut the cake if you would all like to gather around," he invited.

Everyone left their seats and milled around the cake area, Karen right in front. "Smash it into her face, Samuel!" she goaded him loudly.

Rachel gave him a warning look. "If you get one drop of cake on this gorgeous dress, I will be *merciless*."

Samuel gawked at her in amusement.

"I'm dead serious," she cautioned him.

Emma handed Samuel the knife. "I'd listen to her if I were you," she whispered.

"Come here," he beckoned, sliding his arm about Rachel's waist. With his hand over hers they cut off a hunk of the cake and put it onto the little China plate. He forked a spoonful and held it in front of her mouth like a gentleman. The photographer and guests all snapped photos.

Rachel ate and did the same for him.

"*Awww* you two are no fun at all!" Karen complained from the sidelines.

Rachel wiped her mouth. "When it's your turn, you can have a knockdown, drag out, food fight it you want but I'm not ruining this dress!"

The servers came and ushered the wedding cake into the kitchen to cut it up into serving pieces while others went around the room pouring the guests a glass of champagne for the toast.

In addition to the champagne there was also craft beer made locally by a local Amish brewery called Rumspringa. Samuel lifted a small glass to his lips of the amber liquid and took a sip.

"I thought the Amish were tea-totallers," Rachel chided him.

He grinned at her and lifted his glass in a toast. "German heritage."

The day was slowly ending, and night was settling upon the farm. The food and cake had all been consumed and now the only tradition left to take care of was tossing the wedding bouquet. After that, it would just be her and Samuel. Rachel was becoming increasingly nervous. It was her wedding night! She had no clue where they were going to spend it, but upmost in her mind was the fact that she had never been with another man besides her deceased husband, Barry, and she was feeling overcome with shyness.

Karen and Emma sought her out. "Mom, here! Time to toss the bouquet!" She shoved it into Rachel's hands. "Try to aim for me!" she added.

"Single women to the front!" shouted Karen to the milling crowd while Rachel mounted the stairs to the loft area. She stopped on the first landing which was about ten feet above their heads and turned her back, ready to toss the bouquet.

"One, two…three!" Karen called out.

Rachel made to toss but stopped, faking everyone out.

Groans of disappointment all around.

"This time for sure!" she giggled, raising her arms again. "One, two-"

Rachel tossed the bouquet over her head and turned around to see who the lucky girl was.

Emma stood there grasping the bouquet, looking both shocked and pleasantly surprised.

"You're next!!" Karen congratulated her.

Rachel didn't miss the look Emma shot at Josef Eicher under her lashes, her face blushing crimson.

"Hey, what about the garter?" Herb called out.

Rachel shook her head. "Sorry, no garter." She didn't want to put Samuel on the spot and embarrass him like that. Tossing a bouquet was one thing but removing the garter seemed a bit too raunchy a tradition to observe.

Rachel watched Josef make his way over to Emma to offer her congratulations on catching the bouquet. Emma stared back up at him and nodded, the look in her eyes unmistakable. She was completely infatuated, and Josef was blind to it.

He stepped away and picked up the microphone again and made a last announcement. "Our bride and groom will now share their first dance as a married couple together."

Samuel led Rachel out onto the cleared dance floor and took her into his arms. "I've been practicing a little," he reassured her.

The Way You Look Tonight filled the room, and the lights were lowered so that they were all bathed in only candlelight.

"You look absolutely breathtaking," Samuel whispered into her ear, sending chills down her spine.

Rachel looked up into his face which had become so familiar and dear to her, her heart swelling with emotion. "I love you," she whispered.

Samuel pressed her closer to himself and bent down to place a tender kiss upon her lips, "and I love you," he whispered. "No more lonely nights aching for you."

Rachel nodded, her nerves amplifying four-fold. They finished their dance to the applause of all the guests. Janet approached them, a brilliant smile upon her face.

"Okay you two, whenever you're ready I have a car waiting to take you to a local B&B for the next couple of nights until you leave for Leavenworth, Washington."

"You booked a Bed & Breakfast Inn for us?" Rachel exclaimed in relief. She hadn't been too keen on having her wedding night in the Inn where Emma and Karen shared a room above her bedroom.

Janet nodded. "You're staying at the King's Cottage Inn nearby," she told them. "I let them know it would be a late check-in."

"I thought Leavenworth was a high security prison in Kansas," Samuel joked.

"This is in Washington State," Rachel smiled, jumping up and down in excitement. "I've always wanted to go there at Christmas time!" She turned to Samuel. "It's a German village in the Cascade Mountains that looks like it is 200 years old."

"I should feel right at home, then!" Samuel grinned, pleased with Janet's arrangements. "How long will it take by train to get there?"

"Oh, it would take several days," Janet replied. "I booked you a nonstop flight which shouldn't take more than six hours."

Samuel froze. "We're flying?"

Janet nodded.

"On an airplane?"

Rachel grasped his hand, watching him turn pale. "Are you okay?"

Samuel gulped. "I've never been on an airplane."

"Well then this will be a new experience for you!" Janet patted his hand and walked away, leaving him to Rachel.

"Look, I don't much like flying either," Rachel confided in him. "I usually have to get a prescription from the doctor to keep me calm."

Samuel's face went from nervous to alarmed. "It's that bad?" he asked.

"Well, only if there's bad turbulence," Rachel replied lamely, realizing too late that she was just digging her hole deeper.

"*Was ist turbulenz?* He wanted to know, lapsing into his Pennsylvania Dutch out of sheer fear.

"It's air pockets that make the plane bounce a little,"

"*BOUNCE?*" Samuel shook his head. "I would prefer to take the train."

"Honestly, it's fine!" Rachel tried to reassure him.

"How can it be fine if you need to take drugs to calm down?" he wanted to know.

"Look, I have hardly ever flown, but when I have it's always been fine, I just get nervous is all."

Samuel stared back at her, unconvinced.

"Look, just sleep on it tonight," she suggested.

Hearing those words, he pulled her close and nuzzled her neck. "I don't think either of us will be getting much sleep tonight *meine Geliebte*[38]."

His words both thrilled and terrified her.

The barn was dark, and everything had fallen quiet. The last of their family and friends had departed to their rooms or accommodations and were settling down for the night.

Rachel was keenly aware of Samuel walking behind her as he followed her into the Inn to change their clothes and retrieve their suitcases; their driver patiently waiting in the driveway with the motor running. He followed her into the bedroom and closed the door behind him.

---

[38] My beloved

"I'm going to need your help getting this off," Rachel gestured to her back with all the tiny buttons. Her voice was at least half an octave higher. She cleared her throat nervously.

Samuel nodded, giving no indication that he noticed her escalating anxiety. "Turn around," he said quietly.

Rachel turned and waited as his fingers fumbled with the tiny buttons. He struggled for a few moments, muttering with frustration until he finally got the hang of it. Tortuously slow, he continued to unbutton the dress, his warm breath upon her neck. His warm lips blazed a scorching trail down her back as the dress unfastened. Rachel was becoming woozy, a warmth spreading down from her neck to her feet. She swayed a bit then righted herself. The dress dropped onto the floor, and she carefully stepped out of it and handed it to him to hang up.

Samuel took the dress, but his eyes were fixated upon her. He tossed it onto the bed and stepped forward, reaching for her.

"Not yet, Samuel. The driver is waiting for us!"

"Let him wait." His arms encircled her, his lips fastening upon hers.

She straight-armed him back. "*Emma and Karen are upstairs!!!*" she hissed.

Samuel stopped instantly, her words effectively throwing cold water over him. He nodded, "*Jah.*"

Rachel grabbed a pair of flannel lined jeans, a thermal, long-sleeved shirt and sweater and her Uggs and swiftly changed, casting furtive glances at Samuel who removed his nice black suit and white shirt in exchange for warmer, more casual clothing.

He grabbed their already packed suitcases. "Let's go," he said.

Together they walked out into the frigid air and into the warmth of the waiting car. It was a short, twenty-minute ride before they pulled up before the brightly lit, two-story, Spanish revival building that was built in 1915 and converted from a home into the King's Cottage Inn in 1990.

"*Danki*," Samuel thanked the driver as he retrieved their luggage.

Rachel followed him inside where the Inn Keeper greeted them.

"Mr. and Mrs. Miller, welcome!" she smiled. "The room is ready for you, yours is number 8 upstairs." She handed them the room key. "Enjoy your stay with us, if there's anything you need, just use the in-room phone."

"*Danki*," Samuel nodded.

They ascended the stairs and Rachel had the fleeting sensation that she was climbing to a hangman's noose. *Knock it off!* She reprimanded herself. She was trembling all over and it wasn't from the cold air.

They entered the room and stopped to admire its simple beauty. The walls and ceiling were white except for over the windows where a beautiful wisteria tree had been hand painted on the ceiling. The king-sized bed was covered with a simple, white chenille bedspread with pink rose petals scattered on top. On the wooden side table stood a silver bucket with a bottle of champagne chilling in it, and a little silver tray with chocolate truffles. A crystal vase filled with pink; long-stemmed roses stood on one of the nightstands. Soft music played in the background from a blue-tooth speaker and candlelight illuminated the room. Janet had thought of everything!

Samuel set the suitcases down and took Rachel in his arms. "At long last," he murmured, cradling her face and kissing her tenderly.

Rachel couldn't help but melt, her nerves and fears dissolving away as his lips trailed from her earlobe and down her neck and to the sensitive spot between her neck and shoulder, delicious shivers running down her spine.

Mustering her courage, she wrapped her arms around his neck and gazed into his blue eyes. "At long last," she agreed. He lifted her in his arms and carried her to the bed.

Chapter Twenty-Four

"A Small, Unwanted Visitor"

Rachel cracked open an eye and looked at the clock on the nightstand. It was 9:30 am. They had almost slept past the time for the all-inclusive breakfast in the dining room. She could smell coffee and the scent of bacon and cinnamon rolls wafting up the stairs and into their room. Her stomach grumbled but she was effectively trapped in the circle of Samuel's arms, warm and safe, and feeling thoroughly loved and adored. True to his word, they had gotten very little sleep until way past midnight. She stifled a self-conscious giggle, not wanting to wake him up.

Samuel stirred and tightened his grip about her, caressing her arm and nuzzling her neck.

"We're missing breakfast," she informed him. "Aren't you hungry?" She twisted around in his arms to face him.

"Yes," he growled, pulling her closer.

"I meant for food," she giggled.

His gentle hands reached up under her arms, grazing the side of her breast. He stopped.

"What's this?" he asked.

"What's what?" Rachel asked.

He sat up on one elbow, all playfulness gone. He touched the spot under her arm near her breast, his face concerned. "This. It feels like a bump."

Rachel raised her arm and strained her neck to see where he was poking her. "I can't see it."

"Here," Samuel took her hand and put it where he felt the bump. "Can you feel that?"

"Sort of," Rachel said, not sure she could really feel anything. She probed around some more and then found it. "That's funny, I never noticed this before," she admitted.

"*Ach,* so, you don't know how long it's been there?" Samuel asked, his brows furrowing. He pressed on it again. "Does this hurt?"

Rachel shook her head. "Nope, maybe it's just a cyst or something." She sat up. "Can we get breakfast now before they put everything away and deal with this later? I'm starving."

Samuel nodded; his face still creased with concern. They dressed hurriedly and went down to the dining room.

"Good morning did you sleep well?" Asked the hostess as a matter of courtesy.

Rachel almost choked but nodded instead. "Yup," she replied, although it was a bald-faced lie. She'd hardly slept a wink all night. She just hoped her face wasn't flaming red with embarrassment. They were shown to a small round table for two.

"Please help yourself, it's buffet style, I'll be by to get your beverage order. We have juices, Mimosas, regular coffee or specialty coffee drinks available."

Rachel loaded her plate with one of the nut-covered sticky buns, scrambled eggs and fresh berries. Samuel's plate had a ham steak, eggs, sausage and a cinnamon roll slathered with a thick, cream cheese frosting. They took their seats, clasped hands, and bowed their heads.

"*Danki, Der Herr…for all thy blessings,*" Samuel murmured, his double-meaning clear.

"Please also bless this *food,*" Rachel added with a grin, just to make sure all their bases were covered.

Their hostess reappeared. "What may I get you?"

"Coffee with cream, *bitte*" Samuel replied.

"And you, Mrs. Miller?"

Rachel paused then remembered that she was now Mrs. Miller, not Winston. It sounded weird. "May I have a coffee mocha, extra hot with no whip?" she requested. It was her favorite beverage from her local Starbucks.

The hostess nodded. "Of course, I'll be back in a few minutes."

They ate in silence for a few moments.

"What would you like to do today?" Rachel asked Samuel.

"Today is Monday, *jah?*"

"Yes, why?"

"I want to go to a local clinic and have that bump checked out," he replied, deadly serious.

Rachel set her fork down. "I'm sure it's nothing! Can't it wait until after our trip?"

Samuel shook his head. "I would not be able to relax and enjoy myself worrying about it the entire time," he replied.

The hostess returned with their coffee order.

"Is there a local Urgent Care near here?" he asked, ignoring Rachel's protesting expression.

"Why yes, there's one just a few miles from here," she replied looking concerned. "I can get you the information if you can wait a few minutes."

"*Danki,*" Samuel replied. He picked at his food; a sure sign that he was worried.

"Please eat, Samuel," Rachel urged him, taking a bite out of her Sticky Bun. "*Mmmmmm* it's really good!"

He acquiesced and took a token bite of his then sat back and looked for the hostess. "What is taking so long?" he muttered aloud.

"I'm not leaving until I finish my breakfast," Rachel informed him stubbornly. "Honestly, you're worse than a woman…"

Samuel leaned forward and grasped her hand, his blue eyes stern. "My oldest sister died of breast cancer in her forties," he told her in a low voice. "I'm not taking any chances with you, *verstehen sie mich*[39]?"

---

[39] Do you understand me?

Rachel stared back at him in shock and nodded obediently. "Yes, but why haven't you ever spoken of her before?" The look of pain in his eyes was her answer.

"What was her name?" Rachel asked.

"Hannah," Samuel replied. "She ignored the lump for months until it became too painful and by the time she was diagnosed she had stage 4 cancer that had spread everywhere. She passed in agony a month after she was finally diagnosed."

Rachel dropped her fork, her appetite gone; replaced by fear. "Okay, we'll go as soon as she returns with the address."

The hostess returned and handed Samuel a slip of paper. "I took the liberty of ordering you an Uber, they should be out front in a few minutes."

"*Danki!*" Samuel replied, pulling Rachel's chair out so she could stand.

"I'll just get our coats and my purse, and be right down," she said, running upstairs to their room. She grabbed their things and ran back down to meet him out front. The Uber arrived and they got into the backseat.

They said nothing to each other on the ride over. They just held hands and stared out the window, not knowing what to think and anticipating the worst.

They reached the clinic and clambered out. Snow flurries had begun, and their feet crunched on the thin coating of ice on the pavement. They entered the clinic to find it relatively empty.

"Please sign in here," the receptionist pushed a clipboard to her. "May I have your insurance card and identification please?"

"I'm self-employed," Rachel replied, pushing her driver's license forward. "I have Cigna," She pushed the card forward.

"Please have a seat it will be a few minutes." She gave her another clipboard. "Please fill this out and bring it back up when it's completed."

Rachel took the clipboard to a chair and plopped down morosely next to Samuel. "Not the way I wanted to spend my honeymoon," she muttered, filling out the intake form. She answered all the questions and brought it back up to the receptionist.

"It'll just be a few minutes," was the response.

Rachel sat back down next to Samuel. They clasped hands and waited...and waited...and waited.

"We should have finished our breakfast," Rachel muttered, jiggling her legs with impatience. She looked around the empty room, getting more agitated by the moment. "There's no one here! What on earth is taking so long?"

The receptionist overheard her. "The physician just arrived; I'll take you to your room."

Rachel stood and looked down at Samuel. "Do you want to come in with me?" she asked.

He looked torn in two. "I want to be by your side but I'm not sure how I will handle watching another man touch you," he replied.

"There's always a female nurse in there as well," Rachel replied, "if that makes any difference?"

Samuel shook his head. "I'll wait here, too many people in such a small exam room."

Rachel bent down and looked him in the eyes. "It's going to be okay," she said confidently and went through the exam doors.

The nurse led her into a small room. "You can put your things there, please take a seat." She read over Rachel's questionnaire. "You say you discovered a lump under your left breast near your armpit?"

"A bump, yes...well my husband did."

The nurse gave her a smile. "It's usually the husband who finds them first." She checked the chart. "When did he find it?"

"This morning," Rachel replied. "We are newlyweds and just started our honeymoon."

"Congratulations and I'm sorry that this has ruined it for you." The nurse took out the blood pressure cuff and oxygen reader and pinned it over her index finger. "Hold out your arm and uncross your legs so I get an accurate read," she instructed. She pumped on the blood pressure cuff until Rachel thought her arm would burst. "One-forty over one hundred, a little high." She said then checked Rachel's pulse. "One hundred beats per minute, a bit fast."

"Well, I'm really stressed out over this whole thing!" Rachel replied. "I just got married yesterday and we're supposed to leave for Leavenworth the day after tom…"

"The prison?" The nurse blinked at her, thinking she was serious. "No wonder you stressed!"

Rachel resisted the impulse to face palm and roll her eyes. "No, Leavenworth in Washington State…Christmas town!"

"Oh," replied the nurse, shaking her head. "You had me going there for a minute." She put away the blood pressure cuff and handed Rachel a paper gown. "Remove everything from the waist up and put this on, open in the front. The doctor will be in in a few…"

"Minutes or hours?" Rachel wanted to clarify. "Because we've already sat in that empty waiting room for over an hour."

"I'm so sorry for your wait. It will just be a few minutes," she replied and closed the door.

Rachel removed her sweater, shirt and bra and placed them on her chair, donning the scratchy paper gown. She crawled up on the examining table and swung her legs back and forth because they didn't quite reach the step and looked around. "Hmmm, no magazines to look at anymore," she observed. "Probably because of smart phones."

A knock came upon the door and the doctor entered followed by the nurse. "Mrs. Miller? I'm doctor Hastings." He said, looking over her questionnaire. "You found a lump under your left breast?"

"My husband did," Rachel explained again, starting to feel sheepish.

The doctor nodded, "that's how they usually are discovered," he replied, "and 75% of them usually involve the left breast."

"That's weird, why is that?" Rached wanted to know.

The doctor shrugged. "No clue. Now, could you lay back for me and lift your left arm over your head?"

Rachel laid back and was thankful for the fact that she had shaved her underarms in anticipation of her wedding two days earlier.

The doctor thoroughly kneaded her breast from the top to bottom and from the center to the outside and then focused on the lump at the base of her left breast. "Does this hurt?"

"Nope, that's a good sign, right?" Rachel replied. The doctor didn't answer but instead turned to the nurse. "Has the ultrasound technician arrived yet?"

"I'll go check," she said, waiting for him.

"Mrs. Miller, you're in luck, we have an excellent ultrasound technician on the premises today. I'd like to have her do a thorough examination on you."

"Is it really necessary?" Rachel asked, the escalating medical bills flashing through her mind's eye.

"Yes, it is." Doctor Hastings replied. "The nurse will come to get you in a few minutes; make sure to bring all your belongings with you." They left the room.

Rachel's empty stomach grumbled again. *Wish I'd eaten breakfast!*

A few minutes later she was escorted back to the dark ultrasound room.

"Mrs. Miller?"

"Yes."

"Please state your full name and birth date."

"Rachel Elizabeth Wi...I mean Miller, April 18th, 1990."

"I'm Jenna," the technician introduced herself. "Please lay back on the table and lift your left arm over your head, please."

Rachel laid back and shivered as a cool, gel-like substance was squirted over the area in question. The technician took her time, going back and forth, clicking her mouse, measuring and pressing the probe into her armpit and breast. Rachel tried to relax and not let her imagination run wild. After a good half hour, the technician was satisfied. "Can you wait here while I show the doctor the results?"

Rachel nodded and closed her eyes, praying silently. *"Okay, Lord, I'm a bit freaked out and very upset at the timing of all this. Please bring peace to Samuel's heart no matter what the results are and to me too. Into thy hands I commend my body and my spirit."*

She waited another ten minutes until both the doctor and ultrasound technician reentered the room.

"Would you like your husband to be present, Mrs. Miller?"

Rachel's heart dropped. *This doesn't sound good.* She nodded her head. The doctor left and came back in moments with Samuel in tow. He had bitten his fingernails down to the quick.

"Mr. Miller, we've done a thorough scan on your wife and believe that a biopsy is in order. I've called Penn State Lancaster Medical Center. You're in luck, they've had a last-minute cancellation, so I was able to get you an appointment for 9:00 am tomorrow to get a biopsy."

Samuel looked in alarm at Rachel, his eyes wide. "Is it that serious?" he asked, the fear in his voice palpable.

"No, it's not urgent but we know it's your honeymoon and we wanted to get this done before you left so you can still enjoy your trip while we await the results," explained the doctor. "You're not traveling outside the country, right?"

"Leavenworth," Samuel muttered.

"The prison in Kansas?" The doctor exclaimed.

The joke was getting old.

"It's in Washington State." Samuel explained.

"Oh," he handed Samuel and Rachel a raft of papers. "Your preparation instructions are on top. Please report to the hospital at least a half hour before your appointment time. You can get dressed now and go home." He and the nurse left, leaving just the two of them.

Rachel clutched the thin paper gown about her that was sodden with gel, suddenly bashful.

"Do you want me to turn around?" Samuel asked her gently.

Rachel nodded, using the dry parts of the gown to wipe off the remaining gel from her underarm and breast area. She put back on all her clothes and snaked her arms about Samuel's waist, resting her head upon his chest.

"Are you okay?" he asked gently.

Rachel nodded; she could feel his entire body trembling with pent up fear.

"Just hold me," she whispered.

Chapter Twenty-Five

"Testing"

They returned to the hotel, arriving shortly after noon, hungry, exhausted and apprehensive. Most of the other guests had left for the day, gone on various outings. The host greeted them at the reception desk.

"I can reheat your breakfast if you haven't eaten yet," she offered, her face genuinely concerned. "I hope everything went okay?"

"That would be wonderful," Rachel said, giving her a grateful smile. "So considerate of you."

"*Jah, danki.*" Samuel nodded, avoiding the question.

"I'll just reheat it and bring it into the dining room for you if you want to take a seat."

Rachel and Samuel went into the dining room. The fireplace was ablaze and crackling, filling the room with warmth and cheer. They took their seats and just stared at one another for a long moment.

Rachel took Samuel's hand. It was still trembling. For some odd reason, she felt strangely calm. "Are you okay?"

Samuel shook his head. "*Nee,* it reminds me too much of what happened with Hannah." He hid his face in his hands, his voice agonized. "I've only been your husband for one day and now I'm terrified of losing you." He looked up at her, his eyes brimming with tears.

Rachel picked up her chair and sat it next to him. She cast her arms about his shoulders. "Look at me," she commanded. Samuel struggled to do so. "*Samuel Miller, look at me.*"

His eyes met hers.

"I want you to listen carefully, okay?"

He nodded.

"Breast cancer is not the death sentence it used to be," Rachel began. "If caught early enough I can go on to lead a very normal, healthy, long life with you."

"How do you know?"

"I did some research in the Uber on the way back," she replied. "The survival rate is much greater than it used to be and for much longer. So…don't panic until I give the order to panic!" She gave him a heroic smile.

At that moment the host returned with their plates. She set them down, pretending not to notice Samuel's blotchy face and tears. "Enjoy," she said, her voice gentle. She gave Rachel's shoulder a little squeeze and smiled at her before she left.

"Nice woman," Rachel commented. "Scoot over a little." She pushed her seat closer to his so they could both eat on the same side of the table. She took a big bite of her reheated sticky bun and rolled her eyes dramatically. "I've been craving this all morning!"

Samuel pushed his eggs around the plate. "I'm hungrig[40], but my stomach is in knots." He looked imploringly at her.

Rachel set down her fork and took his hands in hers. "Let's pray," she said, and not waiting for him, launched into her own prayer. "Dearest Lord, you said that in this world we would have tribulation but to be of good cheer because You have overcome the world. You know our situation and You alone know what the future holds for us. Whatever may come, we will trust in You and Your goodness and rest in Your peace that passes all understanding, amen."

"Amen," whispered Samuel. He leaned his forehead against hers and closed his eyes. A great shuddering sigh issued from his lungs. "I surrender," he whispered.

---

[40] hungry

They spent the remainder of the day in their room with the fireplace on, just cuddling and not speaking; drawing comfort from each other's closeness. When it came time for supper they went downstairs and sought out the Innkeeper. They found her at the front desk.

"Hi," Rachel smiled at her. "We were wondering if there's a restaurant within walking distance from here you would recommend?"

"Why, yes there is! Do you like Greek food?" she smiled.

Rachel nodded, "I do but he's never had it. Is it good?"

"I eat there at least once a month," she smiled. "It's Conestoga's restaurant."

Rachel input the name into her Google Maps and found it. "Thank you so much." She turned to Samuel, "It should only take us fifteen minutes to walk there at the most."

"*Danki,*" he said to the Innkeeper. He whispered in Rachel's ear. "Are you sure you feel up to walking?"

"I'm not on my deathbed yet! I think I'll be just fine!" she reassured him, not realizing she'd chosen the exact wrong words to use.

Both the Innkeeper and Samuel shot her horrified looks.

She grabbed his arm, "Let's go!" she insisted, dragging him out the door. They got out onto the street and began walking. The snow flurries had turned into a real snowfall. "Boy we got married in the nick of time!" Rachel commented. "It's starting to come down hard. I wonder if it's snowing in Leavenworth yet?" She kept up a running, one-sided, light-hearted dialogue the entire way until they reached the restaurant after crossing over a bridge. They entered, shaking the snow off their winter coats.

"Welcome!" smiled the host, "Party of two?"

Samuel nodded, looking around with a doubtful eye.

"Follow me, please." The host led them to a table for two and dropped the menus. "Your waiter will be by in just a few minutes."

They sat. Samuel looked over the menu, looking more confused by the moment. "I don't understand a word of this," he confessed.

"Because it's all Greek to you!" Rachel burst out laughing, unable to help herself.

Samuel cracked a smile, a very *small* smile. "You know what I like, you order for us."

Rachel rubbed her hands together in glee. Greek was one of her favorite foods. "Okay, you're in for it now!" She looked over the menu. "I think we should start with the Feta Cheese Bake, that's baked feta with honey and thyme served with a grilled pita."

"*Was ist* pita?"

"It's like a tortilla, only the Greek version."

Samuel rolled his eyes at her. "*Was ist* tortilla?"

"Oops, I forgot that you were culinarily challenged when it came to international cuisine," she grinned at him. "Pita is a delicious flat bread that you can dip into sauces or roll up with amazing meat and vegetables to eat with your hands."

"Okay," Samuel nodded.

"Then I think we should share the traditional Greek salad, it has tomatoes, cucumbers, feta cheese, olives, onions and stuffed grape leaves because the portions look enormous," she said, ogling a large salad that was carried past their table to another.

"Anything else?" Samuel asked, clearly enjoying her enthusiasm.

"Yes, we should definitely get the Gyro too."

"*Was ist* euro?"

"It's a blend of beef and lamb with Mediterranean seasonings, tzatziki sauce with cucumbers, tomato, red onion, and feta."

"Tazitski?" Samuel mispronounced.

"Tzatziki," Rachel corrected him. "It's yogurt mixed with cucumber, olive oil and Greek spices and absolutely amazing."

"Yogurt on meat?" Samuel shook his head in disgust.

"Trust me, you will love it." Rachel assured him.

The waitress arrived. "May I take your order please?"

Rachel smiled at her. "Yes, we would like to share the Feta Cheese Bake, Greek Salad and Gyro with fries please."

"Anything to drink?"

"Just club soda with lime for me. Samuel?"

"Sweet tea," he replied.

Samuel waited until the waitress left, then leaned forward. "Do you need to fast for this procedure tomorrow?" he asked, his worries hovering over him like a black cloud.

Rachel withdrew the preparation sheet from her purse and looked it over. "Nope, it just says not to put on deodorant and to wear loose fitting, comfortable clothes and a sports bra."

Samuel nodded and patted her hand. "I love you," he whispered.

"I love you too," Rachel replied.

The waitress returned with their drinks. "Your food will be out shortly," she smiled. "I assume you want the baked feta first and the salad and gyro later?"

Rachel nodded. "That would be great, thank you." She took Samuel's hand, "let's pray."

They bowed their heads and Samuel gave thanks.

Moments later, the baked feta arrived. Rachel spread a warm hunk onto a slice of pita and handed it to him. "You first!"

He put it into his mouth and an enormous smile spread over his face. He nodded at her, chewing.

"It's always a good sign when you nod like that," Rachel grinned. She popped some into her mouth. "*Mmmm* this is so good! I'm going to have to offer this at the Inn as part of the charcuterie course! I wonder if they'd share the recipe. I wonder if they'd deliver their pita bread?"

Samuel chuckled for the first time in over 24 hours. "Always thinking of the future and the Inn," he smiled. "Life almost seems normal at the moment."

Rachel leaned forward and took his hand. "Samuel, there is no such thing as normal in this fallen world. There will always be poverty, sin, sickness, and death but I don't plan to wallow in self-pity. We will get through this. I totally trust the Lord with my life. If I must undergo a bunch of tortuous medical procedures, then we'll just take it as they come. I'd much rather go through this than watch it happen to you like I did with Barry."

"I feel the same way," he replied quietly. "I was with Hannah in her last moments when I was helpless to do anything about her suffering."

"She wasn't married?"

Samuel shook his head no. "*Nee,* she never married so it was a mercy that she had no children to orphan."

They both fell silent, alone with their thoughts and finished their meal in relative quiet. They paid the bill and rose to leave. Samuel helped Rachel on with her winter coat. "I liked the Gyro very much, by the way."

Rachel smiled at him. "We have a lifetime of new experiences to look forward to, together, Samuel."

Samuel nodded and smiled but his eyes were sad. "That's what I'm praying for."

The following morning, they got up early, dressed, ate and were out front waiting for the Uber to take them to the Medical Center by 7:30 am.

They weren't scheduled to leave for the airport until later that day, but it was still cutting it close. They arrived by 8:00 am and Rachel was soon ushered into the room where the biopsy was to be performed. She undressed from the waist up and put on the standard hospital gown open in the front and waited. Soon a nurse entered the room.

"May I have your name and birthdate?" she requested, looking at Rachel's admittance papers.

"Rachel Elizabeth Miller, April 18th, 1990."

"Hello, Rachel, I'm Amy," smiled the nurse. "Did you apply the numbing cream this morning?"

Rachel nodded. "Yes, at 6:00 am and again at 7:00 am."

"Good, now if you lay back and turn onto your right side, I'm going to inject you with some local anesthetic before we perform the biopsy. It's going to sting a little bit."

Rachel turned onto her right side so her left breast was facing up. She shut her eyes.

"Ready?"

She nodded. There was a quick sting then nothing.

"We're going to wait about five minutes for the numbness to spread and then we'll begin." Amy checked her chart. "We're going to take about five biopsies."

"Five? I thought there was only one lump?"

"We have to check the surrounding tissue and lymph nodes." Amy explained.

"Oh…okay."

Amy checked her watch. "Ready, Rachel?"

Rachel nodded.

"Okay here is the first one, you're going to feel some pressure and hear a click."

Rachel waited then heard what sounded like a staple gun. She felt no pain.

"You're doing great!" Amy encouraged her. "Here's the next one." Another push and click. It was over within ten minutes. "Now lay still while I put some bandages over the wounds, we're almost done." Rachel waited, relieved that the first phase was over with. "Okay you can sit up and get dressed now. You did fantastic!" Amy patted her arm and gave her an encouraging smile.

Rachel reached for her clothes. "How long does it take to get the results back?"

"No more than a week," Amy replied. "We'll give you a call either way."

Rachel nodded, "Okay." That would give her and Samuel at least one week of blissful ignorance while they spent their honeymoon in Washington.

"I heard that you're a newlywed, congratulations!"

"Thank you," Rachel replied, buttoning up her flannel shirt.

"I'm so glad we could fit you in before you left on your honeymoon! Where are you going?"

Rachel hesitated for a moment. "Leavenworth," she replied, waiting for the typical shocked reaction about the state penitentiary.

"Oh, I love Leavenworth!" Amy gushed. "I was there three years ago in December, and it was just *magical!* Enjoy every moment and make sure to eat at Mozart's and order the schnitzel!"

"I sure will," Rachel smiled at her. She found her way to the exit and grabbed Samuel's arm, hauling him outside to the waiting Uber. "You and I have a date with schnitzel!" she informed him.

Chapter Twenty-Six

"Come Fly with Me"

Rachel leaned forward in her seat and looked at Samuel. "Are you okay?" she asked.

They were sitting in the Airbus, waiting on the tarmac for their turn to take off.

He turned to her. "Are you? We had no time to get a prescription to calm you down."

Rachel nodded. "For some reason, the fact that you're such a nervous wreck has brought out the calm and stoic Rachel in me." She squeezed his hand. "Just be glad we're not taking off out of John Wayne Airport in Orange County where I used to live."

"Why?" he wanted to know.

"Well, the City of Newport Beach put in a noise restriction, so the planes take off from a much shorter runway, at a very steep ascent and power down the engines right at the apex of their climb. It can be quite unnerving. First you take off like an F-18 fighter jet and then it seems like they turn off the engines. The first time they did that I practically mangled Barry's poor hand."

Samuel closed his eyes and gulped.

"Deep breaths," Rachel advised him.

The stewardess entered the aisle, a deflated life vest around her neck and sample seatbelt in her hand.

Samuel stiffened in fear.

"It's okay, this is just standard safety protocol, they have to do it on every flight."

The stewardess went through all the safety features. Samuel the only one paying her rapt attention, mimicking her every move to make sure he had it all memorized. Everyone else on the plane either had their eyes closed or were setting up their phones for the in-flight movie.

"Why don't they pay attention?" he hissed under his breath.

"Familiarity breeds contempt," Rachel replied. She leaned over and whispered in his ear. "Besides, in the unlikely event of a water landing, I seriously doubt we'd survive the landing to actually get into the life rafts." She couldn't believe how calm she was feeling but Samuel's jitters seemed to have that effect upon her.

"Water landing?" He went pale.

"No water from here to Washington State unless we fly over the great lakes,"

"You're not helping," he said.

The plane began to taxi then took a sharp turn onto the runway. The engines powered up.

Rachel grasped Samuel's hand, "hold on to your pantyhose!"

The plane lurched forward and swiftly picked up speed, careening down the runway.

Samuel's hand was a vise.

"Ouch, let up a bit! Hey, look out the window, we're climbing!"

Samuel turned his head to peek out the window and his eyes grew as big as saucers as they climbed above the clouds, the ground falling away beneath them. He jerked at the sound of clunking coming from under their feet. "*Was war das?*" He was starting to panic.

"Relax, it was just the landing gear folding up inside the plane."

He nodded and took another look outside. "Everything looks so tiny," he marveled, his death grip relaxed a little bit.

Rachel extricated her hand and massaged it. "Remind me never to arm wrestle you," she joked, wincing.

"*Ach,* did I hurt you?"

"I'm fine, no permanent damage, but if there's any turbulence, I'm getting you a stick to bite on."

The movie reference was completely lost on him.

"I'm so sorry," Samuel said, catching her hand and kissing it tenderly.

Rachel smiled at him. "All better now."

"You may now recline your seats and put down your tray tables. The stewards will be by with drinks and food available for purchase."

"They serve food and drink?"

Rachel nodded. "Yes, it's subpar from what it used to be and now you have to pay for it." She passed him the menu. "See anything you want?"

The plane rumbled and pitched a little bit.

"Turbulence?" Samuel asked.

Rachel nodded.

"I think I want something to calm my nerves," he replied, sitting back and gripping the armrests.

The stewardess arrived. "What can I get you?" she smiled.

"Ginger ale for me and a high alcohol content IPA for him, please."

The Stewardess glanced at Samuel who had gone a little pale. She poured the beer into a plastic cup and handed Rachel the can. "Make sure he drinks all of it, Captain says it's going to get bumpy over Montana."

Rachel handed Samuel the cup who downed it in one long draught. She refilled his cup and watched as he swigged the rest down as if it were medicinal.

"Careful, you're drinking on an empty stomach," she warned, sipping her ginger ale.

It wasn't long before his jaw was hanging slack, and he was snoring loud enough to wake the dead.

The plane bucked and Rachel tensed up. Without Samuel's fear to distract her, her own fears took over. She pushed the overhead button to summon the stewardess. The plane bucked again.

"Do you happen to have port?" She asked. Rachel normally couldn't stomach the taste of wine, but port was sweet and high in alcohol content. "I need something for my… OH!"

The plane dropped a bit, making her stomach rise into her mouth.

"I'll be right back," the stewardess nodded, recognizing terror when she saw it.

Rachel grabbed Samuel's limp hand and squeezed every time the plane shuddered or bucked. He was out like a light, snoring loudly. Occasionally, the passenger sitting in front of him would turn around and give him a filthy look.

The stewardess soon returned with three airplane sized bottles of port. "That will be $35."

Rachel handed over her credit card and as soon as the transaction went through, she twisted off the cap and sucked down the contents. A delicious feeling of warmth and wooziness enveloped her, calming her nerves. She drank half of the second bottle and laid back, closing her eyes.

Rachel woke up with a jerk, Samuel was shaking her arm. "We're landing," he told her.

She peered out the window and took in the deep emerald green of Washington State meadows and farmlands. It looked like a vast park from the air. Her head was throbbing. "Uhh! Too much port on an empty stomach!" she groaned.

Samuel grinned at her. "Well at least you slept through the worst of it. I woke up just in time to enjoy the turbulence over Montana."

"Please secure your tray tables. All seats should be on the upright position and your seatbelts fastened."

Samuel gripped her hand. "Is landing as frightening as taking off?"

Rachel shook her head. "Not to me, I always find it comforting to return to earth."

Soon the plane landed and taxied up to their gate. Everyone in the cabin stood and stretched and took their cell phones off airplane mode so they could let people know they had landed safely. Samuel reached overhead and brought down their suitcases, waiting for the cabin doors to open and the passengers to start moving.

Rachel's head was swimming, and she worried that a migraine was coming on. She needed her migraine medicine soon or to eat something.

Soon they were shuffling off the plane and out into the terminal.

"Samuel, can you wait a moment?" Rachel took a seat and rummaged through her purse for her migraine pills.

"Are you well? Do you have a headache coming on?"

"I'm not sure, I just want to be prepared. Can you get me some kind of cookie and a bottle of water so I'm not taking it on an empty stomach?"

He nodded and walked off to the first airport shop he saw that was selling books, snacks, beverages, and other items. He was back in minutes. "They wouldn't take cash," he said, shaking his head in disgust.

Rachel unwrapped the oatmeal cookie and wolfed it down with some water. The food made her feel better. "Okay, I'm good now. Let's find the driver and go to our B&B."

Rachel slung her down winter coat over her arm and began walking to the airport Uber/Taxi/Limousine pick up area with Samuel right behind her, rolling both suitcases. They walked for about ten minutes and found a well-dressed man holding a sign that read MR AND MRS SAMUEL MILLER.

Rachel walked right up to him and smiled. "That's us."

"Welcome to Washington, Mr. and Mrs. Miller." He smiled. "I'm Joe, your driver. You might want to put on your coats, it started snowing earlier today."

They did as he suggested.

"Just follow me," he said and led them out of the terminal doors.

"Whoa!" Rachel exclaimed as she was hit with a blast of artic air. She zipped up her coat. "Thanks for the warning!"

"I'm right over there, we're the green Land Rover."

"I was expecting a Limousine," Rachel said.

"Well, we thought a Land Rover would be better in this weather. The highway leading to Leavenworth can be icy and very steep. This is all wheel drive with superior traction. Safety first!"

Rachel exchanged a nervous smile with Samuel and climbed into the vehicle. It was luxurious inside with full grain leather seats that had heating elements in them and a fully stocked snack and beverage bar.

Joe got in and turned around. "Please help yourself to anything you want, it's all complimentary." He started the engine which roared to life and waited while Samuel and Rachel buckled their seatbelts. "It's about a three-hour drive so let me know if you need to use the facilities at any time."

They started off.

"I should have gone before we got into the car," Rachel whispered to Samuel.

"I had two beers," he replied. "It's going to be a short trip before the next stop!"

After several pitstops they finally arrived at their destination in Leavenworth, the Enzian Inn.

"Wow, that's gorgeous!" Rachel exclaimed. "It looks like a Swiss Alpine Lodge!"

Joe drove up to the front, got out and removed their suitcases. "Congratulations and have a wonderful time," he smiled.

Rachel dug in her purse for her wallet to tip him, but he waved her off. "I've been well taken care of by your friend, Janet," he assured her. He waved and got back into the car.

"Let's get inside before you catch cold," Samuel said, rolling their suitcases into the lobby.

They walked inside the two-story lobby and looked around.

"*I use antlers in all of my decorating…*" sung Rachel under her breath.

Samuel looked at her, perplexed. "No, we don't, there are no antlers at the Inn or barn."

"It's from a Disney movie," Rachel explained. "We'll watch Beauty and the Beast tonight, you'll love it!"

They approached the front desk.

The receptionist greeted them in German. "*Willkommen!*" She was wearing a traditional Swiss dirndl in sage green with a white lace blouse and matching apron. She checked her computer. "Mr. and Mrs. Miller?"

"How did you know?" asked Samuel, impressed.

"Your driver called ahead just a few minutes ago." She replied. "Your room is all ready, George here will take you to the Bridal Room."

A smartly dressed bellhop in authentic lederhosen grabbed their suitcases and led them to the elevator. "If you will follow me?"

They trailed after him, admiring the huge, two-story common room with the enormous stone fireplace and more taxidermized mule deer on the walls. He opened the door to reveal a tasteful room all in colors of cream and white and set their luggage down. He went to the windows and opened the gossamer white drapes. "Your room overlooks the pool courtyard, and the fireplace turns on with a switch." He walked to the bathroom. You have a jetted tub with separate shower and double vanity, and your room has been fully stocked with personal hygiene items."

"Your friend really does think of everything," Samuel whispered to Rachel, staring at the king-size poster bed with the white curtains hanging down. This time the snowy white coverlet had red rose petals all over it.

George continued. "Breakfast is served in the main dining room. There is a daily assortment of pastries freshly baked on site, golden pancakes, omelets made to order, fresh fruits and yogurt and a cereal bar."

"Do they have Honeynut Cheerios?" Rachel quipped.

George merely smiled at her. "Breakfast is served from 7:00 am – 9:30 am. Will there be anything else?"

"*Nee,*" Samuel said. "*Danki,* I'll take it from here." He pressed a ten-dollar bill into his hands.

"Thank you!" George grinned and left the room.

They were alone.

Samuel gathered Rachel into his arms and held her. "How are you feeling, *mein liebling?*"

Rachel snuggled into his arms. He felt warm and solid. "Tired, hungry…a little hung over."

Samuel tilted her chin up to meet his eyes. "Is there anything I can do for you?" he whispered, kissing her eyelids, her nose and finally her lips.

Rachel gazed longingly into his eyes. "I'm sure you'll think of something," she murmured.

Chapter Twenty-Seven

"Leavenworth – the Town not the Prison"

Rachel and Samuel awoke hours later. She got up and peered out the window and down to the lighted courtyard and pool which was vacant. The pool was covered with a heavy tarp and coated with snow. The temperature on her phone indicated it had fallen into the low teens, way too cold for a dip in the pool.

Samuel stirred and rolled over to stare lovingly at her. "What time is it?"

"Almost 7pm," Rachel replied. "Between the jet lag and our schedule these last few days, my body clock is all messed up."

"It looked fine to me," he joked.

She chucked a pillow at him. "I stink and I'm hungry. I need a shower and food!"

Samuel got out of bed, grabbed her hand and led her into the bathroom. "I'll shave while you get cleaned up." Then he swatted her behind playfully.

Rachel giggled, glad that he wasn't consumed with worry over her for the moment. She wanted to enjoy her honeymoon with him.

She went into the shower and turned it on to heat up, soon steam was filling the air. She dropped her robe and stepped in. She lathered her hair with the lavender shampoo that had been provided and then the rest of herself. She wrapped a towel around herself and stepped out. "Do you want me to leave the water on for you?" she asked as Samuel also dropped his robe onto the floor.

He nodded, "*Jah,* I'll just be a few minutes."

Samuel Miller, you are a fine specimen of a man! She thought to herself with a smile.

She blew dry her hair then got dressed in her warmest clothing, layering for the frigid weather and waited for him. The sight of the rose petals all over the floor brought a blush to her cheeks. She picked them up and placed them in a decorative wooden bowl on the nightstand.

Samuel stepped into the room, toweling his hair dry.

"Better dress warm," Rachel told him. "It's *EIGHTEEN* degrees outside and snowing!"

Samuel bundled up and together they walked downstairs to the front desk.

"Hi! Which way to Mozart's restaurant from here please?" Rachel asked.

"Just turn right out the door and it will be on your right," smiled the receptionist.

"Could you make reservations for us?"

"Of course, but it's Christmas and last minute so there may not be anything available. What name shall I request it under?"

"Miller, Samuel and Rachel Miller." Samuel replied.

"Oh! I believe we've already made that reservation for you days ago! Your friend, Janet, requested it before your arrival. Your reservation is for 8:00 pm, you should have just enough time to make it."

"Okay great!"

They headed out the door and into a winter wonderland. The entire Bavarian town was lit up with Christmas lights and outdoor speakers were playing sacred Christmas music. Couples walked arm in arm along the streets despite the freezing temperature, peering into closed shop windows at the fabulous displays.

They walked/ran, their breath coming out in billowing clouds from their mouths like they were steam engines. They arrived just in time to make their reservation.

"Samuel and Rachel Miller for 8pm" Samuel told the hostess, removing his throat scarf.

The hostess checked her computer. "Ah yes, the newly-weds…we've been expecting you! Right this way."

She led them into the cozy dining room and to a small table. On it was a welcome card and a small vase of red roses.

Rachel removed her bulky winter coat and got out her cell phone.

"What are you doing?" Samuel asked curiously.

"I'm thanking Janet for all she has done for us and letting her know that we arrived safely." Rachel said, texting her friend.

"Are you going to tell her about…you know?"

Rachel shook her head. "No, I'm not telling anyone until we get the results and know what's what. I plan to enjoy every moment of this honeymoon with you and not think about you know what until I have to…so *FIDDLE DEE DEE!*"

"I'm still waiting for an explanation on this fiddle faddle," Samuel intentionally mispronounced it with a grin.

Rachel set her phone down and favored him with a sweet smile. "*Fiddle faddle*, my darling husband, is salty fat laden popcorn. Fiddle dee dee was a saying made famous by one Scarlet O'Hara from Gone with the Wind; another movie I must introduce you to."

Their waiter approached the table. "Welcome Mr. & Mrs. Miller to Mozart's Steakhouse. Is this your first-time dining with us?"

"First time in Leavenworth," Samuel replied, looking over the menu with relief. "You have many familiar foods!"

"Oh really? Where are you from?" replied the waiter.

"Lancaster County, Pennsylvania," Samuel replied.

"How wonderful! I've always wanted to visit there and see the Amish."

"You're looking at one now," Rachel grinned, pointing to Samuel.

"Really?" The waiter gave Samuel a dubious once over then digressed. "May I get you anything to drink while you look at the menu?"

"Club soda with lime," Rached replied.

"Sweet tea," said Samuel.

"I'm afraid we only have unsweetened herbal tea, sir," apologized the waiter. "But I can bring you some artificial sweeteners if you like."

"Plain sugar will be *gut*," Samuel replied.

"Right away, sir!"

"What looks good to you?" Rachel asked, scanning the menu.

"I would like Mozart's Platter for two," Samuel replied. "What do you think?"

Rachel read aloud, "*Roasted pork hock, Käsekrainer & Bratwurst, hand-breaded pork schnitzel, buttered fingerling potatoes, roasted red cabbage wedge, signature Andreas Keller mustard & Austrian horseradish.* Everything sounds good to me except for the horseradish. It's going to have to be on the side. I was traumatized as a child by horseradish."

"How could you have been traumatized?" Samuel was curious.

"Well, I was in fourth grade in Hebrew School, and they were passing around the Passover Plate."

"*Was ist* Passover plate?"

"You know, from the book of Exodus, when the angel of death passed over all those who put lamb's blood on their lintels."

Samuel nodded. "*Ach*, yes. I remember. Go on."

The waiter returned with their drinks and a canister of granulated sugar. "Are we ready to order yet?" He watched in silent horror as Samuel poured a ton of sugar into his glass of tea.

"Yes, we'll have the Mozart Platter for two, *bitte.*" Samuel handed him back the menus. "Horseradish on the side."

"Excellent choice!" The waiter smiled and left.

Rachel leaned forward and whispered. "Do you think that they ever tell their patrons that their choice stinks?" she joked.

Samuel stared at her, the humor going over his head. He hadn't dined in fine restaurants before now and was unfamiliar with their etiquette. "Back to your story," he encouraged.

"Right, well the Passover plate contains different elements to remind the Jewish people of the events on Passover. The shank bone represents the Passover lamb, *charoset* resembles the mortar and brick made by the Jews when they were slaves in Egypt under Pharaoh and is made with apples, walnuts, and wine; *Karpas* is parsley and is a symbol of spring and new beginnings. It is dipped in salt water before eating to remember the tears the Jews shed when they were enslaved. *Beitzah* is a hard-boiled egg (I forget what it symbolized) and then of course there is the dreaded *maror. Maror* is the bitter herb, which reminds the Jews of the bitterness of the slavery their forefathers endured in Egypt and is represented on the Seder plate with horseradish."

"Continue, this is interesting," Samuel encouraged her. "What happened when they passed around this plate to you?"

"Well, my mom had been feeding me turnips at the time and the raw horseradish looked like a turnip to me."

Samuel could see where this was going. "Oh, no – tell me you didn't?"

Rachel nodded. "Oh yes, I did. The teacher told us to take just a tiny nibble on it and I remember thinking *hah! I eat this every night at dinner, watch this!*" I took a huge bite of raw horseradish, screamed, spit it out onto the floor and ran out of the classroom. I found the nearest water fountain and stood there crying, rinsing my mouth out for over half an hour."

Samuel's shoulders began to shake with laughter.

"It's not funny!" Rachel protested. "I couldn't stand the smell of it ever since. That and Tabasco sauce!"

"What happened with the sauce?"

"It was punishment for mouthing off to my mother," Rachel explained. "She would put it on my tongue when I got sassy."

Samuel leaned forward, a stern expression on his face. "I would have taken the belt to your *hintern* and there would have been no further need of Tabasco sauce."

Rachel opened her mouth to make a snarky comment, but their food arrived, thankfully distracting him.

Samuel leaned back in his chair and belched loudly, drawing disapproving looks from those sitting nearest. "That was *gut!*" He patted his stomach.

"I'm so full!" Rachel moaned. "I ate way too much!"
The waiter appeared with a huge smile. "Did we save room for dessert?"

"No!" Rachel replied.

"*Jah!*" Samuel countered.

They exchanged looks. "I'm on vacation," he quoted her.

"Well, we have Apple Strudel, Sacher torte, cream puffs and fresh berries."

Samuel's brows furrowed, "what is Sacher torte?"

"It's a famous Austrian dessert. It's two layers of spongy chocolate cake, with a layer of cherries inside, covered entirely in a dark chocolate glaze.

"I'll have that and some coffee *bitte.*"

The waiter turned to Rachel. "And for you?"

"I'll just have a bite of his," she smiled. She glanced at Samuel who was smiling at her. "Aren't you worried about chocolate and caffeine keeping you awake all night?"

The look he gave her answered her question. Heat began spreading from her feet up to her head. "*Oh.*"

They finished their meal and walked hand in hand down the street towards their Inn. All the buildings and Christmas lights were still on, including those on the Christmas tree in the town square. It had stopped snowing but was bitterly cold.

"It's so beautiful here," Rachel whispered, admiring the tree. "I never want this to end."

Samuel took her into his arms and held her. "It will forever be a cherished memory," he reassured her.

The next morning, they awoke at a decent hour, wrapped in each other's arms. Although Rachel was awake, she kept her eyes closed as Samuel tried to kiss her awake, enjoying his attentions. "Wake up, I'm hungry," he whispered.

"You're *always* hungry!" Rachel grinned at him.

"Get up now and get dressed, we can shower after breakfast, *jah?*"

"*Jah,*" Rachel agreed, clambering out of bed. Her cell phone rang. "Now who could that be?" She picked it up and the Caller ID said HEALTHCARE. Her heart began to pound. "Hello?"

"Is this Rachel Miller?" asked the voice.

"Yes," she put the phone on speaker and sat next to Samuel on the bed.

"This is Dr. Hastings's nurse, Mrs. Cole. We just got the results of your biopsy in."

"That was fast," Rachel muttered, starting to tremble.

"Your biopsies were positive for cancer, I'm so sorry."

Rachel sat frozen in shock. "What?" She glanced at Samuel who looked like he'd just been punched in the gut. "How…how bad is it?"

"It's stage 2, HR positive."

"In plain English please. What is stage 2?"

"Stage 1 means the tumor hasn't spread anywhere. Stage 2 means it has spread to some lymph nodes. HR positive means it is fed by your hormones."

"I'm on my honeymoon," Rachel bleated. "Do I have to rush home for this?"

"No, there's no need. We won't be able to schedule you for your surgical or oncology appointments until after the Christmas holidays."

"*WHAT?!*" Samuel bellowed, frightening Rachel. He grabbed the phone and yelled into it. "Why is there such a long delay when she has cancer?" His hand was shaking.

"Is this Mr. Miller?"

"*Jah,*"

"Please understand Mr. Miller, she is still in the early stage. If there was any immediate threat, we would get her in at once."

Samuel handed the phone back to Rachel, still angry and pacing the floor.

"Our first available appointment is December 28th at 10:00 am. Can you make that?"

"Yes," Rachel nodded, jotting it down on a piece of paper.

"Great, I will both text and email you the information before then. Try to relax and enjoy yourself, you're in no immediate danger."

Rachel stared at Samuel who looked devastated. "Are you okay?"

His jaw dropped. "You were just diagnosed with cancer and you're asking me if I'm okay?"

Rachel nodded.

Samuel crossed the room and lifted her face to his, looking deeply into her eyes, trying to read her thoughts. "What do you want to do?"

Rachel wrapped her arms about him, "I want to enjoy my honeymoon with you. I want to go home and celebrate Christmas with everyone like nothing has happened."

"Are you afraid, *mein liebling?*"

Rachel nodded, "I honestly don't know what to expect next or what kind of ordeal I'm going to have to go through." She buried her face in his chest, letting the tears seep from her eyes. "It's so unfair to you…to us, especially after all we have already gone through."

Samuel held her tightly and murmured in her ear, "*Though He slay me, yet will I trust Him,*" he quoted. "No matter what happens, we will trust in *Der Herr's* goodness."

Chapter Twenty-Eight

"Homecoming"

"Look, Rachel!" Samuel pointed.

The lights of the Inn were glowing as if to welcome them home. Christmas lights had been strung all over the Inn and Event Barn and twinkling in the late afternoon twilight. There had been a snowfall the night before, blanketing the entire property so that it looked like a Currier and Ives lithograph. Emma, Karen, Josef, Aaron, Amos, and Abram all stood on the front porch waving excitedly to welcome them home. Karen was holding a struggling Buddy in her arms who clearly knew that Rachel was coming home.

"Do you still wish to keep your diagnosis a secret until after Christmas?" Samuel asked as the car pulled up in front.

"Yes, I don't want to dampen everyone's Christmas; it can wait."

The car stopped and everyone rushed forward to greet them. Karen set Buddy down and he ran to Rachel, wagging furiously and whining to be picked up. Rachel scooped him up and let him give her a tongue bath.

"*Willkommen* home!" Emma smiled, opening her arms wide to embrace Rachel.

"Did you have a good time? What was it like?" Karen asked. "Did you bring me back a snow globe from there?"

Rachel shifted Buddy to one arm and fished the snow globe out of her pocket, handing it to Karen.

"This looks like a prison!" Karen complained. "I thought you went to Washington?!"

They all burst out laughing.

"I couldn't resist," Rachel giggled, fishing another globe out of her pocket, this time from Leavenworth, Washington. She pushed it into Karen's hands and resumed loving on Buddy.

The boys helped Samuel with the luggage. "Looks like you came back with two extra suitcases!"

"Rachel insisted on buying you all Christmas presents from there." Samuel explained, lifting them out.

"Welcome home!" Josef greeted them, genuinely happy to see them. He grasped Samuel's hand then pulled him into a side hug. They clapped each other on the back, smiling.

Rachel followed Emma up the porch stairs and into the main room, setting Buddy on the floor. A cheerful fire was blazing on the hearth and the reclaimed wooden mantel had been festooned with fresh cedar boughs, popcorn and cranberry garland. The air was filled with the scent of cedar, cinnamon, orange peel and beef barley soup.

Samuel wheeled the suitcases into the master bedroom, feeling a bit strange that he was moving into it in front of everyone. He caught Karen looking at him out of the corner of his eye.

"Too weird," she said, even though she had been the first to say *I do* at the wedding ceremony on who was giving Rachel away. "Do I need to call you dad now?"

Samuel shook his head. "*Samuel will be just fine,*" he reassured her.

"You two get settled, I made Beef Barley Soup, popovers and roasted vegetables for supper," said Emma.

"What is the cinnamon and orange peel I'm smelling?" Rachel asked.

"I made a simmer pot of aromatics to welcome you," she grinned. "It also has juniper berries, star anise, and cloves, do you like it?"

Rachel nodded then yawned, "It smells like Christmas. Sorry, we had to get up at the crack of down to make our flight and I'm super jet lagged."

"Go lay down, take a nap! Supper can wait for a few hours," Emma urged her.

Rachel nodded and went into her bedroom which she would now share with Samuel. The sheets had all been changed to red plaid flannel with a complimentary duvet and pillowcases. He followed her in and closed the door behind them.

"Feels weird, huh?" Rachel asked him, suddenly shy.

"We'll all get used to it," he said, taking her into his arms. "How are you doing?"

"I'm tired, a nap sounds really good." She yawned again.

"Sit down," Samuel said.

Rachel sat on the edge of the bed, the yawns taking over.

Samuel went down on one knee and removed her heavy snow boots, then he pulled her up and pulled back the duvet, "you first."

Rachel smiled at him, "Samuel, I need to ask you the all-important question."

He cocked an eyebrow at her, wondering what it could be.

"What side of the bed do you sleep on?"

"What side do you sleep on?" He countered.

Rachel fell back onto the bed and spread out her arms, giggling. "The middle!"

She was irresistible. Samuel climbed in, forcing her to scoot over to the far side. He put his arms around her and kissed her on the nose. "I take this side."

Rachel snuggled into him, "Well, if you insist…" then she dropped off to sleep, snoring softly in his arms.

Rachel awoke, still wrapped around Samuel, who was snoring. The room was dark. She looked around, disoriented for a moment then checked her watch. It was 7:30 pm. They'd napped for two hours! She stared at Samuel, his face peaceful in sleep and traced the contours of his cheeks and chin with her fingers. *Who knew that under that scraggly beard lurked an Adonis!* She kissed his full lips and was greeted with another snore. She pressed her lips against his more firmly hoping that would wake him up. His arms and legs tightened about her body like a Python.

"If this is your way of waking me up, it's having a completely different effect." He told her, his voice croaky from sleep.

"I think we should get up and have some dinner, sweetheart, darling…light of my life…" She tried to move but he held her fast.

"One more kiss first," he insisted, pulling her underneath him.

"Oh, all right," Rachel deadpanned and gave him a little smack on the lips. She wriggled out of bed and stood up, holding out her hand for him.

"*Ach,* that's not what I meant! I'll just have to deal with you later," he wagged a finger at her and got up, taking her hand.

They went out to the dining room and found everyone milling about. Buddy trotted up to greet her.

"Well *finally!* We're all starving!" Karen exclaimed. "Emma wouldn't let us eat without you since it's your first night back."

"Oh, Emma, honey, that was so sweet of you but not necessary," Rachel said, giving her a hug.

Emma favored Karen with a look, "Karen exaggerates, they've all been pigging out on chips and dip and raw vegetables for the past hour!"

"*Jah,* but we want dinner!" Aaron seconded.

"*Jah!*" seconded Amos and Abram.

A knock came upon the front door and Josef entered. "Glad to see you're both up!" he grinned, "Let's eat!"

They all took their places at the long wooden table and held hands.

"Josef, would you please lead the blessing?" Samuel asked him.

They all bowed their heads.

"*Der Herr,* we give thee thanks for the safe return of Samuel and Rachel. We ask that You bless this food and the hands that prepared it,"

"Short and sweet, he must be starving too," Rachel whispered in an aside to Samuel.

Emma lifted the lid off the soup tureen and began ladling out generous portions of thick, beef barley soup while everyone passed around the bowl of rolls and popovers.

"Emma this is just delicious!" Josef complimented her. "I thought Rachel was a great cook, but you are giving her a run for her money!"

Rachel watched Emma's face go crimson with pleasure at Josef's praise and nodded. "Yup! She's definitely a wonderful cook," she added, "but whereas I stink at baking, she is also a fabulous pastry chef. Emma, that wedding cake you made for us was just spectacular and so yummy! I especially loved the chocolate layer with Chantilly filling!"

Karen leaned over and whispered in her ear, "laying it on a little thick, aren't you, mom?"

"Hush!" Rachel hissed, hoping Josef was oblivious to their conversation.

"Just saying..." Karen hissed back.

"We waited for you both to return so we could all pick out and cut down the Christmas tree together," Emma said.

"Can we have a tree decorating party, mom?" Karen asked.

Rachel was about to say no, she didn't want to fuss but

thought better of it. *This will be the last normal Christmas we all get to have together; treasure every moment of it.* "That sounds like a wonderful idea, honey," she replied.

The next morning everyone got up early and met in the Inn to break their fast together. The livestock and chickens had all been attended to, snug in the barn and coop.

Rachel and Emma worked together in the kitchen, mixing the batter for waffles, frying bacon, sausage, eggs and cottage potatoes. Two large carafes of hot coffee stood ready at the coffee station. Samuel and the boys entered through the service porch, removing their shoes and washing up at the large sink. Buddy was running to and fro, the smell of sizzling pork driving him to distraction.

Karen also walked in, her collecting basket laden with beautiful blue and brown eggs. "They aren't laying as much as they usually do, probably because it's so cold" she said to no one in particular, setting the basket on the counter. She carefully transferred the eggs into cartons.

"Everything is almost ready," Rachel said over her shoulder, filling platters with waffles, meats, potatoes, and eggs. Emma took them to the table as everyone took their seats.

"Where's Josef?" Rachel asked, looking around the room. "He's usually the first one here for breakfast."

"He's still in bed, said he wasn't feeling well," Amos replied.

Rachel didn't miss the worried expression on Emma's face. "Why don't you go check on him?" she suggested.

Emma nodded and wasted no time going out the door to the *dawdi haus.* She knocked on the door and when there was no answer, she let herself in. She found Josef in his bed, shivering with a fever, covered with half a dozen quilts.

He barely acknowledged her.

She put her hand upon his forehead, he was burning up! She threw off his covers and began rubbing down his bare feet to draw the fever down. His teeth began to chatter, and he fought to recover himself. She slapped his hands away. "I need to bring your fever down!"

She poured some water into the washstand bowl, dipped in a towel, wrung it out and began wiping his face, arms and feet down with the tepid water. She heard the front door open, and slam shut.

"What's wrong?" Karen asked her, entering the room.

"He has a high temperature," Emma explained. "Can you please get me some Ibuprofen and Rubbing Alcohol?"

"Okay," Karen replied, turning to leave.

"Tell everyone to eat without me,"

Karen ran out the door. Emma turned back to Josef who was still shaking with fever. His strawberry blond hair was plastered to his scalp and his fair skin was red and hot to the touch.

"*Danki,*" he whispered, taking her hand in his for a moment, then he fell asleep.

Karen returned with all the needed items as well as a covered plate with Emma's breakfast on it.

"Help me get him up," Emma asked Karen.

Together they brought Josef up to a sitting position so he could take the Ibuprofen. Emma shook him awake. "Josef! Josef! Wake up! I need you to take these pills."

Josef's eyes opened for a brief moment and opened his mouth as though he were a little boy. Emma put three Ibuprofen in his mouth and held a glass of water to his mouth. "Drink all of it," she commanded. He swallowed the pills, drank half the glass then fell unconscious again. They laid him back on the pillows.

"Karen, can you stay for a few moments while I give him a sponge bath?"

"What?"

"*Ach!* I'm not going to undress him except from the waist up. I need to sponge him down with the rubbing alcohol."

"Oh! Good!" Karen exhaled, relieved.

"I just want you here for decency's sake, it will only take me a few moments."

Emma poured some of the Rubbing Alcohol into the wash basin, dipped the towel in again and wiped his bare chest and armpits down. She could feel his temperature coming down.

"Go ahead now and eat with your family," Emma urged Karen. "I'll stay here and watch over him for a bit." She covered him back up with the quilt.

"Okay, thanks," Karen said.

"How's Josef?" Rachel asked Karen when she returned to the kitchen.

Karen sat down, stuffing a large bit of waffle into her mouth, "I think he's doing better; she got his fever down a bit before I left."

"Karen! Don't talk with your mouth full! I'll go check on him after breakfast," Rachel said. Samuel took her hand from under the table and shook his head "no" at her.

"Let Emma handle this," he whispered.

Rachel was about to protest then perceived the reasoning behind his words. *He doesn't want me exposed to his germs and compromise my health.* Then another thought came into her mind: *maybe this fever will work in Emma's favor like it did for me and Samuel!*

Emma returned an hour later, bringing her empty plate back with her.

"How is he doing?" Rachel asked over her shoulder as she rinsed off the dishes.

"Better, his fever is down and he's sleeping," Emma replied, adding her plate to the pile. "I think I better stay around the house so I can check on him while you're out getting the tree. I'm going to make him some white willow bark tea."

"And chicken soup!" Rached added. "Nothing like good old fashioned chicken soup to cure whatever ails you."

Emma smiled, "*Jah,* that too." She was clearly enjoying her role as Florence Nightingale.

Chapter Twenty-Nine

"Last Christmas"

Rachel, Samuel, Karen, Emma, Josef and the boys were all gathered around the tree in the living room Christmas morning, drinking hot cocoa and unwrapping the myriads of practical gifts she and Samuel had picked out for each of them on their trip to Leavenworth. Rachel looked at each face in turn, seeing the joy and happiness in their eyes and grateful that she had gotten to play a small part in providing them not only a place of refuge but a surrogate family and home as well. For a woman who was unable to have children, her quiver was quite full.

Except for their tattoos, their appearances had all drastically changed for the better. Gone were the piercings, the strange haircuts, crazy colors and weird clothing. They all looked happy, healthy, and wholesome and truly had grown to be family.

Each of them in their own way had been a Godsend, starting with Emma, then the boys, and finally Josef who had recovered enough from the flu to spend Christmas with them. Rachel squirmed in her chair, anxious and nervous about the news she was about to share with them. She hated to ruin their happy morning, but it could not be put off any longer. In three days' time she had to go to Lancaster Medical Center and meet with the surgeon and oncologist and endure a battery of tests.

She cleared her throat for attention. "I have an announcement," she said loudly.

Everyone quieted, except Karen.

"You're pregnant!?" she guessed.

Rachel almost choked. "I wish, no, I'm not pregnant."

They all stared at her, their smiles fading into looks of apprehension when they saw the tears rolling down her cheeks.

Rachel looked down at her cocoa mug and took a deep, shuddering breath. Samuel gripped her hand and gave it a squeeze. Her throat was constricting with tears. "I found a lump on my breast on our honeymoon," she began. "It's cancer."

No one moved. No one said a word. They just all stared at her in astonishment and dismay, ignoring the song of *Chestnuts Roasting on an Open Fire* playing in the background.

"You've known this since your honeymoon and kept it quiet this entire month?" Emma finally cried, tears flooding her eyes.

Rachel smiled through her tears, "I didn't want to ruin your Christmas." She looked around the room. Everyone had tears in their eyes, but Aaron was openly weeping. Karen was mute with horror. "I have an appointment with an oncologist and surgeon on the 28th. Until then, that's all I can tell you."

Samuel stood up, drawing Rachel up with him. "We would cherish all your prayers," he choked, his pent-up grief unable to be suppressed any longer. He bowed his head, covered his face with his hands and began to weep.

They were both immediately surrounded by all, arms reaching out to comfort and empathize.

"You are our family," Josef said, speaking for all of them. "Of course, we will pray for you, but we will also support you both in any way we can. We will take care of everything needed while Rachel fights this disease! No task is too small or too great."

Everyone nodded in agreement and embraced, finally giving vent to their sorrow.

"Thank you," whispered Rachel, "God has indeed been kind to me to have gifted me with all of you."

Rachel and Samuel sat in the doctor's office, waiting for the surgeon to return with the report of all her test results. In the past several days they had poked, prodded and scanned her to within an inch of her life and it was only the beginning…

The door abruptly opened, and the doctor entered, her chart with the test results in his hands.

Rachel and Samuel gripped each other's hands, their hearts pounding, fearful of what they were going to find out.

"Good morning," he greeted them, his face unreadable. "We've run all the tests and your Onco score is 50 which puts you at an intermediate risk and for which I am going to recommend we start with chemotherapy to shrink the tumor,"

"Oh *nooooo,*" wailed Rachel, covering her face with her hands; it was the treatment she had dreaded the most. She began to sob uncontrollably and to shake. She had seen what chemotherapy had done to others and it was horrifying.

"After six weeks of chemo, you will need to make a choice between a single mastectomy with no radiation treatment or a lumpectomy and eight weeks of radiation treatment. After that, we will have to put you on hormone inhibitors which will effectively send you into menopause. I'm so sorry."

Rachel collapsed against Samuel, the reality of her prognosis finally hitting her. She had *cancer.* He did his best to comfort her, but she dissolved into tears. For the third time in her life, she was face to face with death. First Barry's, second when she had despaired of life and crashed the buggy and now cancer, at what should have been the happiest moment in her life.

Samuel held her in his arms as she wept and wept right along with her. "We will get through this, Rachel, for better or for worse, in sickness or in health…"

"Til death us do part," she whispered.

THE END

Greetings from the author!

Greetings Second Chance Inn fans!

By popular demand, here is the sequel to Second Chance Inn, *A Place of Refuge.*

If you haven't read the first book (Second Chance Inn), you will want to read it before reading *A Place of Refuge.*

I invite you to sit down with your favorite hot (or cold) beverage and fur baby (if you have one) and join me, Rachel, Samuel and Karen for the next installment of their journey.

If you would ever like to connect with me, you are more than welcome to email me at: mmgiron@yahoo.com (I won't share your information with anyone.)

Follow me on Facebook: Author Marlayne Giron
Instagram: #mmgiron.

I'd also be VERY grateful if you could write a review online. Getting feedback from readers is both very exciting and gratifying and one of the best rewards for an author!

You can also check out my website named after my first book: https://thevictorbook.com

I hope to hear from YOU!
Marlayne

ACKNOWLEDGEMENTS

I would like to express my deep gratitude to Kim Denando, my graphic designer, who has taken my ideas and turned them into a gorgeous reality! She designed this cover as well as Second Chance Inn and did all the interior layouts that make the books look so professional.

I would also like to thank Joan Gamwell, my editor extraordinaire, who did such a fabulous job in editing this book and getting it back to me in such record time.

I would also be remiss not to express my deep and heartfelt gratitude to each member of my street team who never failed to encourage me, post reviews, and share about my books all over social media with such genuine enthusiasm. I truly wish I could meet and hug every one of you!

Most of all, I would like to thank my sissy (you know who you are) without whom I never would have written five books! Your passion and enthusiasm kept me going even when I wanted to give up.